Staged

Staged

ELSIE G. BEYA

atmosphere press

Published by Atmosphere Press

Cover design by Beste Miray

Atmospherepress.com

To my investor and friend - I would be quite lost without you as both.

1

Fuck.

I missed my opening bar.

Never ever have I done that before. Never.

And I have performed while high as a kite, drunk as a fucking skunk, and hungover as a student in Freshers' week. Plus while battling a sickness bug, waist deep in grief, heartbreak, everything. My mind is frozen, totally blank. This is worse than when I did that dodgy sniff of coke and forgot my own fucking name

Lyrics run around my head, I chase them, but as if I'm trapped in a maze, I can't reach them. I lick my lips, paste on my charming smile and hold out the microphone towards the adoring fans. By now I've completely skipped the first three lines of our debut single. A song I wrote at sixteen years of age. The lyrics to which I have tattooed on my fucking arm. I know those words in several languages, off by heart. Backwards, anagrammed. You name it, I know those words. Yet now, nothing. I'm not even that drunk.

I pick it up, of course; style it out in true Hayden

Fucking Coulthard style. I totally ignore the amused daggers that Jordan is shooting me from behind his bass. It was an honest mistake. Like he's never missed a note.

The end of the song comes, cool sweat pools on my hairline under my curls, I turn round to get a drink, of water (no alcohol on stage, spoilsports), and Jordan laughs at me.

"Fucking idiot!" He laughs again, a high tinkling sound akin to a glockenspiel. It doesn't match his rectangular six-foot frame at all, nor his zombie apocalypse gamer tattoos. He may be one of my oldest friends, but what a twat. Everything is a joke to Jordan. Forgetting lyrics, falling over in the gym, my first and only love getting engaged; all a source of fucking hilarity.

"Fuck off!" I half laugh, keeping the microphone covered. The fans don't need to hear us arguing, kidding or not.

Max, our drummer, kicks off the next song with a heavy beat, all seems to be moving on just fine.

I sing the first verse, chorus. I love the crowd screaming the words at me. I love how hysterical the fans get, their loud screams show that we really are their everything. It does fill my heart with love. And it does wonders for my ego, as I see in their tear glossed eyes that I'm their fucking hero.

A woman in the crowd catches my eye, nothing new there. Yet she looks exactly like my ex. Not the model I've just split up with, nor the countless others who have spent nights in my bed. The ex. The only woman I've ever loved. The same woman who just got engaged. Lexi. Long black hair the colour of my tattoos, that dusts against her shoulders as she weaves through the crowd. I just missed seeing her face, yet I can still picture her bronze wide eyes and skin as clear as pearls. She turns away and threads herself through the jumble of bodies jumping relentlessly to the drums. I try to track her midnight black hair and catch a glimpse of her eyes that I dream about far more than I'll ever confess. I will her to turn around, to confirm whether it is Lexi, or just my mind playing tricks. I lose her, of course. Just like I lost her ten years ago when she broke my fucking heart. In front of me, all the fans with dark hair or brown eyes transform and morph into the image of my ex. I scrunch my eyes closed, shake my head. But it's too late.

My brain becomes shrouded in a dark cloud, the same colour as the black baby grand piano in my hallway. I drop the microphone as if it's on fire. I feel myself turn away from the audience, who are still singing along as always. I raise my shoulders up to my ears, and shrug.

Jordan looks at me like I've grown another head. He's been my best mate since I was eleven, and bandmate since we hit fifteen. But I can't stay here.

"I'm done, mate," I say to him. The words are out of my mouth before I can process it.

"Fuck off then!" Jordan shouts down his microphone, no giggling this time. His voice drowns out the screaming audience, who have become quiet, and dropped a few octaves. "Fuck off Hayden," he repeats. I can see a vein in his thick neck pulsing, the red tinge of anger colouring his face.

So, I do. I sweep my curls out of my eyes, rip the sound pack from my jeans, pull my in ears out and leave. No going back.

The thing that astounds me, is that no one stops me. Raven, our tour manager, Higgsy, head of security; no one from the band. Not even Marlena, Jordan's latest other half, who I high five as I pass in the wings. They just let me go. I'm pretty damn sure they weren't anticipating it, otherwise surely Pete, our manager, would have been there to stop me.

Maybe they are all dumbfounded. I wonder though, would I have walked back on stage if someone had told me to?

I nudge open the stage door, it doesn't need any force, and just walk.

I can't even say I'm strutting or swaggering. Pretty dull exit for me: Hayden Fucking Coulthard, really.

I head back to my flat in Camden; filled with antiques and art, uncomfortable furniture and empty bottles of champagne I've somehow acquired since moving to London a decade ago. I drink myself into oblivion, staring at the blank TV screen, watching my reflection. Waiting for the whiskey to take over so I can't feel anything.

I love my career—making music heard by millions, but I can't fucking breathe.

I run a bath and look out across the Camden skyline. I don't focus on the buildings or clouds high in the blue sky, the exact colour of Bombay Sapphire gin. I find a bird, a pigeon, and follow it. Swooping low, stretching up towards the sun. Wings outspread, flapping delicately. I watch in admiration at that freedom, the ease at which it moves.

If that was me I'd be stuck in a cage. Probably a gold gilded antique cage designed by Gucci, filled with the best organic seeds money can buy. But still, a cage is a cage, no matter how it's dressed up. I'd still be fucking trapped.

I finish the bottle, the whiskey gliding down my throat like liquid satin. The bottle rolls under the bath. I hear the clink as it connects with the others. The cleaner will get them next week.

I close my eyes, as the water, scented with oils of Tuscan flowers according to the deep emerald bottle on the shelf, covers my toned and tattooed body. I have to go to the gym at least five times a week, that's in my fucking contract too, along with dating whoever they send my way.

I picture that I'm the flying bird, wind kissing my face, basking in the sun. Nosediving to the ground, seeing people wander and weave around the streets. Then soaring high again, away from the troubles, the temptations of human life. Free. Following my own path. Making my own way.

Someone far below comes along and shoots me down. Rifle to the heart. I downward spiral to the ground, landing with a thump.

I jolt my eyes open, water sloshing over the rim of the bath. The sky outside is now stained a deeper blue, the sun lower. I shiver, the water is stone cold. I need another drink.

I ignore the hammering on the door, the incessant ringing of my mobile, the beeping email alert which sounds like a constant pedestrian crossing. I wait, for a moment of silence. Now that the sun has risen they've given up, and retreated to bed themselves. I grab a holdall and my guitar and head to London Euston station.

I need to go home; back to Cumbria. I need to see Lexi. There's no point phoning her; she's blocked my number. I need to know if she really is engaged, or if Jordan heard wrong. Has she finally moved on? Am I all in the past for her? Does she not still feel that pull towards me, like I feel to her?

I get myself a pint and call my dad. I realise that I want to see him, that in itself is another unexpected turn of events. We're not especially close. I kind of put him in a box, when I'm working. My whole life, my whole focus is on the stage; and dad is kind of shoved into the lighting box at the back of the venue. Connected to me, but its someone else's issue to deal with. Fuck, that's an awful way to think about my own father.

Maybe I'm like our fans, looking for something to ground me, to give me a place to be, a reason. Is Lexi that reason? Well, she won't be if she's fucking marrying someone else.

Right now, I'm well aware that I'm lost. But no matter what my manager Pete says, I'm not a fucking alcoholic. I'll leave that label with my mother's corpse.

2

It's just after three o' clock on a Wednesday afternoon.

I'm alone on the platform. Sure, there's various people buzzing about, running like pigeons being chased by children, but I am essentially, alone. There's not even a squeal, shout, sexual request or sob from a fan. No one. People pass me by without noticing, it's eerie. Unheard of, unwelcome. Almost.

I've got my newly purchased Louis Vuitton beanie hat pulled down over my trademark curls, and my Ray Ban shades covering half my face; I guess I should be relieved of my unusual anonymity. Yet I do kinda miss it. I didn't think of that when I walked off stage at KOKO last night. I wasn't thinking of anything actually, I just knew I had to fucking leave. I don't wanna let Jordan, my manager, or the fans, down. But I need a fucking break. They don't realise how demanding my life is sometimes. I feel like a triangle in an orchestra. Sat at the back, trying to fit in with the other percussion, but my true purpose is to make up the numbers. Not integral to anything. Just, there. Playing out my nightmares in my head, pretending they're not really there. They usually vanish after a drink or two.

So here I am. Alone. Going home. Back to Cockermouth in sunny old Cumbria.

Cumbria is as dull as the Thames. Boring. Tedious. Bland. A one-way ticket to middle-age and walking in the fells. But I know I need to get out of London, away from this madness. Away from the various rehab clinics that Pete keeps trying to get me to attend.

Moments before the spotlight hit me last night, he declared over video call, for Jordan, and the whole team to witness, that I was booked into another clinic next week.

"This one is not optional, man," Whatever. Pete is a great manager, a good friend, I respect him. However, I don't want or need a stint in rehab. I want a fucking drink in peace, without wondering who is taking a photo of me, or what Jordan will laugh at next.

Hence the reluctant return back to my dad's house, that I have forked out a small fortune for to kit it out again after the whole downstairs was flooded. Twice. That made a dent in the bank balance, I can fucking tell you.

Cockermouth.

Where there's more hairdressers than people, where the bus service is like a broken clock—only working twice a day. Where the landlords, barmaids, shopkeepers, teachers, screeching high school kids, *everyone,* knows me. Where I won't be able to fart without it being the gossip of the fucking town. Let alone have a drink or smoke in peace. Or a shag. Heaven forbid. Still, it's got to be better than pissing London. Surely.

I inhale with closed eyes as a familiar scent floats behind a woman walking past. Clinique's *Happy*. I chuckle to myself. Are they still making that? It was at the height of fashion in the late nineties, along with cargo pants and glitter hair mascara. All of which Lexi used to wear.

Fuck. I wish I could see her right now. I do miss her company, her presence, in my life. Lexi always knew just the right thing to say. While she would be a very welcome distraction from some aspects of my world, her engagement is another of life's issues stacked against me.

I see the woman who I was just thinking of. And then I do see her. Actually her, not a mirage or poor copy. She glances those same, Bambi hazel eyes down the platform. She takes no notice of my good self, then with purpose, strides straight in to Coach G, with a black dog plodding beside her heels.

Her hair is longer, dancing past her slim shoulders. And blonde, no trace of the raven locks I associate with her. She's wearing dark plastic rimmed glasses too, that sit below her now blonde blunt fringe. That is another change, but I'd recognise her anywhere. My Lexi.

I step up into my coach, First Class of course. I might have walked out on my career, but I still have standards.

I stand up as soon as we're out of the station, finally waving goodbye to the cloying city I've lived in for a decade. I pull my shades over my eyes to avoid any distractions, and head down to Coach G. Time to find Lexi. And the onboard shop too, I'm itching for another drink.

I down most of my first can of lager in between carriages, then scan the seats for Lex. The lighter hair throws me; I still always picture her as my own Snow White. Hair as black as a Halloween night, pale skin so smooth and clear. Even at twelve years old, the juxtaposition of dark and light brought her to my attention. I used to tease her and sing *Ebony and Ivory* to her. She didn't appreciate it, but it always made us both laugh.

I see her ahead of me, a table to herself as she stands up to get something from the overhead storage. Glasses. Lexi always hated wearing them, she wore contacts constantly. Apart from first thing in the morning or last thing at night. Then, her NHS prescribed glasses would cling to the bridge of her pale nose, magnifying her bronze eyes and those dark thick lashes. She looked like an adorable baby deer. Precious and beautiful. I have another slurp of lager as I reminisce, it makes me feel more in control.

I decide to sit at her table, going for the bold approach. Even if it's just a Lexi lookalike, I'm sure she won't mind if renowned pop star Hayden Fucking Coulthard makes himself at home opposite her for the duration. I can always pretend it is Lex while I shag her in the toilets.

My stomach churns as I approach, I see a black floppy eared dog under the table, tail wagging like a pendulum. Unlike my usual stage presence swagger, I have a moment of panic. I drop down behind her instead and open another can of lager. That first one slipped down a treat, and I'm not usually a lager man.

The breath stutters out of me like discord notes from a piano. I close my eyes and try to inhale that scent of Lexi's I always loved. Coconuts, limes and lilies, and a lingering after note of roses, like the ones that grew in the parks near my dad's house. It comes floating back from my memories, buried deep.

The cracks in my heart she carved split again, new wounds bursting open. I loved her. No fucking doubt about it, I loved Lexi. The darkness of my heart and mind blankets my core. Strange, it's usually only my dead mother who conjures up these black thoughts.

Lexi. The girl who fucking decided that she was better than my fame, my music. The girl who shunned me, who didn't want me. Broke my heart as I left for London.

The very night we were signed by the record label, Pete threw us a huge local party and Lexi walked out. Just fucked off home. Jordan told me he saw her with someone else. I never found out who. It wasn't important. That guilty look on her features told me Jordan was telling the truth. Why would he not? He's my best mate. Lex didn't even say goodbye, just turned up at my dad's house in the wee hours and broke up with me. As if walking out at my signing party wasn't fucking enough.

In interviews I always say my first love was music, my only love. In a way it's true, although it sounds pretentious as fuck. In private though – in the dark, whenever I'm writing, composing, thinking – it's her. Lexi is the one who gives me constant inspiration. Every song is about Lex, every melody I have floating in my brain, all the lyrics I scribble into notebooks; they're for her.

I shrug it off, play it down when quizzed more by journalists: "high school romance, more like good friends," all that shite.

Yet now I'm faced with her. I should be honest with myself. Keeping secrets has done me fuck all good so far.

When I think of Lex, I always feel a weight of guilt. Guilt that I didn't find out exactly what happened. Guilt that cheating on me, breaking up with me with no explanation: it's not who Lexi is. Was. It was so out of her fucking character.

But instead, I ran with it, let it happen. Didn't read too much into it, except play the heartbroken boy next door. Which I was, my heart was broken, and I along with it. I was in bits, shattered on the floor like the broken bottles under my bath. I turned bitter, towards Lex and Cumbria. I refused to return home from fear of running into her. Not that I ever really have a day off. All of the memories we shared, the fun we had, the love I felt; I masked over them with dark clouds.

I used that unhappiness, that hurt, and had an Alanis moment. Ok, more than one. I wrote some fucking awesome heartbreak tunes. Songs that I screamed out in anger, that teenage girls sang full pelt in their bedrooms, mascara-streaked tears drying on their cheeks. The first Halcyon album is jam packed with angst, harsh riffs and dramatic head banging beats. It was how I dealt with it.

I thought I was over Lex. I thought I was over it. Over her. Yet now, in this pissing train carriage, heading back to where I first laid eyes on her, I was wrong.

There she is: Lexi Louise Blackwood. I watch her as she pulls out a book from her bag, her lightened hair falling over her face. She sighs loudly in frustration as the bookmark slides out. Lexi opens the book with one pale hand, the fluorescent lights overhead reflecting off her clear painted nails. Her red lips purse as she scans the pages, a slight frown on her face, as she struggles to find her place amongst the text. She stretches down to pat at the dog's head, tickles behind the floppy black ears; a smile pushes up her lily-white cheeks, flushed ever so slightly from no doubt not being used to the cloying heat of the Tube. Her amber eyes are even more mesmerising than I recall, now they're magnified by her blocky glasses. The girl who I fell in love with at school. The only girl I've been in love with. The only one I'd want to be with again. Like, have a future with. Lex: the woman I love. I still love her. More so now.

Fuck. I itch at my thigh, my engraved hip flask beckoning me to empty it in one burning gulp. I love her. I've always loved her. I'm still fucking in love with her.

3

I shuffle myself into the seat opposite her, almost tripping over the dog, and accidentally poking my guitar case into Lexi's side.

"Can you be careful please?" She snaps out. "My dog is just here." Always ready with a mouth full of sass.

"Sorry, Lex," I say, directly. No beating around the fucking bush with me.

Her pale skin burns scarlet like the buses I've walked past, and I flash her a charming smile. I ignore the pulsating of my heart, feeling like it might break free from my chest. Lexi's face breaks into a smile. I feel like I'm sixteen again. Giddy.

"Are you here alone?" Lexi blurts out, her brown eyes suddenly dancing around the carriage, as the smile slips from her lips.

"Looks like it."

"That's not answering the question. You're usually surrounded by hoards of screaming admirers or photographers capturing your every move. Where's the whole circus that trails behind you?" Lexi looks bored of me already, avoiding my gaze by focussing on the landscape zooming past the windows

"Not today. Just me, Lex. Lucky you," I wink a blue eye at her, as she rolls her brown ones. "Aww, Lexi! It's so great to see you!" I stand up and lean awkwardly over the table. The chains and charms around my neck clanging on the barrier between us. I follow my heart and place a kiss on her cheek. I inhale her scent, taking me back in time, ten, twelve, fifteen years. The weight of her between my arms feeling as comforting as my guitar. My heart hasn't slowed down in tempo since I saw her on the platform. My brain swirls with countless lyrics and feelings.

She's more beautiful than I remember. She's changed, obviously. Do any of us look the same ten years down the line? Skin so pure and pale, like my silk sheets I left behind. Lips that remind me of red chillies, vivid yet wicked.

Lexi, the woman I love. The only woman I ever will love, if I'm being fucking honest. In a parallel universe we're married and happily living together on the shores of Oban.

Fuck, I've missed her.

"It's so warm on this train," Lexi says, fanning herself with the battered novel. Her skin still clinging to the blush kissing her cheeks.

"Nah Lex, that's the effect I have on women."

"Yes, I see they're flocking round you currently, Hayden."

I flash her a smile, hopefully she doesn't notice how it wobbles slightly, or indeed asks me any questions.

I nudge Lex with my feet, admiring my beloved Gucci boots as I do so. Thank fuck I got proper dressed today, I think I might die of fucking embarrassment if my first meeting with Lexi after ten years was me in my Gucci tracksuit and headband. First (second) impressions count and all that. I can't keep the smile off my lips. Any resentment I held for Lex, for the breakup, has dissolved like sugar in my black coffee. Only sweet memories remain. I want to scoop her up, twirl her around, tell her that everything is in the past and we can move forward.

Until I looked in those hazel eyes of Lexi's, my thoughts of her were always shrouded by the negativity. Not anymore. That doesn't matter, not a fucking bit. Is it too overdramatic if I propose here and now? Surely I'm a better option than Callum. Callum, who we went to school with. He's practically my opposite. Our social circles didn't cross much at school as he was sporty, and I was forever forging notes to skive off from any physical activity so I could hide out in the music room. But we never got on. I imagine he hasn't altered much, still imposing and strong, ready to finish a fight at the drop of a fucking hat. He was shorter than me, but his chest was double the width of mine, even at fifteen. I never quite forgave him for working with Lex on a History project and asking her out, when he knew she was with me.

What sick twist of fate is this? I realise that I love this woman sat opposite me, less than twenty-four hours after I find out she's engaged. Her third finger is bare, but that isn't a definite answer. Maybe she didn't like the ring Callum bought her. Perhaps she said no. Maybe there's still a bit of hope for me. Cliché with curls, that's me; the estranged ex returns and sweeps the first love off her feet. *Fuck*, I'm so pathetic. I sigh in disgust at myself.

Lexi is fiddling with the collar of her very boring black

jumper, she fans herself with the novel, complaining about the heat. Still, her cheeks bloom pink. Lex starts removing her black knit, definitely not Gucci. She's clearly struggling – her arms seem to poke out at angles like a compass as she wriggles free.

I'm about to ask if I can help, insert cheeky wink here, as I'm hit in the fucking chest and chin by several pearl buttons. A grin breaks out on my face, and I choke down a laugh, in both hilarity and embarrassment. Poor Lex. All the buttons have fired off her blouse like popcorn, as she's tried to take off the jumper. Wasn't expecting to see her pretty lace bra on the first meeting in a decade, but I won't fucking complain. The whole of her chest, neck and face lights up like a stop sign. Lexi's mouth gapes like a cave, her eyelashes blink rapidly like hummingbird wings. The dog under the table whimpers in second-hand embarrassment, I guess.

"You always were a bit adventurous, Lex. But shagging on a train table is a bit too exposed even for me," I chuckle.

She scowls as she pulls the blouse off and quickly dresses herself back in the offending black jumper. Lexi's kept her figure, toned and slim. Skin that looks smooth, and I wonder if it still smells of coconut too? It was always her favourite scent. I'm not ashamed to say I've had a few flings with girls who use that scent too. Purely for that reason. Of course I'd never tell that to them, or Lex. Cringe. I flash her a smile. Charming, naturally, just to put her at ease.

"Were you at my gig last night?" I ask her as I open another can of lager. She shakes her head and regards me with a look of distaste.

"No. I was visiting my sister," Lex replies with a scoff.

"I didn't know Aggie lived in London," I murmur. I can't imagine Lexi's little sister as anything other than an annoying shadow with jet black hair the same as Lexi's, and a Barbie clutched in her hand, following us around their Mum's flat.

"There's lots you don't know about me," Lexi mumbles out quietly.

"Promise you weren't there last night? At KOKO?" I ask again, I would've bet my millions on it. Although now I'm faced with the blonde hair, I know I must have been mistaken. Yet part of me was so fucking convinced.

"I haven't been to a Halcyon gig since you got signed. I'm not going to start now," Lexi says with a snarl. Feisty. I always admired her wild streak, even when I was on the receiving end of that sharp bite.

"You mean the night you broke my heart?" I spit out, before I can stop my stream of consciousness. Lex looks offended. Her mouth drops open and she juts her chin forward. I'm too stubborn to apologise. Not that I spoke a word of a fucking lie.

"Nice to see you, H," she starts. My heart speeds up in rhythm as she calls me by the name only she used. No one else ever calls me that. No one else ever did. Only Lexi. The softness of the name sounds so sweet to my ears. "But I was hoping to get this book finished, so if you don't mind?"

It's posed as a question, yet Lexi's face shows there's no room for a discussion. She tucks headphones into her ears, while avoiding all eye contact. The smile slides off my face with the sting of Lexi's dismissal. Her rejection eradicates the comfort of hearing Lex call me H. Despite being physically closer to her than I have in the last ten years, I feel more alone than when we broke up.

Pouting, I drain the can instead of apologising, or asking her if we can start over. Lexi flattens her book on the table, then holds it high, using it as a shield for the rest of the journey.

4

The announcement comes that we're pulling into Penrith, jolting me back to the here and now. I shove a handful of Polos into my mouth, after reading a message that Pete is waiting to collect me. *Fuck*. He'll drag me right back down to London, before I've even got home.

I follow Lexi out of the train and step down onto the platform. I push my conker curls under my knitted hat, sunglasses covering my eyes from any waiting journalists. There's no one. Just Pete.

Lexi and her dog freeze in front of him.

"Lexi Blackwood, is this a happy coincidence, or are you the reason to blame for Hayden's little disappearing act?" Pete asks in his smooth American accent, towering over her like a shire horse to her Shetland pony.

"I wouldn't call it happy, now I've seen you," Lexi fires out. Pete opens his mouth to answer, but she cuts him off. "I have no part in his life, thanks to you."

Pete laughs dryly. I close my eyes. It's these snappy exchanges that remind me how much easier my life is with Pete in it, and Lexi out of it. The two of them never got on. Lexi even begging Jordan and I not to sign with HeadScan

Records. But Pete was the best for the band. He's a world class manager. The best we could've asked for.

"What a shame we can't offer you a lift," Pete says ignoring Lexi's comments.

"I am perfectly capable of driving myself."

"Isn't that lucky?"

"Guys, stop!" I moan out, rubbing my temples, "Some of us have a headache."

Pete places a large, steadying hand on my shoulder.

"That will be the stress, man."

I throw him a small smile. Pete gets how tough my life is, Lex only sees what the press want her to. The glitz and fucking glamour.

"More likely to be the lager," Lexi snorts. I roll my eyes at her behind my shades.

"Mate! You didn't have to collect me," I say franticly. I hope Pete doesn't hear the panic in my voice.

"You're my star act, of course I'd be here to welcome you. Come on, the car is waiting."

I turn to say bye to Lex. To tell her I really hope we can catch up properly, grab a drink and so on. But all I see is her back as she and her dog stride away without another glance in my direction. Fucking great.

The plush leather feels like a calming hug as I sink into the car PMT has brought. That's the not so affectionate name I give him – well no one likes their boss all the time, do they? I should have known he wouldn't be driving. A man like Pete Morris-Turner does not drive himself anywhere. Why have a dog and bark your-fucking-self? Pete is as subtle as a skyscraper in a village. It's a stretch Hummer. As we pull out of the station everyone's head turns to see the monster machine squeeze up the streets. There are ways to sneak about; this is not it. Pete pours me a glass of chilled champagne. It tastes divine. Chilled to perfection.

"We could roll with it. Very clever of you, man," Pete smiles as our glasses clink.

I know I've been drinking pretty much since I woke up this morning, what's new there? But what the fuck is he on about? "It's a good angle," Pete strokes his tanned chin, nodding to himself.

I look at him over the rim of the glass, enjoying the bubbles fizzing on my nose. I still am not following.

"Getting back with the childhood sweetheart," he adds in explanation.

"You don't like Lexi!" I bark out, "You wanted me to break up with her months before we did, before we left for London."

It's true, he advised me to be single as we left for London. 'Girlfriends and bands don't mix,' and that whole spiel. It would better for the image, for the band, if I'm unattached, Pete said. Then I'd be free to be dating the next model, singer or reality star who could boost The Halcyon's publicity and record sales.

"Well, she broke your heart in the end, so you should've got there first. And it's not about disliking or liking someone, it's about knowing what will work for you. For us." Pete might be prattling on, interrupting my snatched moment of bliss with the alcoholic bubbles, but he's trying. He's trying to do the best for me as an artist. I sigh. It's not my manager's fault I'm fucked up in the head and need to escape for a while. I've still got a job to do, I guess.

"You're right," I sigh out in muted agreement. I am too

exhausted for this level of conversation. I need to sleep.

"The only woman you've ever loved," Pete prattles on, tapping notes on his laptop. "Give me a quote about her. How you felt when you saw her again after so long."

"Lexi *is* the only woman I've ever loved. I'm not saying anything, Pete," I gargle, quaffing down chilled champagne without trying to choke and waste the bubbles. The only woman I want to be with, the one person I can imagine leaving this crazy travelling musical-based life for. Not that I'll admit it to him, or Lexi herself. Yet.

"Fine, I'll get someone else to invent a romantic quote. Relocating to your roots to make it work with your first love and that. She's the one to set you on the straight and narrow. I like it. I'll see when we can run a story."

"Pete –" I say as I scrub my hand down my face. I can't think about my career now, about the band, my future, Lexi, and certainly not the fucking press.

"Don't talk, just listen, have a drink," he says, as he tops up my empty champagne flute. "Back to item number one. What a mess you've got us into. Luckily, I've managed to contain some of the damage. We have lost the confidence of the promoters, who can blame them, when their act walks off stage?" Pete sounds livid, his ears have taken on a crimson shade. I expected him to be a bit pissed off at me, but not this extent of anger. I've done far more disruptive things before now. At least Jordan was there to carry on the gig without me. Pete carefully places his empty glass down and leans forward in his seat, removing his shades. The seat belt digging into his shoulder and holding him back. From me? But I'm his star prodigy! I bring him in the most fans, the most record sales, the most cash straight into his bank account.

"Oh, come on, Pete, so I walked off stage," I laugh. I've done worse things in the decade I've been in The Halcyon, surely he'll give me a break on this.

"And what about Jordan? Could he just take over from you? With no advance warning? You left him high and dry to face the masses, Hayden. What happened to the both of you and your 'no going back' bullshit?" Pete's spittle lands on my cheek and Prada top. I subtly wipe it away.

I close my eyes as I remember the looks on my band mate's face. The way Jordan shook his head then threw his bass down in a fit of rage, screaming at me to 'fuck off then'. I guess I should accept that no, he couldn't carry on after that, even if he wanted to. I've always been lead vocalist, main songwriter. Jordan has always been my faithful sidekick. He's always had my back. Ever since we got signed, fuck, ever since we stood on stage for the first time at the school talent show; we've always said, 'No going back.' And now look what I fucking did. Pete's right, as always. I should apologise to Jordan. And I will, but maybe after a sleep.

My whole life seems to have turned into one big soap opera. Not that I'm moaning, I'm not one of those annoying celebrities who begrudges the whole fame game; not at all. I wanted to be a successful musician. I wanted this level of success. I love the lifestyle I've become accustomed to. I guess I've been happy with the cards life has dealt me, mostly. But now I long for a stretch of peace. A slower pace. A fucking holiday for a wee while. Is that too much to ask?

"I've had to pay out a small fortune to terminate future commitments, what good is Jordan without you?" Pete continues in his smooth yankee accent. "You, you're the star! The showman. The leading role. Hayden Coulthard, your name was made to be in lights! You were made to sell out Wembley."

"I just need a break."

"I will give you a break. Six weeks. Six weeks for me to fix your mistakes. Find new promoters, book a new tour, completely revamp the image of The Halcyon."

My heart plummets, I'm still tied down. Well, what did I expect? Our contract is bound and tied up in fucking metal. And only Pete holds the angle grinder. Not that I'd be able to find one myself in my dad's tool box, even if I tried.

"We need to push forward with the new image. The all-new Halcyon." He rubs his hands together greedily; I can see the pound signs flashing in his piercing eyes.

"Pete, I –"

"We're gonna leave the bad boy behind, merely brush it under the carpet. Lexi could really help with the new wholesome image we're going for. The girl next door. She's perfect. She's not too pretty, she's just right. You're of course, way out of her league, so she'll be good to you."

"She's engaged! To someone else!" My words thunder around the car. I tug at my hair in frustration, and only just manage to stop stamping my boots.

Plus, I don't want to drag Lex into this nightmare of a life I've ended up in. Lexi's life is so simple compared to mine. She has no idea the daily battles I have to fight through. The most pressing thing about Cumbria is whether it's going to be dry enough to hang the washing out, or if you need your Big Coat for a walk to the park.

"It's non optional: you sort it out or I will, man."

"How am I meant to do that?!" I snap out. I haven't seen Lexi in ten fucking years! Aside from the train journey today, and that was a fucking coincidence. My heart jumps as if it's on a trampoline, the word 'fate' bounces around my brain. Was it fate?

"Persuade her. Use your charm. Right, so Moms."

"Mums?" The alcohol is buzzing through my blood, my head pounding. I can't keep up. My own mother's face pops into my head. I physically shake it away, squashing my knuckles against my jaw to crack them. The popping noise usually relieves some tension. Not today.

"Stop it with that noise, man! It always gives me the creeps. Moms, they're our new TA."

My head hurts so fucking much. I swear a pneumatic drill has embedded itself into my skull, and I have the heavy pressure of tears behind my eyes.

"TA?"

"Target audience, buddy. You and Jordan are the new crooners in town embracing this next chapter. Bored housewives, full of empty nest syndrome. Stay at home moms wanting a distraction from diapers and washing. Grown women still chasing a teenage fantasy. You know what I mean, man."

"But –"

"Do you know what percentage of buying audiences are women, Hayden?"

I shake my head numbly. I'm used to seeing screaming teenagers lusting after me, not their pissing mothers. Pete really is the best in the business, I shake my head to try and quieten the drilling. I should listen, he's got my best interests at heart. That's why he froze all my bank accounts, to keep me from wasting it all on drugs and drink, women and other disposable vices. With a break though, I'm hoping to get it all back under my control. All I need is a stretch of peace and quiet.

"We're gonna leave the rock vibe, focus more on ballads, the lyrics. Possibly leaving the guitar and pounding bass. Your voice is the star now. I'm thinking short hair, suits –"

"That's so not me," I snicker, already going against my previous thought to listen, my mind being its usual flighty self. I last wore a suit to an awards ceremony six months ago – it was neon floral brocade. I wore it with lashings of silver chains and jewels. Shirtless underneath, obviously. I discarded the jacket half-way through The Halcyon's performance of course. Undid my hair and let it flail around wild and free. Pete said we looked a mess, but I loved it. I hate feeling restricted, all hemmed in. Plus, he's the top manager for music, not for fashion.

"This is the new you, Hayden. If you want to work in this industry again –"

"I just want to get home," I wail like a child, sniffing incessantly to refrain my cries from breaking out. I'm not saying I want to leave it all behind me forever. Music is my life; my heart thrums with lyrics, my lungs work to a melody.

"First of all, your home is in London," Pete stares me down with such an intense look. I swallow down any thoughts of taking an extended break. I'm famous, I can't just put it all in a pissing box while I take a holiday, can I? The music industry is fickle, I can't guarantee that my fans will be waiting for me. I feel my lips pouting. My life is fucking tough. I crack my knuckles again, enjoying the slight squirming of my manager. "Long term the goal is to get you and possibly, Lexi back there. That would add to the story. You are visiting your dad and undergoing another course of rehabilitation. We'll run with that for now. Second –"

Fucking PMT casually slipped that one in, didn't he? "The fuck I am!" I shout.

What is this? I walked off stage and got the train up here to avoid pissing rehab. He's literally just said I can have six weeks off. Pete raises his palm to me then points at my chest with a poker straight finger.

"Yes, the fuck you are. It's a six-week course. No questions. And second, you are still my act. I own you, and Jordan. This is my livelihood too. I don't run my business just for fun. I have bills to pay as much as the next person."

I snort. If I owned at least four houses, a yacht and a private island in the Seychelles I know I'd struggle to pay the bills too. Yet he's right. The number of staff we have on the teams behind the scenes, it was unknown for me until we got signed. They're like shadows, without them I'd be burning myself out like the sun. We need them, I need them to make music, to be an artist, to be successful. The sharp stab of guilt judders my heart again. I walked out on stage, on my career with no consideration to anyone, not my mate, not the team behind the scenes: only myself. Selfish prick I am.

"A reconciliation with the first love will be perfect," Pete says.

"I don't know," I shrug, I don't want to commit to anything. Lexi didn't exactly welcome me with open arms. Or legs. Plus, she's just got fucking engaged.

"I saw the way she looked at you, buddy. She's still sweet on you," Pete winks.

I sit up straighter in my seat, the leather squeaking under my jeans.

"You reckon?" Maybe I've still got a chance after all.

"Definitely. You're Hayden Coulthard, you can make any current man run for the hills," he throws me an eye mask. Silk, oh it feels like heaven. "Now sleep. I'll wake you when we reach your dad's place, dude."

5

Pete drops me off outside my dad's house. "The rehabilitation. You're doing it, Hayden," he says. I'm surprised the enormous car fitted down the potholed street to be honest. He says he has to fly back to London, but hands me a file full of papers.

I look at the street I haven't seen for so long. One on side of the bumpy road, a row of terraced houses in groups of five or six, painted pastel colours like spring flowers – my dad's house a pale yellow like daffodils. They look out across the river. The water babbles over the rocks, racing under one bridge to the next, hurrying to escape the small town and venture out into the freedom of the sea. The rust red coloured walls separate the road and houses from the river. The walls are higher and more defined than I recall, though I guess after the two floods they had to be altered, if not rebuilt.

My dad is waiting with arms folded in the hall of my Cumbrian home; brand new laminate flooring, new striped stair carpet and showroom-esque tones of cream and grey (with navy blue accents, that interior designer I picked was worth every fucking penny) cover the walls. It still smells of burnt toast and shoe polish, making me feel instantly relaxed, and again, on the verge of comforting tears.

"Hi Dad!" I flash him a beaming grin as I reach forward to offer my clammy hand. He shakes it, dutifully. We're not exactly best mates or anything, anymore.

"Hayden, welcome back."

"Yeah, it's good to be back, to escape the madness of the city for a while. The house looks good." I look around, anything to avoid his eye. I know he was grateful for the financial help when the house flooded. Twice. But I also know he wanted me to come up and help him with it. My schedule didn't allow it though. The holiday I took to Monaco during the second flood wasn't a necessity, but Pete said at the time that Jordan and I deserved it. Dad didn't agree.

"Looks better than ever, actually," I hope he doesn't hear the slurring of my words. He tilts his head at me. I finally catch his grey eyes, the colour of storm clouds. I swallow and shuffle my feet nervously.

"Don't play the innocent with me, Son. I have spoken to your manager, and Jordan, at length. I know fine well why you're on this holiday. Or should I say rehabilitation?" Dad snatches the paperwork from my hand.

I gulp. Although I tower over my dad, his careful, level voice and the way his eyes stare into your soul – he is a terrifying man. He's got an even temper; he never raises his voice. Yet again, he never has to. I wish he would scream at me, tell me how much of a fucking screw up I am, but he won't. He never will. His face conveys the disappointment, no words needed. It's worse this way.

"Dad, I –"

"There's no alcohol in this house. I can't stop you buying it, or stealing it, if you've stooped to that level," he doesn't even raise his voice to speak over me, he ignores my attempt at an interruption completely. People usually stop in their tracks to listen to me, their own words lodged in their throat. But not my dad, he's not fazed by my stardom. I also don't think he has the first fucking clue as to my life. You can't teach old tricks to a dog, or some shit like that.

"I'm not an alcoholic. Why won't anyone fucking listen?" I mumble under my breath. The tang of lager lingering on my tongue.

"I hope that you're taking this seriously, Son, and will resist all temptation. I am aware that you have little to no money on your person. I am not going to give you any. You're here, in my house, eating my food, living by my rules. Do you understand?"

"Yes," I nod, feeling, as predicted, like I'm back to being a teenager. He'll ground me once he finds my wallet stuffed full of twenties from the box in my wardrobe in Camden.

"First thing tomorrow morning you have a rehab session. I'll drive you there myself," he speaks quietly, only a hint of his Scottish accent remaining.

I did not traipse all this way to be coerced into another fucking rehab centre. Dad's been in on this too, the fucking backstabber. I wander, not stagger, into the living room. I watch the river, overlooked by tall green grasses and trees touching the sky from the window.

"I was hoping to get back to my roots, do lots of songwriting, composing. Become inspired by the community, the landscape, to rediscover the town," I rattle off. It's a load of bollocks, I was literally wanting to hide out in my teenage bedroom until Pete and the world forgot about me.

"Rehab is the priority, Hayden. And that is final."

Enough of this shit, I think as I sit on my childhood bed. No Egyptian cotton or silk.

I need a fucking drink. I throw on my favourite Gucci boots and sneak out of the back door. Some things never change.

I'm going to the pub. I'm an adult, I am in charge of my own decisions, and no one can stop me. My favourite pub in Cockermouth – well, one of them – has remained the same since I left. I don't know why I'm surprised; this town doesn't change. Unless a raging river rips its soul out. Then these people are forced to rebuild, and start over. Then spend the rest of their days moaning about it, all the pissing time.

Posters advertising Guinness still peel from the tobacco-scented walls, the shamrock stained glass windows cast rainbow lights on the tall wooden bar, the pool table still has a rip in it. I chuckle as I recall the time Big Dave sunk seventeen pints of Guinness one St Patrick's Day. He was fighting fit the next day at school, but hasn't touched the stuff since, or he hadn't last time I saw him.

The landlord pours me a pint of the black stuff and two shots as soon as I perch my arse on a fraying rickety stool.

"Kid," he nods his bald head in greeting. He's been here, behind this bar since I first frequented this place. He must be fucking superglued to the carpet. I don't know his name, mind.

"Sir. Thanks very much," I raise my pint glass and take

a slow drink of the heavy malt liquid. Bliss. "How much do I owe you?" I ask as I make out to be searching my pockets for my wallet. I'm not of course, I know exactly where my wallet is; on my bedside table at my dad's. I'll keep the pockets full of notes for another day.

"Nothing at all, kid. On the house."

"Thanks sir. Very kind of you," I nod in appreciation, though expected the freebie.

I look around the half-empty bar. It's dotted with a middle-aged couple and a group of teenage boys, clearly all underage. Well, the pub didn't get its nickname 'The Creche' for nothing.

"Jordan, you'll never guess where the fuck I am!" I exclaim into the screen of my phone, as I record a video to send to him. "Actually, you will guess! It's still exactly the same!"

The pub becomes quite busy and lively as the night wears on; various people come and say hello. I haven't shaken this many hands since the band won an Ivor Novello award. I'm being bought drinks as quickly as I can drink them, not that I'm fucking complaining about that. My presence has alerted several teenage girls, who in turn throw me their attempts at seductive smiles from their huddle in the corner.

The landlord raises a toast in my name; the local superstar that I am. I stand atop the sticky bar, try not to cringe as stale beer splashes on my Gucci boots, and address my people. I should at least give them something, after all, this is the most excitement they'll get until the Victorian Fayre or whatever it is.

"It's so good to see you all, and to be back here. You've

all been so nice to me. You're such great people! That's why I'm here, you know? To raise awareness of all you great people. To give you all the recognition you deserve. I want my fans, and the wider audience to know where I come from. I want them to see what you've all done; how you've not let the floods break down the community, and more importantly, the community spirit. Cheers!"

Applause, I get a fucking round of applause! One man with a bulging belly actually wipes a tear from his face. Jesus. These people are pathetic.

I'm not denying that the floods were awful, I saw photos of my dad's house after the river ripped through the ground floor and up several stairs; but I mean, they've been and gone. Deal with it. It was only muddy fucking water.

I down my pint and I clamber off the bar. A young couple, clearly incomers with their head to toe sparkling brand-new outdoor attire, buy us all shots, and myself cheese and onion crisps. Bottoms fucking up! It is so fucking nice to have a few drinks without worrying about the fucking paparazzi building a scrapbook of my nights out for the next day's paper. We look after our own in Cockermouth, what stays in the pub happens in the pub, or something. Someone plays The Halcyon through the jukebox. I strum my air guitar and belt out the chorus, a gaggle of teens dressed up to the nines, swoon around me in a circle. They go from giggling to screaming at a rate of knots. I fucking love the reaction I create with my music. I miss it already. Did I make a mistake walking out? I don't have time to ponder, the room spins if I try to concentrate.

The doors open and a gush of fresh air follows in the

couple, hand in hand. The glass falls from my hand. Smashing like a shattered cymbal. All eyes turn to me, but I'm focused on the couple. Lexi and Callum.

Callum rolls his dark eyes as he looks in my direction. He has a frown etched on his largely unchanged features as I expected. Still built like he was made for the rugby field, with his triangle shaped torso and permanent serious face, dark eyes and dark hair. Skin that's tanned from weekend rugby matches with 'the lads'. Hair cropped short and still has a look of disgust to fire in my direction. Lex looks startled, like a deer in headlights. Her brown eyes wide and almost fearful. She throws me a wobbly smile before avoiding my eyes. Callum leading the way into the pub as the door closes behind them. Lexi, so unlike her teenage self, hiding in his shadow.

"Callum, mate," I say with a fake smile as I step over the broken glass and greet him. "Haven't seen you since school!" I extend a tattooed arm. He limply shakes it, not because he's weak, but to show me he couldn't care less about my presence. Callum and his scowl ignore me. I remember Pete saying how he thought Lexi was still into me, and feel my back straighten. I take a step away from Callum, who tuts and approaches the bar. Then lean down to kiss Lex again on the cheek.

"Nice to see you again, Lex." I say, and gently but obviously, and squeeze her shoulder.

She smiles tightly, looking at a place above my head. Maybe Pete was wrong; she can't even look at me.

"Don't mention the train," she whispers as she turns and steps away from Callum.

I raise an eyebrow at her. She hasn't told Callum. Interesting. "Please, Hayden, do this one thing for me,"

Lexi pleads with her eyes as well as tone. I mime zipping my lips like a fucking idiot. Lexi's hand hitches her handbag onto her shoulder. Still no sign of a sparkling ring. The breath catches in my throat as I see a tattooed wing poking out from her short-sleeved top. Instinctively my own hand goes to the top of my arm. She follows my hand, with her wide eyes. She glances quickly towards Callum leaning on the bar, then sighs.

"Yes, I know you covered yours up. No explanation needed," Lexi hisses like a cat, referring to the matching love bird tattoos we got the summer I turned eighteen.

It's not what you think, is what I want to say. *It wasn't my idea, I had no choice.* Instead, the whiskey dives in feet first.

"Yet you've still got yours," I smirk with an eyebrow raise. "Couldn't quite bear to get rid of me?"

I'm such a dick. No wonder she's still with Callum. I bet he wouldn't snipe at her like this.

"I figured the pain of laser removal would be too much. You already caused me enough."

"You broke up with me, Lex." I say quietly to her, so Callum doesn't hear. The harshness isn't lost, despite the whisper. She rolls her eyes, then joins Callum at the bar. Quite the habit she's building; leaving me standing alone in our hometown.

Another song blares from the jukebox. Obviously, it's another one of mine.

It shakes the unease from my brain. I look at the drink, which someone has handed to me, as I try and fail not to watch Lexi and Callum head to the pool table. In another life, that would be me holding her hand. Feeling the weight of her fingers wrapped around mine. Knowing after a few drinks we'd be going home, to our house. Our bed. *Fuck.* I down the drink in one gulp. Fuck knows what it was. Tastes like sour oranges.

The familiar riff and beat call to me, I need a stage, I need to be centre of attention. Drink does this to me; I either need to be performing or I want to run from it. I haven't decided which way is better for me. I climb back onto the bar and fucking own it. This will take my mind away from what ifs involving Lex. My legs seem to have a mind of their own as they kick out in directions I haven't told them about, and a few glasses topple to the floor. I grab a bottle of whiskey and start swigging it, oh sweet relief, in between the verses I've written.

"This one is for Lexi!" I shout out during Jordan's bridge. Not quite moving my thoughts away from Lex then, I realise. Lexi flushes red, matching her chilli red lips. Callum drains his drink before slamming the empty glass down and storms off. Out into the street.

I flash Lexi a smile. She must know this song was always about her. It's definitely one of the less angry ones from our debut album. Much more romantic and flowery. Much to my disbelief – I am after all, the one and only Hayden Coulthard from The Halcyon – Lexi follows Callum outside.

I kick out in frustration. A bowl of peanuts skitters off the bar and smashes into a row of glasses. Not my fucking fault, who still puts bar snacks out?

"This has gone too far! You need to leave!" The landlord shouts as he pulls the plug from the jukebox. The silence is followed by boos from the teenage girls.

"No, I don't!" I shout back, who does he think he is,

telling me what to do? "I'm Hayden Fucking Coulthard!" I can do what I fucking want!

To prove my point, I jump off the bar and pour myself a pint. I give my adoring female fans my whiskey bottle and encourage them to place their glossy, sticky lips around the rim and take a sip of the pure liquid.

"It's like we're kissing," I giggle at them with a cheeky wink. I swear one of them almost wets herself.

"I'm calling the police!" shouts the landlord. "You're not above the law are you, lad?"

"I'm Hayden Fucking Coulthard," I say to him firmly, merely stating my place in the social ranks. I am better than everyone here, and they know it. I don't know how it happened, but I seem to be on the floor, there's a wetness, almost sticky feeling on my head. My fingers come away from it red. Fuck knows what drink that is that's been spilled.

Two pairs of chunky arms help me up then encircle my body as I'm moved somewhere. My feet appear to be dragging. Oh no, they've stuck to the floor.

"My fucking Gucci boots!" I hear myself wail as the cold air of outside smacks me in the face.

My eyes are stuck together, I peel them apart, and everything is blurry. I have no idea where the hell I am. I think I can hear my dad.

I groan. I know I'm not in Camden. He doesn't come to visit anymore. Not since I told him about how my mother died. My head drops to my chest, the blackness clouding me again.

"I'll take him upstairs." That's my dad, for sure. I'd recognise that soft voice anywhere. What's he's on about?

"He's a deadweight, Jock," laughs an unfamiliar man in response.

"You two offering?" I hear my dad laughing.

"Aye, we'll take him, then we'll be off."

"Cheers. First door on the right. Is Michael pressing charges?" That's dad again, I love the Scottish lilt to his accent. It's not as strong as it used to be, but I can hear the Glaswegian dancing on his words. My feet stumble underneath me, those same arms around my waist and shoulders hoist me back up.

"No, don't worry, Jock. He can claim ont' insurance."

"The boy's name will be kept out of it." That's a different voice; it's close to my ear. I don't know why this person is talking to my dad, or what it's about. *Fuck,* stairs. Who put those there? I like the wallpaper, very stylish. Very Graham&Brown. I would have that in my own flat, actually.

"I'm Hayden Fucking Coulthard," I shout.

"Don't we know it, lad," the strange, unfamiliar voice replies.

6

I wake up with a start from a dreamless sleep and feel disorientated, not an unusual feeling. I blink and rub at my eyes. I expect to see the features of my Camden flat, or the white walls of a generic hotel room. My eyes land on my teenage posters, memories jumping back into my fuzzy head. It comes flooding back to me, like the river outside the window. Walking off stage. Lex. The pub. Lexi and Callum. How could I forget that I'm at my dad's in Cockermouth? I taste the tang of alcohol coating my mouth, perhaps that's my answer.

I hear my dad flush the toilet then shut his bedroom door. Not long after, I hear him snoring. I'm feeling quite comforted by the sounds I'd forgotten I knew: the pipes gurgling, the river rolling by outside, and the wind rustling the trees.

Yet, I need to get out. I want to see Lex. I need to see her. I grew up in this house. I've snuck out countless times. I know which stairs creak, where to step to avoid the security light outside, how to push the back door handle down so it doesn't click. I've fucking got this.

"Christ, I'm here," I hear Lexi hiss from behind the wooden front door of her flat. How did I know which flat is hers? My dad told me earlier. See, if I was an alcoholic, I wouldn't be able to retain that kind of knowledge, would I? Hayden Fucking Coulthard: not an alcoholic. Put a tick in that fucking box.

Lex bought the flat two doors down from her mum. I spent days, weeks, round there back in the day. I look towards the weeping willow tree that's swaying, with the wind or my whiskey vision, I can't be one hundred percent certain. The two of us spent hours in this shared garden as teens. Had sex under that tree. Walking here from my house came to me as easy as my name.

"Hayden?" Lexi asks, looking up from under her fringe at me. Fuck, she's beautiful.

"That's me. Hayden Fucking Coulthard!" I flash her a smile, hoping it won't take much to win her over.

"What are you doing here?" Lex asks, as her black dog sniffs around my feet. I keep still to avoid tripping over it.

"Lex, my Darling, come out for a drink," I try to wink, but the temporary loss of vision makes me stumble. I drop my cigarette and accidentally send an empty milk bottle flying.

"I'm not in the mood," she pouts as she wiggles her glasses over her nose.

"Had a row with Callum did you? Never mind Babe, I brought us a bottle. Let's see where the night takes us! The night is young!"

"It's half two, Hayden. You're not living it up in London now, everywhere closed at least two hours ago,"

Fuck me, where did that time go?

It used to take me only twelve minutes to walk to Lexi's

from my dad's. I could do it in eight if I ran. Five on my bike. Fourteen in my Mini, it was worth the extra time in the car; as once we could drive we snuck off everywhere to be together. And no one would walk in on us, like our parents who probably witnessed way too much of their teens' sex lives.

"Can I come in?" I ask, leaning against the wall, trying and failing to light another cigarette.

"For what purpose?"

"To help me drink this," I hold up the bottle of red wine. She always preferred red to white.

"I doubt you need help with that," Lexi sighs, rubbing her forehead under her fringe.

"To catch up then," I shrug. "It's been a while."

"We had four hours on a train together, earlier,"

"You wouldn't speak to me,"

"Perhaps I had nothing to say, especially now you're a high-flying celebrity and all that nonsense."

"Maybe I wanted to speak. *You* wouldn't listen."

"Well, whose fault is that?" Straight to the point is Lex. Always has been. It's not very often she's lost for words. My unlit cigarette hangs uselessly from my fingers.

"Yours," I state, my defences raised. The fucking cheek of her.

"You are the one who left," Lexi fires a flaming arrow towards me.

"You broke up with me," I deflect the flame with a shrug.

"I had my reasons," she says coolly, almost distantly. Her arms fold across her chest. A shield. The fire hits me straight in the heart, my walls crumble. Yes, she fucking did. Cheating on me. *I bet it was Callum.* I turn on my heels and stumble. My feet criss-crossing like busy knitting needles. Lexi steadies me with a grasp around my back. The weight rights me, comforts me instantly. She pulls the front door closed behind her as she steps out barefoot into the night. I stand up on my unstable legs.

"What were you playing at in the pub, the whole rock star performance?" Lex asks with a hushed hiss, confusion clouding her eyes behind her glasses. I shrug as I unscrew the wine.

Having fun. Enjoying myself. Performing. Escaping. Forgetting.

I take a swig of the wine and hold the bottle to Lexi. She takes a quick swig, the wine staining her lips purple. I'm reminded of us sharing wine, vodka, WKD, in the park each summer holiday. A smile tugs at my lips.

"Why did you dedicate a song to me, in front of Callum?" Lexi rephrases the question, mistaking my visit down memory lane as misunderstanding.

"Callum's a twat," I answer without engaging a filter. I despise the bloke. I mean, I don't know him that well, but I know fucking enough. Callum went to the same secondary as Lex and I, so we all mingled through our education. Very occasionally socialised together as teens at the discos and parties. Stick rammed up his arse, growing up in the perfect two-point-four family, living in one of the big houses up on the Moor. He always thought he was better than me. Liked to throw his weight around as top dog at school. Especially as I was the late incomer. The runt from Glasgow with only a dad for company, it was tough to fit in. Until I found music, obviously.

Callum always did have his sneaky eyes on my Lexi. He was just waiting for me to be away, then in he swooped like a falcon and took what was rightfully mine. Fucking pisses me off. Lexi can do so much better than him. I do not know what she sees in him.

"It was a nice gesture. Innocent," I shrug, flashing her another charming smile. She rolls her brown eyes. I'm perhaps not fooling her.

"Innocent? Do you think I'm stupid?"

"Alright. I wanted to piss him off."

"Why?" Lexi snorts with a shake of her head.

"You're dating him. I'm jealous," I say honestly. I see a flicker of confusion dance across Lexi's face, before she settles on exasperation. Though I see a twinkle in her eyes that definitely isn't from the streetlamp. I note she didn't correct me either, by telling me they're engaged. Pete must be right, she must still be into me.

"You're ridiculous, Hayden," Lexi half laughs into the night sky. The stars sparkling above us, the moon covered by a snug blanket of cloud. It's fucking freezing. It never gets this cold down in London.

"Ridiculous or romantic?" I wink.

"Ridiculous."

"A little bit romantic, don't you think? I did write *Without You Here* about you in the first place."

A sharp inhale from Lexi makes me momentarily think she doesn't realise I write everything about her. She can't be that naive. I must be hearing things.

"Can I come in then?"

"No. I'm not one of your groupies or fans falling for your every word. Go home."

"Scared you won't be able to resist me?" I lean an arm above my head, against Lexi's doorframe. I thread my fingers through the ends of her hair. The blonde looks alien, yet feels the same as her darker, natural locks against my calloused digits. As comforting as my guitar strings. My knuckles graze against her collarbones as I weave her hair through my fingers in a rhythm. "You never could turn down a late night visit," I say, another reference to our past relationship. My eyebrows raise as she fights a smile, and I lean down towards her. Her plump lips angle up to mine, we're fractions apart. I can smell the coconut fragrance floating from her skin.

"Alexis?"

Lexi jumps back into the flat, the door swinging open behind her. Callum, barely awake, appears topless in the light from the kitchen. The black dog wagging its tail at his feet. I straighten myself up. So fucking close. At least now I know I've got a fighting chance of getting her back.

"Hey!" I say, waving my wrist awkwardly. *Fuck, they live together? I don't know why I'm so surprised, they are engaged after all.*

"What the fuck, like?" Callum says in my direction, as he scrubs a hand over his short hair, mussed from sleep.

"Mate, I'm just leaving," I hold my hands up in surrender, realising Lexi has the wine bottle clutched to her chest, her cheeks flame almost the same colour as the red liquid inside. "Just wanted to apologise for earlier. I didn't mean to cause any issues."

"The only issue here is you," Callum sneers.

I plaster a smile on my face, grinding my back teeth together. *I could say the same about you.*

"I was just saying it was nice to spend time with Lex earlier, on the train," I say before I can think about it. Lexi's mouth drops open and she sighs.

"You were on the train together?"

"It was a coincidence," Lexi's words rush from her mouth.

"Fate," I correct.

"Fuck's sake," Lexi mumbles quietly. "Callum –"

"I'm going back to bed," he says, the scowl deeper on his face now. "I suggest, Alexis, that you do the same. Unless, there's something going on between you two?"

"I'll just be a minute."

"I'll be counting," Callum grits out. He turns and disappears back into the flat.

"He's got a bit of a complex about you," Lexi whispers with a roll of her bronze eyes. She steps back inside the flat, the door shielding half of her body. I gulp at the wine still in her hands.

"I don't blame him. Who can possibly follow in the footsteps of Hayden Fucking Coulthard, right?"

"Drop the jumped-up celebrity act, Hayden," Lex sighs. "It's not as endearing as you suspect. You ok getting back yourself?" She asks me, looking concerned.

"Course!" I dismiss her with a wave of my hand. "Goodnight, Lex. Can I still call you that or shall I call you by your full name?" I stick my tongue between my teeth. She always hated her full name, refused to respond to her mum or sister whenever they used it. I wonder how Callum gets away with it.

"Please, don't you ever call me that," Lexi says with a sigh and slight smile.

"Night, Lex," I say instead, and smile at her, hoping she can tell how wonderful it is to be able to see her again.

"Night, H," I hear Lexi say as the door clicks shut behind me.

7

My dad graces me with his presence at some fucking ungodly hour. I feel like I've only been asleep for minutes. And these sheets are so fucking scratchy, not a hint of Egyptian cotton or silk pillowcases.

A look of utter disgrace is etched on his grey bearded face, a steaming coffee in his hands. It will no doubt be pissing instant, not beans from the wild jacu bird that I get shipped over from Brazil. I cringe. It's easy to get used to luxury.

"No more arseing around, Hayden. Get yourself up and dressed. You're already late."

Rehab, in Cockermouth? Is he having a laugh? There isn't even a shopping centre or a fucking McDonalds.

"No can do, dad. I left my clothes in London." Yep, I may be an international pop star, but I'm also someone who packs their bag then leaves it on the fucking train. I've only got the clothes I arrived in with me, and the jeans are now ripped at the knees. Dad throws my jeans and one of his jumpers at me. As if I am going to wear that red cable knit. I'll look like a skinny Santa. I text Pete and ask him to get my clothes sent up, instead. Or organise someone to track down my suitcase. Thank fuck I remembered my guitar.

"I'm not wearing that," I snort. I ignore dad's stare as I message Pete. He snatches the phone from my hands. I'm not quick, or awake enough to put up a fight.

"I suggest you wear these, I don't think anyone wants to see you arrive at rehab naked, Son. You're an alcoholic, not a naturist," dad says gently. I can't tell if he's winding me up or not.

I beg to differ, actually. I've had several offers for a naked photoshoot over the years. I've turned them all down of course, I like to keep somethings private.

"I'm not going to rehab. I'm not a fucking alcoholic."

A gush of freezing cold water drenches my head, and chest, causing me to splutter.

"What the fuck?" I gasp as I watch dad place an empty glass on the bedside table.

"That'll count as a shower, now get dressed," dad says evenly.

"No!" I shout from under my soaked duvet, trying to wipe the coldness from my face.

"Right, then I'll phone up Pete, shall I, and tell him this isn't working. First plane to Arizona. Rehabilitation clinic here you come," he says calmly and slowly, in his slight Scottish accent. I roll my eyes as I sit up. Whatever. "And I'll tell the press about your real reason for being here. I'll tell them everything. None of this 'six week break for personal reasons, just a wee touch of exhaustion' nonsense." Dad finishes his threat. At least, I think it's a threat and not a promise. I flop back on the bed, the scent of stale alcohol clouding around me.

"You wouldn't fucking dare," I say towards my ceiling, stained with blu-tack and pin holes from my teenage posters.

"Can you afford to take that risk, Son?"

I groan. I know that dad wouldn't intentionally hurt me, but still. He's right. If I push him too far, I'm guessing he could be tempted to send me away. Or even worse, reveal all my secrets to anyone who walks past a newspaper. I'm not exactly being the model son right now. Actually, I've been a terrible son for years. But in my defence, he doesn't know how hard my life is. He's not fighting the monsters in my head. He'd be no fucking use anyway even if I told him. A cup of chai tea and an hour's fishing can solve everything for him. I shudder. Growing old is fucking horrifying.

So here I am, freshly showered and wearing a Marks and Spencer jumper along with my slightly sticky jeans – as if I was going to wear my dad's chinos. My poor Gucci boots are now battered and scuffed to high hell. I ignore them as best I can, as we stand outside what looks like a very exclusive dog kennels. I can hear various barks and whimpers. What the fuck is this place?

Dad joins me and pushes me gently towards the front door.

"I don't want to do this," I confess. I'm his only child, perhaps he'll just scoop me up and take me home. We can watch Die Hard and eat popcorn like we did at the weekends before I left for London. Dad looks at me and shrugs, he rubs a hand through his beard.

"What, you can walk off stage, make your own way here from London in relative anonymity, get black out pissed in my local, but you can't open a door? Don't talk daft, Hayden."

"I can open the fucking door!" I snap at him, as I instinctively crack my knuckles.

"I bet you can't even give your name at the desk," dad whispers tauntingly as the door closes gently behind us.

"Watch me!" I swagger to the desk, I'm totally owning this jumper by the way. Maybe Prada's new season of knitwear needs checking out when I get back.

"Hayden Coulthard, apparently I'm meant to be here?" I say to the man on the desk.

A glaring sign with the phrase 'Paws2Heal' graces the wall behind him in purple lights. Flanked by photos of dogs with smiling people in the same purple coloured shirts, the tagline description boast of being Cumbria's Canine Therapy Centre. I snort. Canine therapy? Whatever next? Have they been trained to record innermost conversations with their little doggy paws? This world is fucking mad.

The man behind the desk shuffles papers and stands up awkwardly, his knees bumping on the desk as his tea spills over the rim of his mug. Of course it's got a fucking dog on it.

"It might be under my other name?" I clarify. The rotund man's fidgeting is making me feel awkward for him. Privacy and all that, Pete insisted on names for Jordan and me. I needed one I could always remember, so it sounds fucking fake anyway. "Mr Hyde?" I suggest. I picked the name from my favourite book: I'd never forget that. I begged Jordan to be Dr Jekyll, but he wasn't having it.

"Oh! Right, sure! Hayden Coulthard! Oh you're the

client! You're a little late, but we can still book you in now. I'll just go and tell the boss you're here. Sign these forms please," he says hurriedly, like he's going to run out of breath before pushing open double doors. "I'm a big fan by the way!"

I turn to smile smugly at my dad, when I realise he's already left me.

Fuck. No going back now, I guess.

A blonde bouncy woman – she reminds me of a puppy herself, all energetic and rather full on – greets me with the strongest handshake I've ever encountered.

"Hi there, I'm Kimberley. Lexi will be out in a minute."

Lexi? No, no, surely not.

"Sorry, Darling, who?" I ask, flashing her a smile. She giggles a little. Cute.

"The boss, Lexi Blackwood. Paws2Heal is her business, she's very passionate about the canine therapy aspect of our work. You'll love her, she's tough but amazing! Lydia, our in-house therapist will lead your one-to-one counselling sessions. You've signed up to our intensive programme; you'll also have additional sessions with Lexi and your therapy dog. Lexi's sessions will be more relaxed, and focused on a relationship between man and dog than any issues you may discuss with Lydia."

My head is fucking spinning. That's a fuck ton of information to get in a matter of seconds. It basically sounds like it really is just talking to dogs. And Lex is not only the boss, but is running my sessions with said dogs. Well, this ought to be a fucking doddle. Bring it on.

"No guys, I'm sick of that man and he's been back less than

twenty-four hours. I'm fed up of him and his rock star ways, parading around like he's still on a stage and we all have to watch his every move," I hear the familiar snap of Lexi in a temper drift out from a door behind the reception desk. The door swings behind Lexi, who flushes as red as my jumper. The dog, Mavis, I think she is called, instantly runs towards me. Her paws scramble on my legs, pink tongue panting at me. I feel a smirk erupt over my face. I wink at Lexi as her mouth gapes like a fish.

For a moment, I cannot recall why we aren't together. The force of being in love with this woman hits me like a spotlight in the face; it's the only thing I can focus on. I knew deep down that I loved Lex. That I'd never got over us, that we had shit tons of unfinished business. But love? I never realised that I was still in love with her, not just loved her.

You never get over that first love and that shite people say. I took it all with a pinch of salt and a line of coke. At nineteen, living our lives in studios and serviced apartments in London; I fought against feelings. Took full advantage of them as a tool for songs, but largely played on them to produce the angst and honesty in our debut album.

"Mr Coulthard," Kimberley says, fighting back a smile, as she bounces on the balls of her feet. I see her distinctly not looking at her boss. "This is Lexi Blackwood. She'll be leading your canine therapy sessions. Lexi, this is Hayden. Coulthard. Your next client."

"Sorry I'm late, I didn't wanna come," I shrug.

Well, at least I'm honest.

8

“This is your job, Lex?” I ask her with a scoff as we follow the path towards the kennels. Our legs skimming past hydrangeas, geraniums and clematis flowers that sway in the breeze as we pass them. Their heady scent mixing with the lavender and mint from the front of the building and providing a calming, comforting environment. I imagine that’s the suggestion, anyway.

Lexi had always wanted to be a vet. She secured a place to study veterinary science down in London, the same year Jordan and I moved there. She dropped out. I assume it was something to do with me. Or fucking Callum. Literally.

“Obviously,” Lexi snaps out, not turning to face me. "Us normal folks don't make a living being a performing monkey for the masses like you.”

“What happened to becoming a vet?”

“Things change,” she finally turns to look at me, her eyes dancing everywhere but meeting my own. “Wait there. Please.”

I watch Lexi squeeze through a small creak of the open door, quite enjoying how the fabric of her leggings stretches tight over her arse. I look through the glass panelled door and my mouth falls in horror at the size of the dog that jumps up at Lex. She ruffles the giant dogs' ears and jowls before encouraging it back down on all fours. I shudder as I watch a pink tongue leave a slobbery stripe on Lexi's hand.

"Come in then, take a seat on the cushions."

"No, thanks," I shake my head. I will never look at a bottle of whiskey again if it means I can avoid that ginormous dog slobbering all over me. My Gucci boots will be fucking destroyed.

"Hayden," Lexi sighs, her eyes closed in frustration, I think. "She won't bite. Unless I ask her to." A glint dances in her eyes as she laughs quietly at me.

"Don't make jokes like that! It could kill me! How are you so calm?" I realise my voice has jumped up an octave or two in sheer panic.

"Come on, I promise, Anoushka won't hurt you."

I hesitantly take a step inside. Lexi and the monster on four legs, complete with slobber pooling on the floor, are sat on checked green cushions. I really will look like Santa perched on them.

"If you'd like to sit down, so you're more at Anoushka's level, please. She may feel intimidated by your height," Lexi says soothingly, like I'm a client, patient, whatever. Not her ex. Not someone she used to love. Might still love, my heart suggests hopefully.

"She might be intimidated?" I gasp out.

"Sit down, H, don't be a wuss."

I sigh and plop on the cushions, feeling my body deflating like a forgotten balloon, legs sprawling across the floor, like a marionette with cut strings.

“I’m sorry if I caused grief for you with Callum, last night,” I offer, to see if I can crack through Lexi’s professional face. Her hand falters over the head of the horse-like dog for a second, before she allows her eyes to dart to mine.

“We were thrown off guard. I wasn’t expecting to see you in the pub, especially not doing the whole rock star thing.”

“I’m entitled be here you know,” I say, cracking my knuckles and ignoring how her use of ‘we’ cuts my heart. “It’s my home too.”

“What, Cockermouth? The place you grew up in physically but not mentally, because who can realistically function in the real, wider world if you grow up surrounded by lakes and mountains, and not much else? Hidden from the horror and reality of metropolitan life?” Lexi retorts, quoting one of my earlier, more pretentious interviews.

“Someone reads all my interviews then,” I wink at her.

“It’s hard not to sometimes, your face is plastered on every magazine and TV channel going,” Lexi snaps out, then soothes the dog who barked twice, loudly. I nearly jump out of my fucking skin. This dog is as loud a fucking foghorn.

“So, this is Anoushka. She’s a St Bernard. She’s one of our senior dogs, yet still very energetic.”

“Canine therapy Lex, really?” I raise a dark eyebrow, the scar from a skateboard accident above it, pale like a sliver of frost. I see Lexi looking at it, remembering the moment like it was yesterday.

“It’s not a new concept. There’s such places the world

over, that have been running for nearly fifty years. With very successful results. It started out in care homes, and has been transferred into schools, hospitals, prisons and now to assist with recovery for addictions and mental health problems. Dogs are a huge aid in lots of situations to such a variety of people. And horses actually, equine therapy is fascinating. I went on a course –"

I can't stop smiling at Lexi; she blushes under my gaze. I shuffle towards the fluffy mound in the centre of the cushions. My legs folding under myself like elastic. I reach out to tentatively stroke Anoushka's broad back. She feels strong, but also candy floss soft.

"I'd forgotten how passionate you can be about stuff," I say to Lex. "You always loved dogs. Remember your dog walking business? We ran out of school at lunch to walk several of them round the block!"

"You scuppered that business if I remember correctly," Lexi says, her shoulders relaxing at the ease of our old ways.

"My school shoes were soaked, trousers ruined, my dad banned me from helping you. It's not my fault you couldn't manage to walk all those dogs by yourself!"

"Even now, I think single-handedly attempting to walk eleven dogs is asking too much!"

"Your mum still got Rex?" I ask. I loved that dog of her mum's; he used to follow me everywhere in their flat.

"No, we lost him a few years ago. Mam didn't get another after Rex. She got me Mavis though."

Lexi flicks through sheaves of paper on a clipboard. I shudder. *Oh fuck*, it will be an endless stream of my misdemeanours and mistakes over the years. I crack my knuckles to relieve the tension.

"So, with our in-house counsellor, Lydia, you'll be working through the issues surrounding your alcoholism, and I'll sort out someone to run the canine therapy with Anoushka. You two seem a good fit, but if you're not comfortable with her size, I've got a Maltese we can try," Lexi states, not looking at me. Her bronze eyes skimming my notes. She is gonna be so pissed off about the GBH charge, that Pete paid me out of. And if she finds out about my mum's death, fuck, I don't know what I'll say. I wait, holding my breath for her to ask. It doesn't come.

Perhaps Callum is indeed, a good catch after reading the truth about me.

"She's fine."

"In relation to the dependency on alcohol –" Lexi continues.

"I like a drink, Lex. I'm not an alcoholic," I blurt out. Anoushka lets out a solitary deep woof. I startle, I'll never get used to that. She's as loud as fans at my shows. Sort of.

"How much have you drunk this morning? In fact, that's not important, you're probably still drunk from last night," Lexi shrugs.

I laugh, bitterly.

"Whiskey tastes nice. I like it," I say leaning closer to her, Anoushka's brown and white mass between us.

"I like cheesecake; I don't have it for breakfast." Lexi snaps quietly, her body mirroring mine.

"If I brought you a cheesecake round at like eight o'clock you'd fucking eat it," I say, my lip curled in defiance, but my eyes dancing from hers to her lips. Wanting to kiss her.

"I have my breakfast at like six am," Lexi chides back.

I cheer inside, as her eyes stay on my mouth for a fraction too long to be innocent. I watch her swallow. I lean myself across Anoushka, Lexi stays where she is, the distance between our lips just fractional. Lexi clears her throat and leans back, her hands on the ground. All eye contact gone. *Again, so fucking close.*

"With the canine therapy, I think Noel can take over from myself," Lexi says, addressing my left shoulder.

"I thought it was you, leading this?" I ask. I can feel my hands start to shake. I'm actually fucking scared about this whole therapy shit.

"Keep stroking Anoushka, the action is soothing, calming."

I do as Lexi says, and look to her for approval. She smiles. I try my hardest to ignore the fireworks bursting in my heart from her smile and eye contact. Maybe she won't be rushed. We're not teenagers anymore, it's not all jump into bed at the first moment we're alone, like it used to be. Clothes ripping in haste to shed them and –

"I hardly think it's appropriate for me to be your therapist. We're –"

What am I to you, Lexi?

"Please Lex. You know me better than anyone," I actually place my hands together as if in a church and beg. Pathetic.

"I'll do the first one and take it from there. Come on, let's get you signed up inside with Lydia. Anoushka will sit with you in the sessions, after the first one. That is, if she's settled. And you, of course," Lexi says, a small smile fighting its way through her professional mask.

"How long do I get with you each time?" I ask with a

cheeky smirk. Sexual memories of the two of us jumping into my head like popcorn in a pan. Snatched moments of kisses and touches. Half undone clothes, jeans round ankles.

"That depends on how things go. I'm flexible," Lexi shrugs innocently.

"I remember," I wink at her, as she clambers to her feet, clearing her throat and no doubt hoping I don't notice the embarrassment flushing on her cheeks.

9

I follow both Lexi and Anoushka the giant dog to meet my counsellor, Lydia.

I look at Lexi's exposed neck. Her hair swept up in a messy bun. I feel a stab in the heart as I realise she hasn't got on the necklace I bought her for her fifteenth birthday. The one she swore she'd never take off, hanging over her heart. Well, what did I fucking expect? My heart plummets to my toes. Of course, Lexi's moved on. Just pathetic little me stuck in the fucking past.

Lydia, it transpires, is a terrifying woman who incidentally is built like a cart horse. I'm well over six foot, but I feel like a fucking garden gnome next to her. Lexi hands over the clipboard to the woman who makes Anoushka look like a small cat. All my darkest secrets and scandals printed for them to examine.

"Hayden, a pleasure to meet you," Lydia smiles. I shake her shovel like hand and gulp.

Lydia waggles a finger at myself then Lexi, a smile on her face, making her seem one hundred percent more approachable. "I've heard that you two are –"

– Destined to be together. Lexi's the love of my life, the one I never got over. The one I never wanted to get over. She inspires my lyrics, notes dance off the page and form that face in my mind.

I haven't come back to Cumbria since I left, aside from my dad's fiftieth birthday, because it reminds me of Lex so much it pains me. And all I ever wanted was Lexi. We're meant to be. *Please, Lex, tell me you feel it too.*

Fuck. Where did that come from? My subconscious is having a pissing field day today. It must be the alcohol surrounding my clarity like low-lying mist in the autumn mornings.

"Old mates, aren't we Lex?" I chuckle half-heartedly. Lexi wiggles her glasses over her nose, as a flush creeps up from her neck towards her ears. She grimaces, I imagine she was hoping for a smile, but it's definitely not. I watch with longing as she walks away, she doesn't even glance back.

Lydia has me sat on a wee chair while she perches on what I can only describe as throne, looking down on me over her glasses. I have flashbacks to being scared witless as a child by Miss Trunchbull in Matilda. I shudder just thinking about that book. If there was ever a time I wanted to plunge myself in a bathtub of whiskey, now would be it. It is hell.

Luckily, we don't have Anoushka, the horse in disguise as a dog, with us. I'm certainly not one to shy away from anything new, but rehab with dogs – are you having a fucking laugh?

Lydia's office is in like a glorified summer house, or shed. It's built from strong-smelling wood, practically held up by rows and rows of dogeared books and boxes. The grey metal filing cabinet in the corner is disguised by trailing leaves of green plants, growing down and towering tall against the sides. The windows to the back of the room look out towards the kennels and grounds. I can see dogs of various sizes chasing balls and running free in the close-shorn grass. There are plants on every available surface, making me feel like I'm in either a jungle or a garden centre. Dad would fucking love it.

"I'm Lydia, Hayden, I've been a therapist for –"

"Lydia, I am not an alcoholic, I just want to get that straight," I cut her off with a raised palm, admiring my latest Gucci rings sparkling in the light as I do so.

"Do you feel you have any issues surrounding alcohol?" She asks. I ignore her knowing smile.

"I like a drink," I shrug. "It helps."

"Helps with what?" Lydia asks, her head tilting to the side, inquisitively.

"Helps me get through the day. Clears my mind. I'm a creative soul, Lydia. My mind is constantly on the go. Filled to bursting with lyrics, melodies, plans for stages, music videos. You know, the alcohol enables me to unwind, to silence my busy head for a while," I sound quite poetic in my ramblings, I wonder if she'll fall for it?

Lydia scribbles in a notebook. She could sell that for a fair whack. Maybe I could get a copy for my autobiography. I might write it, now I'm not touring. It's just like a long extended song, can't be too hard.

"That's interesting, Hayden."

Yep, she's falling for my tale: hook, line and fucking sinker. This rehab will be a piece of piss.

"So, a day without alcohol – what would that be like, Hayden?" Lydia asks me. The smile slips from my face, when was the last time I had a full day without a drink? It was a while ago, I guess. I probably couldn't recall the date, if we're trying to be that specific. But so what? It doesn't mean anything, it certainly doesn't make me a fucking alcoholic. It just means I like a drink, that I have a high tolerance for whiskey. I can still do my job, in fact I can usually do it better after a drink or two.

"I dunno," I shrug and sniff. Lydia looks at me, expecting a better answer. I have nothing. I crack my knuckles, it doesn't calm me.

"So you drink every day, Hayden? As soon as you wake up?"

I snort, I see what she's doing, trying to put words in my mouth. She's like the fucking press. Twisting whatever snippet I say into a full blown drama or confession.

"Not as soon as I fucking wake up, no. I have a drink after my breakfast, usually," I don't add that my breakfast is often a protein shake or a black coffee with a shot of whiskey in.

"Ok," she says. I watch Lydia's hand jot it all down. Stillness fills the air, rushes into my ears. I feel like I should fill it. My life is never this quiet.

"If I don't have a drink, they –" I stop myself. I'm gonna sound like a fucking nutter. They'll lock me up. Please, subconscious, please shut the fuck up.

"What will happen?" Despite her harsh exterior, Lydia is sweet. She has a voice like a hand knit scarf, soothing and relaxing. I've only been here a few minutes and I feel like she cares for me. I haven't felt that way for so long. Dad tries, but his face is always wearing a mask of disappointment. I sigh and scrunch my eyes closed.

"I get like, bogged down with stuff. Not like the music shite I told you before," I sigh and take a big breath. "My head is fucking full."

"Life is very stressful. I can't imagine the things that you deal with every day," Lydia smiles gently. I feel my shoulders relax as I lean back into the squashed cushions. I nod. Finally, someone ready to listen. Maybe this time it could work, I could be honest with a therapist. Lydia is by far the best one yet.

"When did you realise you were drinking more? More than usual, Hayden?"

I shrug. I know the answer, of course I fucking do. I know when life started to become a bother for me. I can recall the exact date when I started needing an extra drink or three to drown out my thoughts. That doesn't make me a fucking alcoholic.

"Maybe two years ago," I reply eventually. Guarded. I might feel cared for, but I still don't know if I want to trust Lydia with all my secrets and truths. Pete has hammered it into me that I can't trust anyone. People always want something in return. I lean forward, my elbows resting on my legs. I look up through my messy curls to Lydia on her throne, already hating that I want approval from this almost stranger.

"That's good that you can pinpoint it. Hayden, can I ask do you drink the same amount now as you did then, two years ago?" Lydia smiles, she doesn't force anything from me. Her silence isn't weighted with expectation. I must learn to trust the quiet. To not try and fill it with noise. I shake my head in response.

“I do drink a bit more now, if I’m honest.” A bit. A bottle more. Perhaps sometimes two. Who’s fucking counting?

I can hear the sound of dogs barking happily, and the odd lilt of voices floats through the windows. I wonder what Lexi is doing while I'm trapped in here. I'm determined not to fill the silence, I'll wait for Lydia to speak before I reveal anything else about myself, or indeed my drinking habits. I crack my knuckles, then tap out a rhythm with my palms onto my thighs. I will not break first. This is Lydia's domain, if she wants me to jump through hoops, she's gotta lead me to them. Not that I want to tell her anything else.

“Did this coincide with your mother’s death, Hayden?”

I fold my arms across my chest and lean back in the chair. Lydia snuck that right fucking in there didn’t she? Trying to make me feel calm and loved. Safe and protected, like she’d actually listen to me. Like she would trust the words from my actual mouth instead of believing whatever nonsense is in the papers and glossy magazines. Then boom, she blows the whole thing out of the fucking water with a sawn-off fucking shot gun.

“Just when I was starting to like you, Lydia,” I respond, the words spitting out of my gritted teeth. “You fuck it up by mentioning my mum. I thought you were better than that.”

“I’m sorry, Hayden. If you don’t feel ready to address your mother’s death –”

“I’m not ready? She’s dead. I saw her in the morgue with my own eyes. Watched her wooden coffin slide behind the velvet curtains. I collected the pathetic little box thing with her ashes in it. I think, Lydia, that I've accepted she's dead."

The breath pants out of me like I've just attended an all-night rave whilst high on acid. That is an experience neither Jordan nor I want to repeat. My heart is stomping in my chest. My feet, in their Gucci sleeping bags, jiggle up and down. I start scratching my thighs through my jeans. I want a drink. My thigh burns where my etched hip flask is usually nestled. The room swirls around my eyes, visions of my mum peek out from the bookshelves. I gag a little, the scent of the hospital morgue – antiseptic and metallic tangs – tap dance on my tongue.

"Hayden, can you name me five things you can see?" Lydia asks, her concerned eyes boring into mine.

"What?" I roll my eyes under a frown, my head falling to my hands, my fingers pushing and pulling at my skin. "You, books, the window, door, that plant."

"Good work, Hayden. What about four things you can feel?"

I look up at her, she's smiling gently. She's not furiously cross at me for purposefully disagreeing with everything she said, like the very first therapist that I was sent to. It wasn't entirely my fault. I didn't want to be there, and I was still high on lines of coke, so I thought the whole thing was fucking hilarious. I was making the best of a bad situation. Nor is Lydia crying and claiming that she's not cut out for the job, like the most recent therapist Pete palmed me off to. I do feel a little guilty about her, now she's popped back into my head. I flat out refused to say anything, or even acknowledge her presence, or indeed my own existence. I almost convinced her that I was a figment of her own imagination. But you know, not my fault. I was just making sure her very first client was one she'd never forget. I look back at Lydia. She holds up four fingers for me to count, as if I'm a fucking child.

"My jeans, the breeze from that freezing fan, these cushions, this jumper. It's not mine, it's my dad's by the way."

"Tell me three things you can hear," Lydia continues, smiling, probably eyeing up the jumper. Bad idea, red would not be her colour.

"Dogs, cars, birds." It's a world away from what usually filters into my ear drums: screams, instruments being tuned, cameras clicking, backing tracks repeated, the overlapping of Jordan and our team.

"Very good. Two things you can smell."

"Coconuts," I say instantly, as I focus on two fingers encased in golden rings Lydia is holding aloft, like a fucking sacrificial lamb. Lex isn't even in the fucking room, so fuck knows why I said that first. "Fresh air."

"Tell me one thing you can taste."

"Polos."

"Good, very well done, Hayden," Lydia smiles as she places her hands on her lap. "How are you feeling?"

I pick at the midnight blue nail varnish before cracking my knuckles. I exhale, my breath feels steadier. I feel more grounded. More present. I nod. I still want a fucking drink, though.

"No one knows," I sniff. "About my mother," I wipe my eyes with the heels of my hands.

"Sorry, no one knows what Hayden?" Lydia asks, her pen scratching again on her notebook, engraving it with my personal, secret information.

"About how my mum died."

"No one?"

"My dad and manager know," I shrug. The fans, the press, Jordan – they don't know. That's what matters. And Pete, well he knows fucking everything. But he was a friend to me more than a manager during that time, and kept a lot out of the papers. For my sake.

"Was that your choice not to tell anyone else?" Lydia questions.

"I didn't want a big fuss about it. She isn't," I clear my throat. "She wasn't a great mum. Not a good person really." I just wanted to deal with it and lock it the fuck away. Quickly, before it was splashed over the internet, before she became a topic up for discussion. It was my way of having a little piece of privacy. Pete issued a statement; saying it was a death of natural causes after a long illness. The usual stuff that brings in sympathy and privacy. '*Pop star behind his mother's death*' isn't exactly the thing to keep the fans onside. Pete felt it wouldn't help with the record sales. '*Hayden Fucking Coulthard kills his mother in his penthouse*' doesn't exactly sell tickets. I got his point.

"I'm sure she had some good qualities," Lydia says. I snort. I swipe the tears from my eyes as soon as they start running down my cheeks. It pisses me right off that I still cry about her.

"Tell me, Hayden, how did she die? What do I not know?" Lydia asks gently, tapping her fingers on my files nestled on her lap.

"Can we fucking stop? Please?" I ask the woman on her throne. I can't take any more of this shit right now. "This is like, strictly confidential, right?"

Lydia scribbles on her clipboard. She passes me a box

of crisp white tissues. I take a few and loudly blow my nose. Attractive.

“Absolutely, Hayden. Not even Lexi or any of the Paws2Heal workers have access to my files, unless it’s an emergency,” Lydia smiles, I kind of forgive her for bringing up my mother. I guess it is her job. I nod. Good.

“Next time would you like Anoushka in with us?” Lydia asks.

“I dunno,” I shrug. I don’t really see the point. What difference will a dog make? Will I have to throw it a fucking bone every now and then?

“Let’s try it, and see how things feel with her here,” Lydia smiles, almost knowingly.

“Sure, bring it on.” I say, defeat pounding in my veins.

10

I watch the river from over one of the many, many bridges Cockermouth boasts. The current rolls like a snare drum, constant, murmuring. The water bubbles over the rocks and stones, and the stray rusted shopping trolley. The sound is quite soothing, the visual making me feel a little dizzy as the water carries my thoughts with it. I feel like I could topple in and be carried away quite easily.

I shudder again as a recurring image of my mother appears and is washed under the curved bridge. Her curled hair the colour of straw and wide, empty eyes that haunt my nightmares. Floating by as if she belongs there. Just like the floods that burst the banks, my mother's face with hair exactly like mine but blonde, shatters the life I've built around me: the fans, the music, the money and bottles of gin that usually surround my life on stage. Akin to the wild waters, her image haunts me, breaking out from being trapped beneath the bridge of my professional career. I scratch at my face with my fingertips, anything to try and snap me out of it.

I breathe out and stand up, turn to face the sky like I would do in London. My eyes chase a small bird as it flutters from branch to branch, singing as it goes. I smile. Usually I trace the overhead wires or aeroplanes through the sky. Things are more natural here.

My phone rings. Pete. Back to my cage I go.

"Hayden, man! How are things going in your quaint little hometown?"

Shit. Lexi's still with Callum and resisting my advances. My dad is barely speaking to me, and my therapist has made me sob uncontrollably for forty fucking minutes.

"Quiet," I reply out loud.

"Great," Pete laughs, I can hear pounding music in the background. "We're just at the studio, laying down the tracks ready for your vocals."

"You're working without me?" I ask, pissed to find I'm hurt. How can they actually produce decent songs without me there? I'm a much stronger musician than Jordan. It might sound cruel, but that's show business.

"Man, we cannot sit around waiting for you! This is for you, Hayden; we're making the transition back into The Halcyon easier for you."

Of course they can't wait. But still, it's *my* band. My songs have always done better in the charts, they get a better response from a live crowd than Jordan's. It's just the way it is. The way it's always been. Why are they fucking with a well-oiled machine?

"Jordan has really got his spark back. Seeing how you nearly blew it for you both; it's been a blessing in disguise from the musical gods. It's ignited his passion for it again, he's been writing non-stop," Pete says down the line. I can hear his smile. He's proud, I bet Jordan's fucking preening like a spoilt pedigree cat.

"But I write the lyrics," I whine like a child. "I'm the better lyricist."

Aren't I? Even Jordan says that. *'Words are his bag,'* Jordan repeats in all interviews.

"This is a new direction that you have led us to take, man," Pete says, his accent as smooth as silk. "We're just trying a few things out. Experimenting, as it were. And the sooner you get yourself sorted, the quicker you can join us, man." The echoing pop of champagne and the high tinkle of glasses toasting cascades down the line. My mouth waters. "I've lined up a few gigs, very small, intimate. We're going for an anonymous release with the next single. Of course, everyone will know it's you with that distinctive gravel in your tone," Pete tells me. So I'm allowed to fucking sing these songs I have nothing to do with, how fucking polite. "No one else can sing like you, Hayden. You've got that raw talent and emotion that can't be trained."

I run my fingers through my spiralled hair. Flattery will indeed get you everywhere. I stand taller on the bridge, it's nice to feel admired.

"I'll have the demos sent to you, man," Pete says.

"Thanks, I guess," I mumble out. This break is going to be over way before I'm ready for it. It's not like I can really enjoy or embrace it when I'm at fucking rehab most days.

"Though to be honest man, Jordan's vocals sound on point!" Pete muses. "We might go for shared leads this time around. Really shake things up."

What the fuck? If they can make the damn songs without me, what's the fucking point of me even going back to fucking London?

"Sending the demos up to you as we speak man, let me know your thoughts. Jordan thinks they're the best songs we've done for years."

I bet he fucking does. I turn my phone off and start the walk back to my teenage bedroom, envy filling my pores.

***

My feet hang off the end of my bed. Downsizing from a super king to a single is a slight culture shock. I've smoked a full packet of fags, and drank one bottle of whiskey that I nicked from the off license. I am bored.

So fucking bored that I want to walk Anoushka. But without the therapy. Dad is out at work. Lexi is at Paws2Heal, and probably wouldn't answer me even if I phoned her.

I pull the photo albums off the shelf. I can't stop thinking of this summer dress Lex used to have. It was white with little blue flowers on. It was her favourite thing to wear, when we weren't floating lazily down the river on old tyres.

A photo of my dad jumps out at me. He's in a brown corduroy suit with a paisley shirt underneath, I chuckle, that must be where I get my distinct fashion taste from. He's beaming, ear to ear, clean shaven and dark brown hair. A look I can't recall ever witnessing. Yet there I am, chubby hand clutching his. My mop of curls hanging low over my eyes. My beloved elephant toy in my other hand. I've still got that teddy somewhere, probably shoved under the bed upstairs.

I turn the page, and my mother's face smiles up at me.

"Fuck!" I drop the album in shock. There she is. Blonde

curls skimming her shoulders, like my chestnut ones do now. A simple cream dress, satin heels and a short veil pushed back from her face. Fingers curled round an empty wine glass.

The last time I saw her, she looked asleep. At peace. Almost smiling. If only I had that image come visit me at night, instead of the one that always appears. Why my brain conjures up the worst memories is a mystery. One I hope I can solve and tell to fuck off.

Fuck this. I shove my feet back in my trainers and grab my dad's credit card from his not-so-secret -hiding place behind the golden clock on the mantel.

After picking up bottles of spirits, polos, and cheese and onion crisps from Sainsbury's – followed by a quick scout for the local talent, resulting in the company of two skinny women with nothing better to do than well, me – the party can begin back at my teenage home. Nirvana blares from the stereo. Whiskey burns my throat, and my fingers keep failing to light the cigarette hanging from my lips. Two girls, who I think I met in the supermarket, or perhaps in the pub are dancing round the living room. Who says you can't dance naked at half fucking one during weekdays? Hang on, naked?

"Follow me ladies," I say smoothly, I assume, as they titter behind me. I lead them into my teenage bedroom. Not quite as impressive as my Camden flat, I must confess. Yet I doubt they're here for the interior design. Smirk.

One of the girls, I can't even pretend to know their names, starts tugging at my jumper. It's Gucci thank fuck, not my dad's M&S one. My suitcase arrived safe and sound, and Pete added a few extra pieces from Prada's next season too. Divine.

I ease her hands off.

"Give me a sec, Sweetheart," I say as I bend down, and stick my arms under my pine bed.

I'm on my knees, head in the cavernous space beneath my bed. I pull out old notebooks, socks, a few books, some vinyl singles, and at last, my elephant teddy. Pale blue he is, so pale and worn in places that he's almost white. Patches of his ears are threadbare. I hug him to my chest. "My dad bought me this when I was born, y'know?"

I see the girls exchange glances, before they start attempting to clutch hold of my clothes. It's a team effort, one on the hem of my jumper, the other fiddling with my belt.

I ignore them both as my glazed eyes fix on my mirror; photos line the edge. There it is, Lexi in that white and blue floral dress. The sunlight behind framing her head like a halo. Her jet-black hair looking almost petrol coloured in the light. Her brown eyes the exact colour of Galaxy chocolate (I checked one day at school) smiling at the camera, her petite nose scrunched up in laughter, all her teeth on show as if they're sunbathing. Perfectly beautiful. Innocently in love. I wonder if my dad ever felt this way about mum?

"Are you ok, like?" A screechy voice coming from one of the girls, infiltrates my thoughts, I realise that the storm clouds have blocked out the light. I no longer feel like the invincible Hayden Fucking Coulthard I've been for years, nor do I feel safe in my teenage bedroom. I'm in a narrow cave, as black as my tattoos. Pinhole vision darkens my mind, as the walls crush me down. I can only see my mother's dead body on a silver slab.

"I need a drink!" I roar out. That will lift my spirits. Or at least help to fucking forget.

"I'll get you one," the girl replies, and I hear both sets of feet patter down the stairs. It feels like hours later when the girls appear, fully dressed, and hand me a bottle of vodka. It's not my first choice, but needs must and all. During their absence I've put on The Halcyon's first album. It fills each crevice of my room and mind.

"I'm a fucking good singer, right?" I ask the women, who now look a tad out of place. I don't wait for an answer. "Jordan can't do this without me. It's my band. My vision. These are my fucking lyrics, my feelings."

"We're gonna go," one of the women says through her slick bubblegum pink lips.

"Do you know what?" I say to them, as they fasten up their coats. "People think I'm all arrogant and big headed, just because I'm a singer. I mean, I'm fucking good at my job. But I have to strip myself bare to be able to perform those songs. They're my innermost thoughts, the things I can't bring up in conversation. Singing is the only way for my brain to compute, to communicate, d'you know what I mean?"

I'm met with blank stares. Fucking typical. The vinyl finishes, the silence replaced by the songs of Nirvana still blasting from downstairs. I'd forgotten about that.

"But how can I write about her? No one wants to hear me sing about my dead mum. Or about an ex who clearly doesn't still love me. What else have I fucking got?"

I already fucked up big time with that. If I sing about what happened, the truth, is it speaking ill of the dead? Will it backfire onto me? Of course it will. Pete looked at my lyrics, scrawled in my notebooks, and dismissed them.

They wouldn't fit with the image; it would add a different dimension. Take us into territory that wasn't right. Must try harder, stick to the formula that makes our records go platinum. I swallow down gulps of vodka, fighting back from the instinct to hurl it back up. Writing them down isn't enough, they need to be performed for me to deal with my thoughts. I've written nonstop since I got back to Cumbria. But I know none of the songs will ever be released. Pete wouldn't even want them as album tracks.

"I should just stick to writing aggressively about Lex," I sigh, am I destined to forever be trapped by a nineteen-year-old's heartache?

I hear the blare of Nirvana abruptly come to an end. *What the fuck?* The girls look at each other in a slight panic.

"Hayden?" My dad pushes my bedroom door open, and I inhale sharply at his look of pure disappointment. His shoulders actually drop and a frustrated sigh releases from his lips. "Ok girls, fun's over, let me call you a taxi," he says and scrolls through his phone.

"You don't understand me, do you?" I shout at them all. The girls shake their heads, moving in sync like puppets. Why did I bring them back here? I rake my eyes up their slender bare legs. I know fine well why I brought them here, thinking with my dick instead of my brain. Dad has left me, and I can hear him friendly chattering, as if this is a normal day occurrence on the phone. He's probably best mates with the fucking taxi driver.

"Do you know who does understand me? Lexi. She gets me." Or she would, if I actually spoke to her instead of trying to force my lips onto hers. Would she fucking understand if I told her everything? I don't fucking know anymore. Does it matter?

"Maybe speak to this Lexi? You're in a right state here," the same screechy voice says, patronisingly.

"Why thank you, for being so fucking observant," drunk I may be, but I can still spit out sarcasm. I hear a rapid knock on the door downstairs. "Your taxi's here," I state. I point the half empty vodka bottle towards the door. Part of my mind is screaming to be nice to them, so they keep quiet to the press about this incident. Pete would skin me alive if he could hear me. But he's not here. Him and Jordan don't even fucking need me down there in the fucking studio. Therefore, I don't give a flying fuck what these women say about me.

Lex doesn't want me. Jordan doesn't need me. What have I got left without them? Fucking nothing. I throw the bottle at the mirror, they both smash. Splinters of clear and mirrored glass cover the corner of my room. The clear liquid runs down and stains the photos of a past life.

11

"Lexi –" I hear my dad say from downstairs. *Am I dreaming? Lexi is at my dad's? What for?*

"I have a reputation to uphold, a business, Jock. Right now he's funding my staff wages."

Oh fuck.

She's realised that I've missed another session with Noel today, who she fucking palmed me off with. No wonder she sounds fucking furious. I smooth down my wayward curls and wipe my smudged eyeliner from the bags lining my eyes. I should prepare myself for a charm offensive.

"You've got five minutes to get up, shower and scrub the stench of sex off your skin, then you're coming with me," Lexi snaps at me as I hear her stomping up the stairs. Lex pushes open my bedroom door, like she must have done thousands of times. I still expect her dark hair to be framing her face, I falter for a second at the blonde tendrils, then smile. I light myself another fag, lean myself back on the bed. Exhale the smoke in her direction, raising an eyebrow.

"Oh," she fiddles with her glasses, taking account of

my fully clothed figure. “I was under the impression you were busy.”

“Saving myself for you, my Darling,” I wink. I can’t let her know my insecurities. For all I know she’ll run off and share them with Callum. I watch her brown chocolate eyes roll. The scent of coconut and a linger of dog treats fills my nostrils. Comforting. The walls of the cave open up, light starts shining in.

“Don’t be a dick,” Lexi huffs, her hands on her hips, eyebrows raised in an unimpressed stare. "You're not on stage, there's no fans here to swoon over your every word, just stop it with the act, Hayden."

“Missing me?” I ask, ignoring her demand, as the smoke encircles my curls.

“Actually, you were missing from a session,” Lexi sits down on the bed, her eyes tracing memories stuck to the blue walls. “Come on, Lydia can squeeze you in now.”

“What about Noel?” I ask. I missed a session or two with Noel, which she’s obviously discovered. What good is walking a fucking dog anyway? But I haven’t dared skip a session with my very own Miss Trunchbull. Lydia is lovely, but for all I know she could have her own version of the chokey hiding behind her abundance of fucking plants.

“Noel is obviously swayed by your fame and fortune. He can clearly not handle you, and no, that wasn’t a compliment.”

The smile, as fake as it all is, falls off my face. Maybe the exaggerated charm offensive isn’t doing it for Lexi.

“Come on, Hayden, let’s get you a coffee before we go up to Paws2Heal,” dad says, poking his head around the door.

“Lex?” I ask, leaning forward and placing a palm on

her thigh. She doesn't push it off. "Can we walk back up together? Just me and you?"

"Sure," she smiles. "You smell like the brewery though. Go get a shower and I'll make you a drink. Coffee."

"Dare I ask Son?" Dad says above the whoosh of the shower. It's not as soothing as mine in London, but it's not bad. Scalding hot, just what I need. I can almost see the alcohol and bad memories whirling down the plug hole. Or at least if I imagine it, it might be true, maybe I can just pretend.

"I can't explain," I start, as I scrub my skin with extra rigour. "I don't know who they were. Nothing happened."

"Nothing happened? The police rang me to complain about the noise. I daren't count how many empty bottles there are in your room, nor downstairs. And I see my credit card has funded your habit. Again," dad reprimands, I can feel the mortification of his tone. I am fucking useless.

"Ok, nothing sexual happened with those girls. I'll pay you back once Pete has unfrozen my bank account." Problems can easily be solved with money. That's what this is about, right?

"It's not about the money, Hayden."

"Then what is your pissing problem?" I shout through the water, as I rub shampoo through the tendrils of my hair.

"You lied to me, Son. I brought you up better than this."

"I must get lying from my mother then," I spit out in anger. Dad sighs, I cringe at the words I keep firing at him, like a constant machine gun. The patter of the shower, drops falling like rain on a car roof, mingling with the shaky yet steady breath of my dad makes guilt swell in my chest. I can almost hear the constant thrum of it along with the distant twittering of birds in the trees. The happy squeals of children back at the infant school.

"Have you spoken to Lydia about your mum? The truth?" Dad asks, the soft accent sounding so comforting.

"Yes!" I snap at him as I shut off the water. "That's why I feel so fucking shit today! And also because Jordan doesn't fucking need me anymore!"

"Have you really told Lydia?"

"I told her mum's dead if that's what you mean."

"No, Son, that's not what I mean, and you know it."

I rip open the shower curtain, it sticks to my legs and makes me even more aggravated.

"Pass me the fucking towel," I gulp, see the hurt in my dad's blue eyes. "Please."

"Jordan loves you like a brother, of course he needs you, Son," dad says, as soothingly as he can. "Where has this come from?"

He carried on just fine without me when I was burying my mother. Doing interviews by himself. '*Hayden's taking a few days' vocal rest*' and all that shite he spewed. And now Jordan's stepping into my fucking Gucci boots without a glance in my direction. He hasn't even fucking called to ask how I am. Maybe I just won't go back. He can do it all without me. See how he fucking copes without me there full time. See if he's really as fucking good as Pete says.

"Pete told me," I mumble.

"Pete will say anything to get you back to London."

"Pete Morris-Turner has my fucking best interests at

heart," I snap out in defence.

"And I don't?" Dad asks, a look of sorrow etched on his face. "Don't you dare answer that in anger, Hayden. Words are hard to take back, especially when your actions back them up."

Fucking hell. I feel fourteen again, at least this time he didn't ground me for swearing at him.

"Do you want to talk to me about your mum? I know she's why you drink," dad starts again. He's not letting this go today, for fuck's sake.

"I like a drink. So fucking shoot me," I laugh, but its hollow.

Dad sighs and rubs his hands over his short curls.

"You need to tell Lydia, Son. It's not good for you to be keeping it all inside. Maybe she can help you understand what happened –"

"I told *you* what fucking happened, and you said you didn't want to see me again," I hiss at him quietly, in case Lexi can hear us. I throw the grey towel in the bath and stalk, naked across to my room. Dad follows, I can hear his work boots creaking behind me.

"I have apologised for that. It was said in anger, in shock. You know I didn't mean it. Hayden, I love you more than anything."

"You blame me, said it was my fucking fault!"

"No, Son, that's what *you* think."

"I think it, because its fucking true," I snarl. "You wish I was dead, not her!" I shout, the words filling my bedroom, as I pull clothes from the same pine dresser I've had since we left Glasgow. Not caring anymore if Lex, or next door, or the whole fucking town hears. Dad looks as if I've punched him.

"Is that what you believe?"

I shrug as I ease my jeans over my feet. He wanders out of my room and returns with the towel draped over his arm.

"Hayden, you have always come first. Always. I left – we left – for you. To give you a better life, to put some distance between you and your mother. I thought it was best," dad says, rubbing his forehead.

"Do you regret it? Leaving Glasgow?" I ask him, fear of the response causing my voice to wobble.

"No, it was the best thing I did for you. You were suffering, struggling with how she was. You needed a new start," he replies as he starts to mop up the vodka below my mirror with the towel.

"Do you miss her?" I ask, thinking back to the wedding photo I found earlier. They looked so happy. But then I know how a single photograph doesn't always tell the full story.

"I miss her now I know I can never see her again, yes. But seeing you settled, and happy, being a child free of responsibility – that was far more important than how I felt for your mother. Maybe we left too late. I gave her too many chances. It's my fault you're like this, Hayden." Dad sighs, guilt drowning his features. I'm too selfish, too caught up in my own world to comfort him.

"Did she love me?" I ask instead. I bite down tears pushing against my eyes. Sobs try to force their way up my throat.

"Yes, of course she loved you. But she knew she couldn't put you first. She was ill, so ill," he looks so sad, so lost, but of course I break the fucking moment.

"She was a fucking alcoholic!"

Dad's head snaps up, shards of broken glass nestle in his palm.

"Yes, it's an illness. Ask Lydia."

"Whatever. I'm going for that fucking coffee, even if it's only fucking instant."

I leave my dad to clean up the mess I made in my teenage room and trudge downstairs. I treat him like shit, but I just can't forgive myself for what I did to him. I can't forget his words, his look of disgust when I told him about my mother. It's easier if I keep at a distance. I don't have to consider his feelings if I push him away. It becomes his issue, not mine. Harsh, but life's no fucking picnic.

12

Lexi and I walk slowly – well, as slowly as an energetic St Bernard will allow – the long way up to Paws2Heal. We take turns and twists over bumpy paths, stopping to look down to the fast-flowing river from varying heights of the bridges.

"Would it kill you if you jumped off this bridge?" I ask, musing aloud, as my eyes track fallen leaves floating like boats on their way to the sea. The birds swoop past us, twittering about Anoushka's presence as they flit from branch to branch. Their wings fluttering by in the last few hours of summer sun, before autumn arrives with her chill and darker days.

"Do you have suicidal thoughts, Hayden?" Lexi asks, concern in her words.

"I just wondered," I shrug. If it was good enough for Lexi's all-time favourite singer Michael Hutchence (and including the legend of Kurt Cobain and Ian Curtis amongst too many others to note) maybe it's good enough for Hayden Fucking Coulthard. *Fuck.* I want to slap myself. No. No, I don't want to die. Sometimes, when sleep alludes me despite an empty whiskey bottle on the pillow, I feel it would be easier if I just slept and didn't awaken. If I just disappeared. Just stayed laying in my bed until the breath escaped me. But no, I wouldn't ever actually fucking kill myself.

"Favourite sandwich?" Lexi asks, clearly just to break the tension building between us.

"Bacon, lettuce and tomato, on white bread, butter and a pinch of salt, from your mum's shop. You?" I would have imagined I'd spout off something like hot smoked trout and pickled cucumber, or pesto and salami, but no. Turns out my favourite was one from home. I look at Lexi's profile. Figures.

"Cheese and pickle."

"Still the same," I smile, looking down at her, as she sits on the bench. Her legs cross at the ankles, toes against the ground, heels raised; ballet lessons from her childhood instilled in her muscles.

"Favourite song?" Lexi asks next. Her eyes gleam beneath the low sun reflecting off her large glasses. I sigh. *Fuck*, she's so beautiful.

"Of mine?"

Lexi shrugs, encouraging me to loosen Anoushka's tight leash. I do, tentatively, then a laugh bubbles out of me as she darts off with her extra metre of freedom, jerking me backwards.

"Without You Here," I answer, referring to the song from the pub the other night. I follow Anoushka in circles around the bench, the across to the bridge railings. "Same question?"

"*Tear Us Apart*," Lexi answers, a smile pushing her cheeks under her blocky glasses. I snort. Trust her to name an INXS song. She always did have a thing for Michael

Hutchence.

"I didn't write that! I wish I fucking had. Favourite one of mine?"

Lex stands up, joins me by the iron railings as Anoushka sniffs a lamppost. We both look down to the water below. Our hands gripping the black iron railings. She's so close that I can feel the weight of her against my legs, my side. I can hear her breathing, hear her hesitation before she answers.

"*Join The Dots,*" Lexi finally replies. I turn to look at her, my eyes dancing over her pale skin. The curls whip round my head, lifting up like smoke from a chimney.

"Really?" I ask her, I wasn't expecting that one to be a favourite. "That was like, the first song I wrote."

"It was always my favourite," she says. She might try, but Lex can't hide the happy emotion on her face. I wonder if she's remembering me singing it to her that very first time? Under the willow tree in the shared garden, that her mum and now her own kitchen window looks out at. My bony fingers stopping every now and then on my guitar as I changed chords, strummed to find the right key and my place in scribbled lyrics.

I feel like all pretences have dropped like stones into the river. With a slightly shaking and a touch clammy, hand, I cover Lexi's. Knowing already what it will feel like. I run my fingers back and forth over the bumps of her knuckles. My rings with their rainbow stones, and nails showing remnants of blue nail varnish, look gaudy compared to her bare skin. Automatically, my fingers seem to make a point of caressing her third finger. Naked. Again.

"Do you not wear your ring for work, then?" I ask her,

trying for nonchalant, but my heart ready to break at the answer.

"What ring?"

"I heard you and Callum are engaged,"

"We're not." She says with finality.

"You're not?"

"No."

"What would you say if I proposed to you?" I ask. Lexi laughs, the short melody fills my heart with lightness.

"Here?"

"Yeah," I shrug. *Is there a good enough reason not to try again? To remain in this weird not dating but not doing anything about the fucking obvious chemistry between us situation?* "Why not? You know I love you, Lex."

"You're maybe more drunk than I thought," Lexi laughs again.

I join in, the two of us giggling, until it peters out. Our happy sounds taken away by the wind. I realise she hasn't responded to my questions.

"You won't really marry Callum, will you, Lex?" I implore, though I have no fucking right.

"I turned him down," Lexi says, not looking in my direction. She turns her back to the view, her eyes following Anoushka, who is merrily sniffing nearby.

"What?" I ask. This is news. What a fucking relief. A weight slides off my shoulders instantly. That's another reason to actually do it, to ask her to marry me instead.

"Twice, actually," her deep brown eyes flicker to mine then away again, she swallows loudly, as if a bitter pill is lodged in her throat. She offers Anoushka a treat, increasing the distance between us.

"He's asked you to marry him twice? You've said no –

both fucking times? Why?" I find myself wanting to laugh and punch the air. It's arrogant as fuck, yet I expected Lexi would be there for me. For us, as a couple, when I eventually left the London life behind. Maybe I didn't quite picture her waiting in a white dress, staring longingly out of her bedroom window, but I did always imagine the two of us getting back together. I guess I expected her to just wait. *Fuck.* That is pathetic of me. That is a helluva expectation. Still, knowing she's not committed to marrying Callum, that does give me some hope.

"We've split up, actually,"

"You have? When? Why? Has he moved out? Did you end things? What happened? Are you ok?" The questions shoot out of me, like I'm beating a timpani drum in excitement. Lex half smiles at me but doesn't answer.

"Come on, Hayden," she says, pushing herself off the railings. "Lydia will think we've got lost."

The snuffling and happy woofs filter through the chilly air. They mingle with the heady scent of lavender and florals, and a hint of meaty food jumps into my nose, as we walk up the path to Paws2Heal. I feel my shoulders deflate, swooping to touch my toes. I shuffle with resistance as if wading through glue, the closer I get to Lydia's office. I know I have to be open and honest if this therapy is going to work. And to be fucking fair, I do quite like Lydia. Well, I respect her, which is more than I can say for all the dozens of other therapists I've come into contact with.

"She's here to help you, H," Lexi says, as she rubs my back. She reaches around me, one hand on the handle of Lydia's office door, when I place my hand on her arm. I squeeze it gently and she pauses, looking up at me from under her fringe.

"Lex," I say quietly, feeling my eyes glistening like a summer puddle. I tug her gently away, Lydia's door swinging slowly open with a loud creak. "Lex," I repeat, like her name is the chorus of my own song. I talk straight into her eyes, heart and soul. My hands, larger and scarred with bumpy callouses from my constant guitar, than the last time I cupped her face. I caress Lexi's skin like she's the last and most precious golden egg on Earth.

"Why did you turn Callum down?"

Our foreheads touch, breath mixing together, our lips millimetres apart. I feel my heart melting, the soldiers defending to keep her away, downing their tools.

"He's not the one," Lexi replies with a shrug and a small smile. I open my mouth to speak, to ask more. To ask if I'm her one instead, but then, I can't bear anything else. Lexi shuts off my brain answering questions for me. She tilts her head, up towards my mouth. The feel of her lips against mine is like muscle memory. I know her body better than I know my own. The taste of her skin, the feel of her raised moles on her back. The way her eyes twitch when she's tired, and how her fingers shake when she's stressed. My arms reach around her fully, so I can feel the weight of her as I pull her closer.

"Hayden," Lydia's voice breaks our kiss, our moment. We jump apart, like teenagers caught behind the bike sheds by the teacher. "Come on, let's have a chat. Bring Anoushka."

13

"Hayden, set up a date with Lexi. You have been out of the public eye for too long," Pete's American drawl echoes around my dad's car as he drives me up to Paws2Heal for my next session with Lydia.

I'm now on three sessions a week with the modern-day Miss Trunchbull. It's fucking tough going. But I am starting to actually tell Lydia my shit. She's the first therapist, counsellor, guru, delete as appropriate; I really feel connected to. I almost feel like she's actually there to help and not just piss around and be nosey.

I see dad's jaw set from the corner of my eye.

"Pete, I don't care," I say to the phone on speaker in my lap, as I try to tame my curls into a bun at the nape of my neck. I should have packed my conditioner. Sainsbury's own that dad has in the shower does nothing for these locks. It's like frizz central today. Thank fuck for my Moroccan oil serum I had in my Gucci messenger bag. It's doing some damage control.

"You should care. This is your career, dude! We need your pretty face back in the papers," Pete's Texan accent bellows from the crinkly speakers. I can't say I've missed the press intrusion at all, which is a fucking revelation, as I do love a bit of attention. I prefer it on a stage, love it. Have done since I first rocked out to INXS at the school talent show aged thirteen. I still get a buzz from stage, from being the front man, the showman. It's fucking exhausting being constantly hounded by press down in London though. Always plastering a smile on my face, or they'll report I'm arrogant and rude. Wailing, sobbing fans that I have to pose with after long-haul flights, or a morning run. They don't care if I'm sweaty, drunk, or sleep deprived. They just want a selfie and to tell me how much they love me. Don't get me wrong, I love the fans. Appreciate them. I'm insanely grateful to each and every one of them and their dedication. But they forget that I'm more than a poster on their wall, a background on their phones. I'm a human, a real fucking human, and I need a fucking break.

It's different up here in Cumbria, refreshing. No one really bats an eye lid, aside from the odd teenager and their mother when I'm in Sainsbury's or at the cashpoint. I've had a few flirty stares in the gym, but I'm not complaining about them. Everyone loves an ego boost. Plus, I fucking need it after hearing the demos from Jordan. It pained me, but they were good. Too fucking good. He could actually do it all without me. Maybe Pete will decide to just leave me up here and let Jordan carry on without me. Maybe it wouldn't be so bad if he did.

"Tonight, at eight. I'll have cameras ready, message me the location. Surely even your little town has a posh restaurant," Pete continues, cutting into my fantasies of moving back up here. Buying an old farmhouse and turning a stable into a recording studio. Walking my own dog out in the fields, Lex and Mavis waking up beside me each day. Breathing in fresh air, instead of exhaust fumes and dripping sweat from bodies packed into our shows.

"Fine," I yawn, already bored of this revisit to the life I always wanted. Out of the corner of my eyes I see dad shake his head. Something else for me to do to disappoint him. "If you think it will really help."

"Of course man! All press is good press. But a reunion with the teenage sweetheart, man, that can be only positive. Actually, I have a surprise for you."

Gucci's latest boots? I glance over at dad, and we both exchange worried glances, before I catch myself and turn away from him, watching the school kids dressed in navy weave their way through the cars on the way to the secondary school.

"Jordan and Marlena are joining you, so text him the location. And we'll talk tomorrow about the show in Carlisle."

Not exactly the best surprise in the world. Jordan, who I haven't heard from since I abandoned him on stage, and his pretend girlfriend. I feel my hands start to shake, my head feels woozy like I had a few too many shots, and I haven't had a fucking drink yet today.

Fake dates, yet another publicity stunt. Both Jordan and I have done that shit a million times. Sure, it'll be different with Lex. Actually being with her, without a dog in between us, will be amazing. That's if she'll agree. If I can persuade her it might be fun, even with Jordan and his latest squeeze. But being back on the stage? *Fuck*. I'm not ready for that shit, even if I love it.

"No, Pete I'm really not ready to do a gig," I speak the words out loud that I've sent to him via email all week.

"We'll see," I scrub my hands down my face and sigh as Pete hangs up.

"I do not like that man," My dad says, his brows furrowed as he indicates into the lane which holds Lydia and all her probing questions at the end.

He doesn't get it. It's not about liking or disliking him. Pete Morris-Turner is a hugely successful manager. He was the best, as a band, that we could wish for. He's what The Halcyon needed, wanted, to make a splash on the music scene. We owe our success to him. Well, that and my talent, my vision for the band. Although apparently Jordan is doing a fucking good job without me.

"Please Hayden, don't go on a fake date with Lexi. She's not like the others," I know he's right. Lexi is the only woman I've loved. Years of dating and shagging models, singers, dancers, whoever; and it's still Lexi Blackwood who holds my heart. But this is my job, how my life works. It won't fucking matter how we got back together in the long run.

Lex and I have been getting on really well recently, and I feel like a date is the next step.

I think professionally, things are going ok. Anoushka seems to be responding well to me, and I enjoy spending time with her. Even if my jeans are stained with her slobber, and my Gucci boots will never fucking recover. As soon as the timer goes, it's like a knife comes down and slices the atmosphere away. A switch is flipped, and there we are. Lex and H; as easy as it always was. She laughs loudly, showing off her teeth packed tightly together, like fans in the front row. We while away hours after our sessions laughing and joking with each other. Our bodies lean into one another, as if we're magnets. Our fingers lace together, tracing patterns on our palms. With Anoushka and all her fluff between us, I sing songs that I used to perform with The Halcyon before we got signed. *Beautiful Girl* by INXS, *Better Day* by Ocean Colour Scene, and *Live Forever* by Oasis to name a few. They're my beautiful moments with Lex. Treasured. Secret. Sacred.

Maybe I should bust out the engagement ring. I chuckle to myself. I haven't actually bought one. But there's time. I could bob down into town after my session with Lydia.

"I was going to ask her out anyway," I shrug in defence of Pete's instructions, which of fucking course I'm going to follow. Lexi would be fucking livid if she ever found out about me having managerial instructions to date her. But I'll just have to ensure she doesn't find out. I'll play the innocence card until it's forgotten about. If I keep Lex in the dark, if she thinks I don't know about the press, then I should get away with it. I'm doing no fucking harm, really.

"It's different, Son. You love Lexi," dad says gently. It must be obvious if he's picked up on it. Though he has always liked her, said she was a good match for me.

"Would I let you down if I asked her out?" I ask, staring straight ahead, even though we're in the car park. I crack my knuckles to fill in the silence that's stretching between us.

"At Pete's request, yes you would, Son."

"Why break the habit of a fucking lifetime?" I scowl.

"You'd be betraying Lexi too, and yourself," dad carries on, as if I haven't spoken. I unclip my seatbelt and stare out of the sunroof. Birds swoop high through the clouds, threading their way across the rectangular window.

"I don't care about myself," I mumble. Why should I? They'd all be fine without me.

"You should Hayden, you're a good soul under all –"

"The shame and distress I cause you? Yeah, thanks a fucking bunch, Dad," I say as I slam the car door too hard.

I stomp like a moody teenager towards the purple doors of reception, the tall swaying lavender and baby skin soft hydrangeas tickling at my legs. I inhale a deep breath; the floral scent calms me.

With one hand on the gleaming glass panel, I see my reflection. Tendrils of curls already escaping the bun, jump around my face like jellyfish tentacles. My eyebrows pulled low, a scowl etched on my face. Angry eyes lined in kohl. Purple bags hanging beneath them like spring fuchsias. I see my hand shaking against the door, and despite the clouds darkening and hiding the sun; I can feel sweat on my forehead, clinging like the last few drops in a whiskey bottle.

I want to ask Lexi out anyway. It was going to happen with or without Pete's encouragement. He's merely giving me the push I need. Right? I don't like the guilty features on the face that is staring back at me. *No going back*, the band's words echo in my brain.

"Fuck!" I snap out to no one, then push the door aggressively. My reflection left behind, like my moral compass.

14

I stand in the doorway of Lexi's office, tapping my feet to an internal, ever present rhythm. I've got four minutes before I'm due to see Lydia. Should be enough time to persuade Lexi to agree to the double date later.

I watch as Lex slams the phone down, Mavis jumps up at her legs and whines. She falls backwards into her chair and puts her head in her hands. Mavis nudges her owner's arms with her glossy snout.

"You ok, Darling?" I ask as I gently rap on the door. Lex jolts up and smiles tightly.

"Sorting out the flat and shit with Callum," she says.

"Why do you let him call you Alexis?" It's been nagging me since the first time I heard him use it. She always hated her full name. She swore if I ever called her Alexis she'd never speak to me again, or at the very least hold off all kisses and sexual advances; which as a teenage boy I was never willing to take the risk on how serious she was. Lexi shrugs, groans a little as she shakes her head.

"He claimed that whenever he called me Lexi, he just pictured you and I together. Association, I guess. We were pretty inseparable at school, me and you,"

I snort a little at Callum's obvious inferiority complex, I push my chest out a little. Maybe he has the right to feel that way.

"And you didn't tell him to get over himself?"

"Trust me, I did. But in the end it wasn't worth the argument." Lexi shrugs. Her shoulders kissing at her ears.

"Aw Lex, you two argued about me? Should I be flattered?" I ask cheekily.

"Trust me on this too, H, not everything I've ever said about you is positive."

Whatever.

"Enough about Callum, you didn't love him anyway," I shrug and chuckle a little, pleased I made her smile.

"Hayden!"

"You were the one who turned down his marriage proposal."

"Twice," Lexi mumbles, though a smile adds a twinkle in her chestnut brown eyes.

"How about an offer you cannot refuse?" I smile as I perch on her desk, my boots swinging back and forth. Her Bambi eyes widen, though they don't look scared.

"Please, Hayden, do not propose to me," Lexi laughs out as Mavis jumps onto her lap.

"Not quite," I muse, scratching at the more grey than black stubble on my chin. "Will you join me for dinner tonight, Lex? The Italian on the bridge, where we used to go."

"That was direct. I would've expected a full-on lyrical prose before going straight to the point."

"I'm not writing a song about me asking you out."

"That's a relief."

"Though maybe I should. You know me, Lex, I'm

honest," I smile, at least I hope it's a smile and not a grimace. Lexi chuckles and shakes her head fondly. Pete would be fucking proud of me.

"I don't want a one-night stand, H," Lexi says suddenly, with colour popping on her cheeks.

I stand up to stretch, like a blossom tree, all skinny lines reaching for the sky. I'll never be as ripped and muscular like Callum. He's definitely more rugby lad, and I'm shaped more like a golf club, long lines and not much weight to my bones.

"I asked you to dinner, Darling. No mention of anything more," I wink, as Lexi rolls her eyes.

Mavis hops down from Lexi's lap and runs off. She returns with her slobbery rope toy between her teeth. She places it on my battered, but still beautiful, pointed boots.

"These are Gucci, Mavis," I say to the dog, before picking up the toy and tugging it for her, anyway. She growls playfully. I mimic her. Who would've thought I'd actually enjoy the canine companions on offer here?

"What does this date mean?" Lexi asks, her face pained.

It's a step back on the path for my plummeting career. I'd be doing it for some peace from Pete, and so Jordan can carry on living out his dreams. It's a job. On the surface.

"If you want me to propose, Lex, I will. I swear it, I'll fucking do it now," I say instead, sidestepping her question like a wayward note in an already written melody.

"I am not marrying you when there's any chance of trashy magazines bartering over official wedding photos, you can get that out of your head."

"There would have to be an engagement shoot first, actually, Babe,"

"Of course, the only way to a successful marriage is through interviews and posed photographs with celebrity guests. Your life is utterly ridiculous, it's not real. I honestly don't know how you do it, H." Lexi murmurs with a shake of her head.

"So what? Am I proposing right now, Lex?"

"Hayden, life isn't like one of your happy love songs," Lexi tilts her head, as she flicks the fringe out from her eyes. She reminds me of Anoushka. Calm, almost soft, but in a nice way. However, I know Lexi. I know she has a wild streak that can be flipped like a switch. Her temper can be as short and brittle as ice.

"It could be. I've written more songs these past few weeks than I ever have," I say as I tug at the auburn curls on my scalp. *Maybe I could pen a happily ever after for us to act out.*

"I'm not asking for a diamond ring or a white dress –"

"Good. White would do nothing for your complexion. You could get away with ivory, but I feel champagne or pearl would work best with your colouring. The gold undertones wouldn't wash you out. Maybe I could go full on nineties boyband and rock up in a cream suit –"

"Be serious!" Lexi says, playfully hitting my arm. "You'd never wear a suit anyway."

"For our wedding I'd wear one. For you," I wink at her from my crouched position on the floor, slobbery rope between my fingers. Not quite the right moment to propose, now I'm faced with it.

"Look, back to the point," Lexi says, with a pink blush rising up her neck. "If this is just a date to fill your spare time, then no thanks. I'll pass. I don't wish to go on a date with the infamous Hayden Coulthard from The Halcyon.

He's not who I'm interested in."

"Lex, it's complicated, I –"

"I know, your absurd celebrity status separates us massively. You live in London. I'm here, you're –"

"Here too," I cut in. I have a feeling she might be trying to get out of this date before Pete's even got a photo of us together in the press. He will be fucking fuming if I fail with this. And Jordan will never forgive me if I screw up the band's success. Even more than I have already. I'll have to turn on the charm. The thought makes me cringe internally; it hasn't fucking worked so far. I feel like a fake, putting on this act for her. It's Lex. I should be able to be honest. I shake the guilt from my head. I was going to ask her out anyway. I want to go on a date with her. The pressure from Pete has merely encouraged me to do so quicker.

"You're only here temporarily. A few weeks left to go," Lexi says, I notice the hint of sadness in her bronzed eyes.

"Things can change," I confess. Being in Cumbria is much better than I ever expected. Would it be the end of the world if I split my time between here and London? I sigh, recalling the upcoming schedule Pete emailed me. I'd never have a night's sleep in my Camden bed, let alone time to travel up here, and wake up in the farmhouse my mind keeps imagining.

"You'd be bored out of your mind here long term, Hayden. Don't deny it. No recording studio for miles, no Gucci stores."

"Online delivery, Lex," I cut in with a chuckle.

"We're getting off track. Am I more to you than the others?" Lexi sighs and rubs at her eyes beneath her glasses. She stands up and flicks the switch on the kettle.

In an action that transports me back in time, she shakes a tea bag before dropping it into the waiting mug. My head tilts to the side as I watch her. Such an inane movement, a silly little thing she's done each time I've ever seen her make a brew; yet it makes my heart feel as warm as a bonfire.

"It's you, Lex. Of course you're not like the others," I reply truthfully. I wander across the small room and study the framed map of Cockermouth hanging on the wall.

"I don't want to be another notch on your bedpost. That's what it boils down to," Lexi says, her back to me as she adds a splash of milk in the mug.

"FYI, I have a sunken bed. You would know that if you ever came down to London to see me."

The metallic sound of the teaspoon clattering on the small worktop startles me. It shouldn't because that comment, even for me, was unnecessary. I know, without looking at her, that Lex is going to take that to heart, and start getting fucking defensive. Lexi was agreeing to this date, job done, as far as Pete would be concerned. And then good old fucked up me, brings up my insecurities. I may have just fucking blown this.

"Some of us have jobs, commitments, which we can't just up and leave," Lexi says, her eyebrows pulled low in a scowl, her smooth, ice calm temper starting to splinter, like I anticipated.

"You can't get a day off once in ten fucking years?" I spit at her to cover up my annoyance of ruining a potential moment.

"You're so over dramatic," Lexi rolls her eyes, and Mavis abandons the toy rope at my feet, and joins Lexi's side. "You're not on stage now, Hayden. Dial it down. This is the real world, not your fake celebrity one."

"Why didn't you ever come to any of my shows?" I bark out, pissed at myself for not thinking for once, what I was fucking saying. Jordan will be so fucking annoyed if he traipses all the way up here from London, for a publicity stunt that isn't even happening.

"I didn't want to," Lexi puts her mug down on her desk, and starts threading her arms through her coat. She doesn't meet my eyes. I know she's lying. But I don't know why. I don't know what about. Didn't want to. Didn't fucking want to? What, did she have a better offer? Was Callum really that much more appealing than me?

"Can you pass me a lead please?" Lexi asks, indicating to her head towards the shelves on the wall. Her change of subject floors me, but at the same time I don't want to end up in a full-blown argument, certainly not before I've secured this date tonight. Time for damage control. I reach out and move a few things then hand her the lead.

"What's this?" Lexi asks, her nose scrunching up, confusion, anger and a touch of humour in her wide eyes.

"A lead, like you fucking asked for," I pout, as I steal a slurp of her abandoned tea.

"A dog's lead, obviously," she says, waving the wired plug around uselessly. Mavis barks once, a pathetic sound in contrast the boom that Anoushka emits. I think she's embarrassed on my fucking behalf. Of course Lexi wanted a fucking dog lead.

"You should've been more fucking specific," I spit out, to hide my embarrassment. "Perhaps tell people how you really feel, what you mean and all that shit. Instead of assuming everyone is a fucking mind reader."

"Perhaps you should use your common fucking sense. Or do they remove that when you're granted celebrity status?" Lexi snaps, only fragments of her calm exterior remain now. Shattered by our exchange. I ignore the desire in me to fight with Lex. We used to argue until we were both red in the face. No longer knowing what it started as, neither of us wanting to give in. It always, *always*, ended in kisses. Begrudgingly or passionate; we never left an argument hanging in the air like kites at the beach. *Aside from the one that resulted in the break up.* I swallow down the hurt that still clings to my heart like bitter nettle stings.

"Are you coming on this date tonight, or what?" I ask, noticing by the clock on the wall that I'm now late for my session with Lydia.

"Pass me the dog lead, and get out of my sight," Lexi spits out as she toes off her shoes and pulls on a pair of mud encrusted wellingtons. Mavis sniffing at her discarded trainers.

"You don't mean that," I say, pushing my curls off my forehead.

"Try me."

The air around us stills. We battle silently through our stubbornness. The tick of the large clock resounding in my ears. Taunting me. I crack first, Lexi always could stare me down. I blink rapidly at her. Fire burns in her eyes like sparks off a poker. I spin on my heel, the chains clanging against my chest like tinkling Christmas bells, and stomp off down the corridor.

As I'm pushing the door open to Lydia's office, I hear Lexi call out. I might have cracked first, but she's keen to glue us back together. Like kintsugi.

"Hayden, wait up!"

"Miss me already?" I ask, knowing I sound like a dick, but not able to drop my facade.

"What time tonight?" She enquires casually, twiddling with her zip on her coat. The blush staining her cheeks showing that it's an anything less than casual question.

"Eight. You'll be there?" I ask, smiling.

Lexi shrugs her eyes focused on the view above my shoulder. Trying to give the impression that she doesn't care. She doesn't want to appear to be easily swayed.

"Please," I say to her, meaning it, yet also playing to her good side. "Please say you'll be there?"

"I'll be there," Lexi replies with a shrug, as she walks back away from me. Her words smoothing over our cracks with gold, making them whole and more beautiful.

15

The clatter of cutlery and babble of other hushed conversations, are our music for the night. The odd raised shout from the kitchen. The scent of roasted tomato and garlic sauces lingers in the air. It's the soundtrack to Lex and I. We used to come here most Friday nights; no mates, no teachers, no parents. Just the two of us.

"It's like we've gone back in time, mate," Jordan laughs as he looks around the restaurant. I admit, the decor hasn't changed, and it does look a little shabby. It certainly is a million fucking miles away from Bob Bob Ricard, where each table comes fitted with a 'press for champagne' button. Yet I like it here, it's comforting. Warm. *Safe,* I think, as I see the photographers and reporters munching their way through garlic bread, checking their cameras as subtly as possible.

"What brought you back up here, Hayden?" Marlena asks. She's got one of her perfectly manicured hands on Jordan's thigh, the other curled around a bread stick, that I bet she won't fucking eat. There's no doubt, she's an attractive woman. She'd have to be. She is the winner of a model competition shown across the nations tv screens.

Redhead, freckles, a little too symmetrical to be natural. Enormous boobs, definitely fake. Tiny waist, and flared fertile hips. She reminds me of a humanised sand timer: a real-life Barbie doll. But Barbie's red-haired, younger sister. The downside is, she fucking knows it. I thought I was fucking arrogant until I met Marlena.

She's been dating Jordan for a few months, after their first publicity stunt went well. I say dating, but it's not for real. They share a bed every now and then, but their relationship is based on gaining publicity for their careers. There are no genuine feelings there. A shag and positive press; win fucking win. Marlena is tolerable company. She makes me slightly on edge though. I don't quite trust those gleaming green eyes of hers. Who would trust her, when she's being paid to be here, and no doubt report back to Pete, and her own manager?

"I wanted peace and quiet," I exhale. "For a while, just a break," I add on quickly, so Jordan knows I'm not giving up on him.

"You should've asked Pete for a holiday then, not run off up the country," Jordan stares at me. I have apologised to him, but I still left him in the lurch, and I can't change that. He might be smiling, the strip lights dancing off his nose, eyebrow and lip piercings, but he's got a right frown in his eyes.

"I wasn't thinking, mate, it just all happened,"

"Bad high?" Marlena enquires bluntly, her perchance for a line of cocaine most nights, also helps her keep her slender figure. "This is why you should stick to reliable dealers, Hayden, I've told you this before,"

"No! Fuck no!" I bark out at her, hoping the reporters aren't listening or recording. Those days are well and truly behind me. "It just got to be too much. I can't explain it."

"Walking off stage mid-gig, mate, I was furious," Jordan states. The frown etched into his forehead.

"Was?"

"Let's see how this next promo tour goes," Jordan answers, then stares me down over the rim of his wine glass. I down a bottle of water, feeling the intense stare of his blue eyes watching my every move.

"It sounds so exciting!" Marlena giggles, as she flicks her perfectly straight red hair off her bare shoulder. "Anonymous launches, secret gigs –"

The bell jangles above the door as Lexi walks in.

My heartbeat dances to a rhythm only reserved for moments like this; it drowns out Marlena's speech.

Lexi pushes her glasses up her nose, fiddles with the buttons on her coat as she refuses to hang it on the rack.

"I'm still a bit cold, but thanks," I hear her say. Gentle yet determined.

She frowns slightly at me as she takes stock of Jordan at our table. Maybe I should've told her it was a double date. The black dress she has on underneath her coat is heavily embroidered with reds and oranges. Nice, but no Prada. It hangs just below her knees, and chunky boots grace her tiny feet. She looks fucking stunning, even without a designer label.

Though I must admit, I love her everyday clothes too. Leggings and fleece tops. They are light years away from sequins and skin-tight denim dresses I see in London, but it's a refreshing change. My eyes glance to Marlena, the black dress practically painted across her hourglass figure. My fucking point exactly.

I stand up to greet Lexi, pulling her into a hug. Like a

fucking pro, I ignore the table across the other side of the restaurant, and place a kiss on her cheeks, then a lingering one on her red lips. I disregard the flash of a camera.

"You look gorgeous," I beam. I mean it.

Lexi blushes.

"I didn't have any shoes to go with this dress, it was these or trainers," she shrugs, embarrassed.

"Hey, Lexi!" Jordan says, awkwardly hugging her. "It's been light years since I last saw you!"

"Hi Jordan, I didn't know you were here too," Lexi throws me a look. I smile tightly back at her.

"This is my girlfriend –"

"Oh my god! You're Marlena Racer!" Lexi gushes, "I voted for you to win! You're so beautiful!"

"That's so sweet," Marlena comments, still in her seat.

"I didn't know you two were dating!" Lexi's eyes dart from the two of them, wide and shining, like my fans'.

"Don't you read the papers?" Jordan smiles as he throws his arm around Marlena's chair. Lexi shakes her head. She was never into celebrity gossip magazines as a teen, and clearly that frame of mind has followed her into adulthood.

"I was actually meant to be dating Hayden, but he wasn't keen," Marlena smiles sweetly. I gulp. Jordan's fingers freeze above her shoulder. Lexi turns her head to me.

"Let's sit down!" I say, too loudly to be natural.

"What does that mean? You weren't keen?" Lexi hisses at me from behind the crinkled menu.

"They're not actually dating Lex, it's all a set-up – good for the image and shit. I wasn't keen on it. On her. So,

Jordan stepped in. It worked out for them though, they're a pretty good match."

"Are you blind? It's Marlena Racer, she's stunning!"

"She's not the one," I shrug, using her words towards Callum.

Colour bursts on Lexi's cheeks and neck. I'm desperate to hold her, to pull her close to me. To feel us chest to chest, and push my tongue into her mouth and taste her. To feel every inch of her skin. That can wait though. We have all night.

If I pretend that the table behind us don't keep standing up to take photos, and ignore the same person walking past outside, then I can state that it is the best time I've had in years. Lexi and I just fit, like the drums and cymbals, together we make each other complete. We laugh far too loud, and - due to our hands being intertwined together - spill more spaghetti than acceptable for a public place.

I can't believe how easy it is between the two of us. The decade apart felt like it was minutes not years. It is just like nothing had changed. Yes, we had different stories to tell, but that was all. I show her that I am the person she fell in love with. It could still work. I know it could. It can. I want it to. *Fuck,* I actually do want to propose.

Jordan and I reminisce about our early shows, how we'd get detention for practising in the sports hall, we even sing a few lines of our older, never released songs. Lexi listens with more interest than I expected as Jordan talks about the next album and the songs he's written. We talk about the places we've toured, and where we want to go to. It feels like we're talking about a dream, it doesn't feel real. I guess I've never taken stock of what my life has been.

Marlena pushes food around her plate, laughing in the right places, asking questions so Lexi feels included when the chat turns to London life; but it's clear she'd much rather be at a champagne bar with dimmed lights than here.

"I'm dying for a fag, I won't be a moment," I say as I kiss Lexi on the lips. It's like heaven, better than alcohol. Even better than the Mcallan whiskey I bought myself to celebrate the release of our latest album. And the best bit, she doesn't even resist.

"I'll come too," says Marlena, squeezing herself out from her seat.

I swagger towards the back door of the Italian, I can feel Lexi watching me. The connection between us feels electric. Not just physically, although I can pretty much guarantee that I'll be waking up in her bed tomorrow morning. But the chemistry, the whole spark. Lex can't fight it. I can't fight it. The universe is screaming at us to be together, I can tell. *No going back.*

I slip out of the back door, holding it open for Marlena, and overlook the river. I feel free. I try to swallow down the guilt of the cameras and press reports tomorrow and the next day. It won't matter in the long run, I convince myself, because Lexi and I will be together. Reunited.

"She's sweet," Marlena says as she exhales smoke in my direction.

I nod at her, but keep watching the river, enjoying the beauty in nature. For possibly the first time.

"She's sweet," Marlena repeats. "But –"

"But what?" I snap out, as if I need relationship advice from a woman who is always paid for her first date.

"She's small town, Hayden. She'd never cope in London, with all the attention you get."

"What?" The word jumps out of my mouth. Instantly on the defensive of Lexi and I as a couple. But I shouldn't be surprised. Of course Marlena isn't going to like or approve of Lexi. A canine therapist living hundreds of miles away from London isn't going to help spur on Marlena's modelling career. And that's all this woman in front of me cares about: success for herself.

"The two of you totally zoned out when me and Jordan were talking about London, like you didn't care."

"There's more to the world than just London," I say wistfully, pulling on the cigarette. Lexi despises London, and I know she'd be reluctant to come and visit me, let alone move there if things work out between us. That's even if I make it back down to London. Right now the thought fills me with weighted dread.

"Yeah, maybe, but it shouldn't be a little town like this. You deserve to be on huge stages, selling out arenas, your faces on all magazines! Not confined to a glorified village."

"I deserve it, or Jordan deserves it?" I ask, wanting some fucking clarification. Knowing her, she's probably thinking about her own press coverage.

"He deserves it, he works hard," Marlena shrugs her tiny shoulders. "You do too, but he's always in your shadow. Don't block out his light. I've heard the new stuff, it's amazing. Let him have his time to shine too."

"You mean it's amazing because Jordan wrote it?" That's what she really fucking means. Well, maybe Jordan would be better off without me. Maybe I should fucking never return to London and let him shoulder it all, for a fucking change.

"I'm just being honest."

"I'd prefer him to be honest, rather than sending his pretend girlfriend to pass on messages."

"Hey, I'm on your side, this works for me too. Jordan just wants what's best for the band, Hayden. He just wants you back where you belong. In the studio, making music."

"I need a break," I repeat. *Fuck,* it's like talking to a female version of Pete. Why don't people fucking listen to me?

"You guys are so close to like, worldwide fame. Jordan doesn't want you to blow it over some girl you used to date, that's all. I don't think she's a good fit," Marlena shrugs.

"Jordan said that?"

"Jordan, Pete, what's the difference? They both have the band at the forefront of their minds, which is what you should be doing," she shrugs her perfectly smooth shoulders, then sashays away back into the restaurant.

The water gurgles and rolls over smooth stones, washing the first autumn leaves away to the sea. I can hear the odd squeal of tires, and clatter of dishes, but compared to my usual night out, it's silent. And I'm shocked to discover that I prefer it.

The guilt sits heavy in my stomach, it rolls round as if I'm on a rollercoaster. Jordan and I are in this together. Yes, I am the one who carries the band more, but I couldn't do it without him. Fuck, I wouldn't do it without him. This is his dream too, and I'm risking shattering it for him. I made a commitment to him when we signed the record deal. He's my oldest friend – he'd never, ever forgive me if I ruin this for him. I feel like a rag doll between two warring siblings. One pulling me away; to rest, recover, deal with my demons, to be with Lexi, the ultimate love of my life. The other dragging me to London, leaving me in recording studios, pushing me on stage to perform. I love the stage, I love my job. I love Jordan, he's like my brother. But my heart, it isn't fucking in it anymore.

The river water gushes past, mirroring my whirling thoughts. The water sounds vexed, in a hurry to get to the sea and be free from the constraints of the now manmade riverbank.

I watch it, I feel empathy with it. I just don't know where my destination is.

I return to the table as Lexi is fastening her coat. I look behind her, the photographers have long gone, thank fuck. I might have just got away with this.

"Where are you two staying?" I ask to Jordan, whose parents left the area a few years ago.

"That hotel on the main road to Carlisle."

"My sister got married there, it's lovely," Lexi says sweetly.

"It's hardly The Ritz, but it's fine for a night," Marlena rolls her eyes. I want to ask if they've booked one or two rooms, but feel it would make me sound pettier than I am.

"Actually, we'd better be off," Jordan says as he stands and stretches. "Some of us have work to get back to."

"Mate –"

"I'm back up next week to start rehearsing, so we'll catch up then," he says as he shakes my hand, then pulls me into a hug. "It's good to see you smiling for a change," Jordan comments in my ear.

"I'm writing, you know? Did Pete tell you?" I ask. Jordan shakes his head, a smile showing his teeth.

"Are you?"

"Yeah, I'm enjoying it,"

"Good for you mate, I can't wait to hear them. Lyrics are always your forte."

"Thanks, mate."

"I mean it, it's good to see you actually proper smiling," I pat him on the back for fear of crying if I verbally reply. I hold the door open for Lexi and Marlena, as Jordan pays the bill.

"We'll get back to it," I confirm, as he joins me and we head out into the street. We will, I can't let him down.

"Damn straight we will," he says, a smile breaking his face almost in half. "Now the question is, where are you sleeping tonight?"

16

We say goodbye with air kisses and hugs. Jordan and Marlena climbing into a waiting taxi, and Lexi waving at Marlena enthusiastically.

"She's so mesmerising to look at!" Lexi smiles.

Not as much as you.

"Can I walk you home, Lex?" I ask, holding out my hand. Her fingers thread through mine, our hands join like Velcro.

"You can," she smiles back, with flirtation dancing in her eyes.

Our laughter follows us down the almost empty street, stopping every now and then to share memories, or kisses under the streetlights. We walk past the start of Lexi's road, and in silent agreement, just keep walking.

We stroll through the posh estate at the edge of town, and towards the park on the hill. Images of Lexi and I, and occasionally Jordan, racing our bikes. Me falling off my skateboard, twirls and twists on scooters, then revving engines of our first cars flash through my mind. I see a memory of myself as a cocky teenager, leaning against a lamppost. Crooked teeth shining under the soft orange light. Mine and Lex's fingers lacing, prints lining up like artwork, feet in perfect sync. Kisses in the rain, the snow, the sun. Taking corners too sharply in my Mini, INXS blaring from the stereo. Screaming with laughter. Everywhere we walk, there's a shadow of us together.

We end up doing a full loop, and our steps slow as we reach Lexi's front door.

"I'm guessing Callum has moved out?" I ask. My head and heart, and my cock full of expectation.

"You'd guess right," Lexi says with a smile.

"Why did you break up?"

"Is this not a cardinal sin? Talking about the ex on a date?"

"I've never been one for following rules."

"I told you already, he's not the one."

"Who is?" I ask with a bit more cheek that I probably needed. I see her mirror a smile back to me.

"You," Lexi shrugs. I study her eyes, the different shades of brown dancing under the stars. I see honesty, and perhaps a touch of embarrassment colour her smiling cheeks. Like the tide, she's coming back to me. Like I always believed, hoped. Fucking longed for.

"Can I propose yet?"

"Certainly not," she laughs out. A light from the opposite side of the shared garden flickers on, bathing the infamous willow tree in a soothing lustre.

"Are you going to invite me in, this time?" I ask with a head tilt, despite knowing the answer. Still, not let's not be too fucking presumptuous. I don't wanna fall at the last hurdle.

"I am," Lexi says as her fingers fumble with her keys.

"But leave the rock star persona outside, yeah?"

My lips attach to her neck, as I kick the door closed behind us. I peel off the coat from her shoulders, and spin Lexi to face me. My phone rings. I jump, but ignore it.

“Your own song is your ring tone?” Lexi asks, her laughter, and the tinny recording of my voice ruining the moment. I sigh loudly. Mavis pads through to join us from, I assume, a bedroom.

“It was a joke. Jordan has the same.” It was a joke, but who doesn't love a good ego boost? I extract the phone from my pocket, it’s Pete. I hang up and turn it onto silent. He can fucking wait. “Sorry, where were we?”

“About here,” Lexi says as she steps closer to me and our lips melt together. Her arms loop around my neck, I know without looking that she’s stood on her tiptoes. My fingers trace down her jawline, to her neck. I expect to find the delicate silver chain I placed around her, on her fifteenth birthday beneath my fingertips. But there’s just silken skin. I shrug it off, I don’t need an old necklace to tell me how she, or I feel. But still, I feel a punch to my pulsing heart. I wonder when she took it off? The vibrating from my pocket interrupts us again.

“Aren’t you Mr Popular?” Lexi smiles, she pushes away from me, and walks into her little kitchen. “Answer your phone, I’m going to feed Mavis.”

I stare at my phone. Pete, again. I throw the offending thing on the table and watch Lexi hang up her coat.

“I need a fag,” I say. Pete’s persistency has killed my mood, though I’m hoping only momentarily.

“You’re not smoking in here,” Lexi says and opens the front door. I head out and sit on the wall opposite her kitchen window. “Don’t be too long,” she adds on, seductively.

I shut the door behind me, the cigarette giving me some space to forget about Pete and focus on Lex. I step over Mavis who is munching loudly. I smile at Lexi, who is sitting cross armed on the small sofa.

"You ok, Babe?" I ask, with a sinking feeling in my stomach. What could have gone so fucking wrong in mere minutes?

"Do not 'Babe' me."

The smug smile falls from my face. What have I missed here? I crack my knuckles.

"Lex, what's going on?" I ask, hoping, praying that she hasn't found out about Pete's involvement.

"What's going on is that this," she spreads her arms out wide. "All this has been a lie."

"Lex, what do you –"

She cuts me off with a stony stare and slight stamp of her foot on her faded grey carpet.

"A little tip for you, Hayden, if setting up a fake date, publicity stunt, whatever it's called," *fuck.* "Either ensure everyone is aware of it, or keep your phone with you at all fucking times!" Lexi blinks, tears threatening behind her glasses, but anger refraining them from breaking her harsh voice. My heart plummets like a stone, my stomach churns and guilt washes over me like I'm in the river. I stare, wide eyed to see my phone on the table, buzzing in circles. I stalk over and snatch it up. I scroll through the new messages Pete has sent me. Can I do damage control on this? Can I still salvage this evening? It was going so fucking well.

I see the latest message, and several photos of me and

Lex throughout the evening. The four of us laughing, and of course, the money shot. Lexi and I kissing. *Fuck.*

Gold dust dude! Great plan to get the ex on board! Hello headline news! Excellent work, proud of you man.

I don't know how I can get back from this.

"Lexi, Lex, I can explain," I start, but actually have no idea what to tell her.

"It was all a set up?" She sounds angry and confused. But it's the hurt that cuts me deep.

"Yes, but I was going to ask you out anyway!" As the words leave my lips I know they're pathetic. Lexi laughs bitterly.

"Well, that's ok then, isn't it?"

"Is it?" I ask, knowing that I'm grasping at the last millimetre of the fucking straw.

"No, you fucking idiot! It isn't ok! You've lied to me, made a show of me, all for your precious band. I should've known it was all fake. What with the whole Jordan and Marlena Racer not actually dating revelation. God, you live in the craziest of realities."

"Pete's right, it is a good move for The Halcyon –"

"You don't even want to be in the band anymore, Hayden!" What? How does she know? Am I that obvious? Lexi flicks her fingers through her fringe, she stands up and starts pacing the room. Mavis follows her. "Each time Jordan mentioned The Halcyon earlier, you flinched. Physically cringed. Every time I see you, you keep repeating how refreshing it is to not be on stage, how you don't miss that life. It's obvious that you want out."

"I can't leave Jordan –"

"Jordan is a grown man. Grow a backbone, H. Stand up for yourself."

It's not that easy.

"I don't always have a choice," I sigh.

"You're in a band, not serving a prison sentence. Get over yourself," Lexi snaps, anger firing out of her mouth, like a dragon. She doesn't understand. Marlena's earlier words about Lexi not being right flitter through my mind. I chase them away like snowflakes in the wind.

"I'm sorry, Lex," I say as I deflate onto the chair. "For dragging you into my shit."

"You should be sorry. Fucking wanker."

"It wasn't a lie, though," I shake my head, pulling at the curls that cover my scalp. "I love you."

"I admit, you played a good game. I totally fell for it," Lexi wipes the tears from her cheeks. "You're a much better liar than you used to be."

I push myself out of the chair, my whole being aching. The anger at Pete, and myself, is coursing through my veins. Humiliation heats my muscles. Frustration buries itself in the marrow of my bones, though who or what is the source of frustration eludes me. Heartbreak, that I'm the reason for Lexi's tears, crackles through my chest.

I cup her face in my hands, gently yet persistently. Lexi struggles, avoiding my gaze, hitting at my wrists, but I hold her there. I implore to her chocolate eyes. She sighs, as her fight leaves her. Tears still tracking down her cheeks. Her shoulders drop and she stares back, it feels like we're the only two people in the world. The tides aligning once more.

"Marry me," I say. I expected another apology to fill the space between us, or possibly a kiss, not a marriage proposal. That doesn't mean I don't mean it. I find I do.

"You're fucking ridiculous."

"Ridiculous or romantic?"

I don't give Lex a chance to answer, instead placing gentle kisses across her face, tasting the salt from her tears. I want to smooth away the frown etched on her face, make the tears dissolve. She takes a step back and shakes her head.

"I don't know what's real, Hayden," Lexi sighs. "I've just been on an amazing double date with you, Jordan and a supermodel, then I find it's all a lie. I can't tell if I'm meant to be talking to a musical messiah or just some guy I used to know."

"It wasn't all lie, this isn't a lie," I grab her hands. Her frown remains. Heavy pulled down eyebrows, lining her face like war paint. "The only thing that was fake about the date were the D cups stuck on Marlena's chest."

Lexi chuckles slightly yet still looks torn, almost.

"I love you, Lex," I'm hoping she'll say it back to me. I wait, feeling like I'm the final note in the concerto. Waiting for the applause to start. The note fades out and silence encases us.

"I think you should go," Lexi says, looking at her feet. The discordant note breaking the weighted silence.

17

"Morning," I say to my dad as I enter the kitchen diner. He's poring over some colourful leaflets, while drinking tea and munching on toast so dark it's almost black.

"Son," he says, his usual greeting. Dad is a man of few words, usually. But at the moment I am so far in the doghouse, I've practically sprouted a fucking tail and might as well have a collar around my neck.

The very next day after the double date of doom, photos of Lexi and I were on every internet site and tabloid paper going. It was indeed, great publicity, had I wanted it to be. Jordan was fucking thrilled. Marlena sent me a string of love heart emojis, and a seductive lingerie pose, both of which I ignored. Pete sent a bottle of champagne. A fucking Solomon bottle, eighteen fucking litres of the stuff. It was grotesque to look at. I was so overcome with guilt at the furore I'd brought on Lex, I gave the obscene bottle to the Italian restaurant.

The photos are pretty good, at least that's something. I couldn't deny that. Lexi and I make a great couple. Our children will be beautiful, that much is a given. If I could only get Lexi to see me, I'm sure she'd agree. I've been to Lexi's office and flat every fucking day since. She's ignored or avoided me each time.

Today though, I've left a present for her on her doorstep. A lemon cheesecake, her very favourite, which I made from scratch yesterday. Wrapped in a box accompanied by a hand-written note. Hopefully that will win her over, and we can get back onto the road which we were travelling down.

"Pete's coming by later."

I drop the mug I've just taken from the cupboard, in shock. Splinters of a faded map of Scotland cover the kitchen floor.

"Shit! Sorry, Dad," I sweep it up, keep myself busy to detract from my managers' impending visit. He's still banging on about getting me back on stage. I have started composing a few new songs, but they're certainly not ready. Lyrically I'm pretty fucking proud of them. They feel more real, my heart jumps. It's probably being back and seeing Lexi again, which is adding to the authenticity. Not that they're anything like Pete and Jordan have produced recently. Theirs are much more polished, perfect. Ready. My lyrics and compositions aside, I am not ready to perform yet. But, I guess I'll have to, or Jordan will take a shredder to my beloved wardrobe, and our friendship.

"What are you reading about?" I ask, anything to delay talking about Pete.

"Grief counselling," he replies, steadily. I empty the dustpan into the bin, and snort.

"Who's died?" I ask.

"Your mother, Hayden."

I snort again. Not exactly a current death, Dad. It was two years ago. I tug on my curls, as I remember her birthday is coming up very soon. Sneaking up on me like frost on the ground in winter.

"She was a fucking alcoholic," I shout at my dad, anger burning through my skin. I don't understand why he has to be so sad about the loss of a woman who caused him nothing but heartache. "Why did you roll your eyes?"

"It's easy for us to say that," he frowns at me. "She was a very ill woman, Hayden."

How can he defend her? She ruined our lives.

"She picked drink over her child and her husband! And you're defending her like some kind of whipped pussy!" I shout. I can't believe this. How can he attempt to justify her actions, after all she put us through?

"I loved your mother, you know I did."

"She could've just fucking stopped. Why didn't she?" I ask, the question burning like hot coffee flavoured with acid on the tip of my tongue.

"Why didn't you when you were getting into trouble in London?" My dad asks me, calmly. The strong, grounded rocks to my waves of furious temper. "Why don't you stop now?"

I open my mouth to respond. Why didn't I? Why don't I? I didn't want to. I don't want to. I wanted to drink. I wanted to let go of everything. I still do now.

"The apple doesn't fall far from the tree, is that what you're saying?!" I bark out, purely in defiance. "You're calling me a fucking alcoholic?"

"You're doing so well, and I want to deal with my own issues so I can support you."

I note that he didn't answer my pissing question.

"Mum and me, both driven to drink. And you're the sober one. Maybe it's you with the fucking problem," I slam the cupboards closed, just to make a noise. I wince at the harshness of my words, and take a step backwards, bumping my arse into the sticky oven, trays clanging loudly inside. I didn't mean it. Any of it.

"Sorry, Dad," I swallow, that was a pathetic excuse of an apology, even by my standards. Lydia would make me apologise again, using proper words of meaning and explanation. But they're trapped in my throat.

"It's ok, Hayden," he says with a shallow smile, as he pushes his chair backwards.

"It's not ok, is it? This is all my fault," tears pool in my eyes, breaths pant out of me as my chest heaves with heavy emotions. The doorbell interrupts the hug my dad is about to pull me into.

"That will be your manager."

Pete Morris-Turner looks totally out of place striding through my dad's narrow hallway. He's a big hot shot American music mogul. Stereotypically he looks exactly how you'd expect. Average height, jet black (I suspect dyed) hair swept back and covered in slick gel. He works out, but he's not slim; more well-built. Sturdy. Bulky.

Dressed in a black pinstriped suit, he looks like he's just attended a funeral in the Florida sunshine. Dark shades nearly always cover his eyes while outside. Inside, they're always clipped over his jacket pocket. He looks like the uncle of the average family, slightly creepy but loaded from carrying out dodgy deals online. Perma-tanned fluorescent orange skin. He's smooth, sleek, but with a rough edge to him that's as cutting as a razor blade. Cutthroat yet professional.

Women fall at his feet; it must be the control and power. I've witnessed countless girls crying over him, swooning over him, being told that he can't commit to them. I don't get the appeal personally. Men, on the other hand want to play golf with him, share a whiskey then punch him. In that order. Or that's what I've observed. To me, he's the best manager we could have asked for. He knows what he's talking about in regard to the music and celebrity world. He's self-absorbed, always has to be right. Even when it's clear he's very wrong. But he knows his stuff.

"I'll leave you two to chat," dad says as he grabs his jacket from the coat hook behind the front door.

"Privacy is no issue of mine, Mr Coulthard," Pete smiles out. I roll my eyes, internally of course. He's also a charming fucker.

"It's at my insistence," dad beams and squeezes my shoulder as he passes. "Stand your ground, Son," he whispers into my ear as he gives me a quick hug.

I watch Pete open his briefcase over the round pine table, and hear the shuffling of papers. What do I have to sign now?

"Hayden, man," Pete doesn't stand up to greet me as I enter the kitchen diner, but he places a bottle of whiskey down on the table, and produces two glasses from the monogrammed crocodile skin briefcase. Pete oozes money, power, wealth. It jars with the homely scents of lingering burnt toast, chai tea and the cling of fish fingers dad and I had for tea last night.

I gulp. My mouth starts watering as I watch the amber liquid glide effortlessly from its tall frosted bottle, into the two vessels on the table. Droplets splashing up the sides and landing like crystals on the table surface. I scrub my hand down my face. *Fuck,* I want to lick the table clean before ripping the bottle from Pete's hands and pour it down my parched throat. I sit down instead, placing my hands under my thighs, and try to recall how to form words.

"I'm discouraged that there hasn't been any further sightings of yourself and the lovely Lexi Blackwood," Pete states. He rarely talks to people; he talks at them. I'm used to it. That's how he gets shit done.

"She won't speak to me," I shrug. Fuck knows I've tried.

"That's not my problem, man. Column inches are exactly what we need. But if she's a no go, I can line up a new love interest. The Halcyon needs press coverage, especially as I have a surprise for you!" Pete smiles fiendishly, his whitened teeth blinding.

Fuck, what now. I was under the impression he's here to discuss contracts, and my finances; at least that's what he told dad.

He slides out a poster with mine and Jordan's silhouettes on.

"I've booked you a show in Carlisle! It's sure to be a sell out," Pete announces, a grin like the Cheshire cat on his face.

"I don't want to do it," I admit. I don't think I could

even if I wanted to. I had hoped that this show of dreams wouldn't ever materialise, that it would forever remain in the pipes. Now it looks set to become a nightmare reality. Pete laughs, a brittle sound. It jars around the room like a shattering glass.

"Oh, is that so?"

"I'm not doing it," I repeat, louder. I need to be clear in my thoughts and opinions, Lydia says, I need to have the conviction to stand up for myself. I still have two more weeks, and countless sessions left with Lydia at Paws2Heal. Pete promised me I'd get six weeks rest from the band. Fucking liar.

"Yes, you are. Jordan is all set; we start rehearsals tomorrow."

"I don't want to be on stage right now," I scrub my hands over my face, pulling at my wayward curls. I was under the impression I had at least another two weeks of this freedom, this new life away from performing.

"The industry won't wait until you're ready, man. We have to move quickly. Jordan's good, but he's no Hayden Coulthard. He's nothing without you, even though he's had offers for a solo deal," Pete says, I know he's trying to both flatter and goad me. My ego inflates, I despise that his words are working on me.

I'm a way better performer than Jordan. And I'm a far superior lyricist. Yet the news that Jordan is being head hunted as a solo artist unsettles me. I know how the media, the industry works. They'll pitch us against one another; bandmates turned rivals. It will be fucking carnage, until one of us succeeds. I don't want that. None of it. I'd prefer to stay on stage forever with my friend, than watch how we become one another's nemesis. I couldn't do it without him. He couldn't do it without me, surely.

"The solo deals won't happen. Yet. You're both bound contractually, to perform, as The Halcyon," Pete smirks.

"I thought we could discuss that, actually. I'm not happy with my contract."

"Do this show, then we'll discuss it," Pete replies instantly – so quickly I'm unsure if he's actually listening. I sulk, my bottom lip jutting outwards like a child, I stare at the ceiling to avoid Pete's eyes.

"I want control of my bank account, give me that and I'll do the show," I counter. Pete holds out a large, orange-coloured hand.

"Deal."

That went well. I'm pleased with that fucking outcome. I snatch the glass closest to me and down it. If that was a test, I have failed. But the fuck I care. I cough, the burning liquid feels harsh, but it soon transforms into a spreading of warmth down my chest. Oh, sweet relief, I've missed it. Pete sips his glass and tilts his head and glass in my direction.

"To you, Hayden Coulthard, and getting back on stage, where you belong."

He pours me another drink as soon as my empty glass leaves my hand. As much as I'm desperate to, I resist picking it up. I can show self-restraint if need be. I pop my knuckles like bubble wrap as a calming distraction instead. I feel sweat fill my armpits and the dips in my spine, as I try to hold off from the whiskey. "I can get the finance department to get in touch with your dad, Hayden. But I can't trust you to regain full access to your accounts, yet," Pete puts up a palm to silence me, as my mouth opens.

"Talk it through with finance."

Not quite as straightforward as I first thought, then. Fucking stupid of me to think it would be that simple, I guess. I sigh, puffing air out of my inflated cheeks.

"I was supposed to be with you here for longer, but things have cropped up, man. I need to head back to London ASAP," Pete says. And yes, he does pronounce 'asap' as a word. Cringe.

"You're not even going to be here for the gig?" I ask. I can hear the pleading tone of my voice. Pete may be trapping me with a contract and control of my money, but he's always got my back. He encourages me and Jordan, always there when we need a push in the right direction.

"Don't worry dude, I've got a full team in place. Raven and Higgsy can hold the fort, and Jordan will be there with you," Pete says dismissively, referring to The Halcyon's tour manager and head of security.

"Why can't you stay?" I ask, and I mentally scold myself as I realise I'm reaching out for the glass of whiskey again, like instinct.

"Because, Hayden, I barely have time to chase after my wayward acts, let alone check if you stay on the goddamn stage! My job involves more than just you," he claps his large hands once, indicating the end of discussion. "My number one lead singer. I'm missing being in the studio with you. Jordan's good, do not get me wrong, but he's not you. You know he'd be lost performing without you. When you go solo, you're going to swallow him whole. How are you doing, man? Are we on the road to recovery or do we need to issue a statement?"

"I'm ok."

"That fifth drink of whiskey says otherwise, man."

I flush, from the alcohol and a faint tinge of embarrassment. The drink was a test as I first thought, and I clearly have failed. Well, what's new there.

"I hear you've had a few moments under the influence at the local free houses too."

Apparently so, the memories elude me still. I crack my knuckles.

"I need more time, Pete. I'm maybe more reliant on alcohol than I thought," I say. *Fuck, please do not send me back to London.*

"It doesn't bode well for the career, Hayden, if you're an addict."

I flinch at that word. Just like my mother.

"I just underestimated the recovery time. I wanna stay here. The fresh air is good for me, I'm getting out. Walking, breathing, you know? I'm thinking about getting a dog." I sound pathetic. He's not gonna roll with me on this. Any of it.

"Dogs and bands don't mix."

"I thought that was girls and bands?" I ask. Fuck, I'm slurring, I can taste the salt of sweat from my upper lip. Pete shrugs.

"Same difference. Though at least you can tell a dog what to do, keep it on a leash," he guffaws, I give out a short, awkward chuckle. "In between your therapy, why don't you start writing your next album. We'll need material to put together with Jordan's, but scale down the angst. Moms don't want angst," Pete says.

"These things can't be rushed," I slur, then clear my throat. If you wanna make a decent album, you can't rush the magic. Songs don't work well under pressure. Unless you're Queen, of course.

"They can be if you're working to a time scale," Pete taps a tanned finger on his glimmering gold watch. "Jordan's writing has come to him as naturally as breathing. If I was you, I'd be worried."

"I have been writing actually," I wriggle in the wooden seat as I slide my battered leather bound notebook across the table. "They're different to what Jordan has come up with, but –"

My words fade out and hang in the air. I watch with desperate, eager eyes as Pete skims through the pages. He sighs, then with a shake of his head he locks it into his briefcase.

"You don't need to take it –"

"These aren't good enough, man," Pete says shaking his head again. I feel a pang of disappointment. Of course he's going to prefer Jordan's. He's not in the fucking doghouse like I am. I could have written the next fucking *Smells Like Teen Spirit*, *Never Tear Us Apart*; this generation's *Heroes* or fucking *Hey Jude*, and Pete would fucking dismiss it, as I wrote it.

"I'll work on them." I hold my shaking palm out. I want my words back.

"No point, they're not right for the new image. Try again, try harder," He points a finger at me, like he's giving commands to a pet.

"Right, so gig on Tuesday –"

"Tuesday?" That's less than a fucking week away. I'll never wriggle out of it in less than seven fucking days.

"And get back with Lexi, if you decide to stick with the girl next door vibe. Both are non-optional," Pete states, no nonsense, no fucking room for discussion.

"You can't make me go on stage! I'm in the middle of rehab, Pete!" I fire out, anger fizzing like champagne through my veins. I'm pissed off about the songs. I know they're decent. And now he's totally taken them from me. Fucking confiscated them like I'm a naughty child.

"I'm not making you do anything, man. It's in your contract to uphold appearances and scheduling that the band have committed to. Technically, you should be in the studio with Jordan, but hey, I'm going easy on you," Pete smiles. I suppose he didn't have to give me this time in rehab. He could have taken me back to London. He can certainly keep easy tabs on me down there. "And arrange a date with Lexi."

"I love Lex. I don't want to bring her into this again."

"Fine, then I'll set you up with someone else. Marlena has just signed a lingerie deal with Ella Egan, she'll fit the bill."

"That's not what I –"

"This is your whole career, man. Not to mention everyone else who is involved with The Halcyon. They don't get paid if there's no one to work with."

"I'm not doing anything on purpose!" I plead. I bang my fists on the table, making the honey-coloured whiskey jump out of the glasses. Pete's largely untouched. I down them both in quick succession. My throat burns, and I grimace.

"I am trying to do the best by you, Hayden. You wanted signed. This is your dream, man, not mine. What is it you say, 'No going back'? Take note of your own words," Pete says.

"I am not ready to go back on stage," I state, clearly. As clearly as I can with a whiskey infused tongue. I cannot even begin to imagine performing yet.

Pete starts packing up his papers into the animal print briefcase, then folds his arms on top of it once locked shut.

"You will be on stage, with Jordan next week. Both of you following every, single instruction I have left for you. Or you, Hayden have got no hope of regaining financial control," he snarls, calmly but laced with venom, the viper coiled to strike. For the first time I think I'm scared of him. "No going back, Hayden."

I swipe my arms across the surface of the table and knock everything off in one fell swoop. Glasses shatter, papers tumble, Pete's closed briefcase lands with an echoing thump on the floor. He stands up, the chair legs scraping on the wooden flooring. I hear myself breathing heavily as Pete's shoes crunch over the broken bottle and glasses. The front door slams, and I'm left alone. With just my screaming, overwhelming thoughts, and a fucking pounding head for company.

18

"Tell me Hayden, was your mum always alcohol dependent?" Lydia asks from her throne in her leafy office. I'm sat on the floor, Anoushka chewing on a squeaky toy. My hand smooths down her back. I'm not even a bit bothered about the drool that is draped over my Gucci trousers. When did I stop caring?

"I don't remember it when I was little, but dad told me she was always drinking," I roll my eyes. I have little sympathy for my mother, dead or not. Though I am perhaps starting to appreciate that when drinking becomes a habit, well, it's fucking hard to stop. To lessen it. Not that I'm ready or willing to admit that out loud to Lydia, or anyone.

I'm struck like a bass drum in the heart with painful realisation. My dad asked me why I didn't just stop drinking. I told him he was being ungrateful. I could be a drug addict, which would be far worse than relying on a drink to get me through the fucking days.

A few years ago, drugs were exciting; the rush was phenomenal. I felt like a superhero surrounded by neon lights and magic. I wanted to chase that high, but I never caught it again. They started affecting my music too much. Both Jordan and I took it a bit far. We couldn't produce or write. My vision was blurry, and I was seeing stars and having random hallucinations. I started drinking more to hide from the demons the drugs created. But by then I had a reputation of life and soul of the party to live up too. It was easier, much easier to function after a few drinks. The alcohol chilled me out, unlike the drugs that made me hyper. And the more I drank, the more I could handle. Until it became a habit, a habit that I thought I could just stop, but it turns out that I –

Can't.

Fuck, I can't. I can't stop.

I gulp as I realise Lydia is addressing me.

"And you were how old when she left?"

"About six."

"Do you know her reasons for leaving?" Lydia asks.

"Dad said she was ill. That's what I was told, that's what I believed for a few years. Me and dad didn't see her until I was about nine, maybe ten. I was excited to see her again. You can only remember good things about people once they've left."

My mind wanders to Lexi. If she never speaks to me again, will she remember the precious gems of moments we've shared; or will she forever be tasting the bitter deceit of my lies?

"There were bad times too?" Lydia probes, as her pen scratches on her paper.

I was left at school a lot, didn't have lunch as she'd spend the money on the way on a bottle of wine. She missed birthday parties, forgot presents. She slept a lot. Threw things when she came back from seeing her friends. Turned up drunk at Christmas. I don't want to tell Lydia all of this, so instead I just nod.

"Did that change when she came back into your life at ten?" Lydia probes.

"No, to be honest it just got worse," I feel a pressure behind my eyes, a throb building in my throat. Anoushka whines at me and I try to concentrate on the feel of her fur, the golden sparkle in her eyes. But I can't block it out. The memory is chiselled into my brain like the tattoos on my skin. I will forever carry it with me.

The straight path that led directly from the bus stop to the flat's main doors. My hands, nose pressed up against the living room window. From six floors up, you get a decent view. Buses came and went, dislodging people like beans from a tin.

None of those beans were my mum though. She'd been poorly for the last three times she was meant to pick me up. The skies turned from blue to dusky grey via orange and pink; she promised she'd be here. I could hear dad pacing the room behind me. Slamming down the phone receiver each time he tried to call.

"She'll be here, Dad. She promised."

I refused to get into my Power Rangers pajamas, refused a bath. Refused to accept it was bedtime, and far too late for a trip to the park and McDonalds with my mum.

"She's here!" I squealed as I spotted a familiar bob of blonde curls exit the bus and wobble her way under the streetlamp. She stumbled and fell onto her knees. I watched as a bottle rolled out of her shopping bag. She promised she was bringing me my favourite crisps and some

chocolate; I didn't ask for any juice.

Dad joined me at the window, I heard his sigh.

"Hayden, stay here," he said quietly, as he left the flat.

Minutes later I saw him jog over towards my mum. She was still on the frosty ground, underneath a lamppost closer to the flat. Now drinking the juice. It wasn't juice, it was wine. She was poorly again. The wine and vodka, other drinks like that, they made her ill. She was poorly because she couldn't stop drinking them.

I opened the window in dad's room and climbed onto the balcony. Voices travel far and high. I could hear them shouting.

"You've let the boy down, again."

"You're a fucking tyrant."

"I want what's best for Hayden."

"You're trying to control me."

"You're an unfit mother."

"You knew this about me."

"Loves drink more than your own child."

"You're trying to turn me into something I'm fucking not."

"He needs you; he wants to see you."

"Let me fucking see him then you self-righteous prick."

"You can't be a mother and an alcoholic."

"You can fucking keep him then."

"You don't mean that, Sheena."

"I fucking well do."

"Come back when you're sober."

"I'll come back when I fucking like; he's my son."

"It's not fair to do this to him."

"Give it a rest, Jock. He's seen me drunk before."

"You need to make more of an effort."

"I'm fucking here, aren't I?"

"Hours too late to take him out; it's not good enough."

"I'm never good enough for you, am I?"

"This isn't about me, Sheena. Did you at least bring him a present? A card?"

"What for? It's not Christmas."

"Sheena, you are unbelievable."

I ran into my bedroom, dived under my covers and cried. I knew dad was there, I could hear him shushing me, promising me that it would all be ok. But I stayed buried under the covers, silently sobbing. My own mum forgot my birthday.

"She forgot my birthday. Didn't even bring me a card round late, nothing, just fuck all," I sigh rubbing the same old tears from my eyes, along with my eyeliner. The pain feels as real and raw as it did when I was ten.

"Do you feel your mother tried her best, Hayden?" Lydia asks, pushing a box of tissues towards me.

"No. She was a fucking alcoholic! She would rather drink than see her family!" I shout. Lydia scowls at me and indicates a finger towards Anoushka, who doesn't like loud voices. She lets out a low howl. I tickle behind her floppy ear in apology. Lydia pushes the pile of leaflets, which she has referred to each and every fucking session towards me.

"There's much more to it than just drinking, Hayden. I really think you'd benefit from reading these." My eyes, blurry from the tears, pick out encouraging words from the leaflets, offering support and understanding for alcoholics, addicts, children raised with such people as parents.

I sigh, blowing air from my cheeks. My cheeks burning in embarrassment. I'm like her. I'm turning into my mother.

"Fine. I'll take them home." But I'm not promising I'll read these apparent helpful and informative brochures. Anoushka nudges my ribs with her nose, I continue tickling her huge ears.

"Do you think your mum was trying to make amends when she came to your house in London?" I shake my head. Wouldn't that have been a lovely joyous reunion, a happy ending for mother and son? The truth is, I never asked. I didn't ask what she wanted. I assumed it was money, and she sure didn't refuse it. I never knew, never understood why my mum drank to excess. I was always scared to ask why, in case I was the reason behind it. I knew, I know, I made her habit easier for her to fund. I have guilt about the financial support I gave her, pressing on my lungs every minute of every fucking day. But I couldn't cut her out. I couldn't. She was still my mum. Plus, Pete said it was best to keep tabs on her. So I bought her a flat, kept her bank account topped up. If she spent it on gin, well, that wasn't my decision.

I slide down onto the floor further towards Anoushka's body, and hide my face in her thick fur. Her tail thumps merrily on the hardwood floor.

"Why do you drink Hayden?" Lydia asks, a question she hasn't repeated since our first session together. I look up at her blue eyes.

"To forget," I shrug, then feel my mouth go slack. I'd never realised that before, I do turn to alcohol to forget memories, to escape from haunting images.

"What are you trying to forget?"

The room is drowned in the loud, hiccupping wails from my core for what feels like hours, until I can finally get the words out. Four words that I've never admitted to. Four words that stoke a fire in me; the flames can only be extinguished with alcohol. Tears stream down my face, and my eyes scrunch shut in pure shame.

"I killed my mum."

19

"Is Lexi here?" I ask Raven. He's been our stage manager, tour manager, general busybody and Pete's favourite minion, since The Halcyon were signed.

Raven runs a pale hand through his platinum hair, the other hand attached to a ringing mobile the size of a family size chocolate bar. He's a short man, barely the same height as Lexi, but he practically runs the show. His jaw, as straight as castle walls, is dotted with yellow hairs like a scrubbing brush.

I pushed a ticket and backstage pass through Lexi's letter box yesterday. I scribbled a note too, telling her that the date wasn't my idea. I shouldn't have fucking agreed to it. I wanted an easy life from Pete, and I wanted a date with Lexi. It's just my fucking luck it backfired on me. I pleaded with her to come tonight too. A pissing fruitless task, if the past ten years are anything to go by.

Not once has Lexi appeared at my shows, and believe me, I have sent her tickets and passes to the majority of our UK gigs. I'm always searching the crowd for those chocolate eyes. I'm the one left alone in hotel rooms, waiting for her to open the door. I'm the one always left hanging, like the last forgotten peg on the fucking washing line.

"If she turns up, I will inform you," Raven replies in a bored tone while he continues looking at his phone, and ever-present clipboard. I watch him in the mirror, giving instructions to a variety of people, most of whom I've never seen before.

Backstage is like a busy airport terminal, but with no perks of duty free. Though there is always an endless supply of alcohol, cigarettes, honey and lemon drinks and cheese and onion crisps. But still, there's no half price Gaultier aftershave to stock up on, nor chocolate bars as big as my fucking guitar. People bustle and tussle to get to the right make up brush, to attach the right wire, tighten the last lightbulb. Echoes and screeches filter from the stage as the sound guys do a final run through. I'm like the hive they all flap their wings to return to, this dizzying fluttering all centres on me. Usually I fucking love it, bask in their dedicated attention, encourage them to inflate my supersize ego more, so I can go out on stage knowing I'm the best in the business. Yet today I'm stood stock still, only moving when requested to.

I notice things expected of me, asked of me: t-shirts and posters thrust in front of my hands for me to sign for competition winners or needy fans. Wires and sound packs are masking-taped to my half-naked body. I'm measured and weighed, poked and prodded like cattle. Foundation smeared on my neck to find the exact shade. Tattoos that 'don't fit the new image' glazed over with layers of make-up.

Everyone is talking to me, at me, across me in voices

one higher octave than the usual. The air fizzes with excitement for the whole crew, adrenaline makes everyone move quicker like worker bees before the pollen runs dry. On a standard gig day these things roll over me as if I'm the lines on a music sheet; here and now I feel like the flat note, the low note in the pissing high section. I'm the one in the wrong. I shouldn't be here. I don't want to be here.

Jordan's loud, brash laugh drifts into the shells of my ears. I turn towards the door, batting off the woman fiddling with my earrings. My lip curls in disgust as I take in his outfit. He looks like a clown playing dress up in a king's robe.

"What the fuck are you wearing?"

"A suit," Jordan shrugs. "Obviously. Here's yours," he holds up a coat hanger draped in a grey suit. It matches his. They're both boring and insipid. Crimes against fashion. A million miles away from my usual designer, bespoke wear.

Marlena trots in on her sky-high heels, that make her toned legs looks endless. She holds up a dark grey tie, the colour of slate that matched the beard that adorned my face, until moments ago. Now it lies rejected by my feet. Abandoned, like reels on the cutting room floor.

"This is Ella," Marlena says, winking a winged Cleopatra eye at me. She gently nudges a tall, beanpole of a woman towards me, who looks like she hasn't eaten a meal in the past five years. Her sunken but dark eyes emphasise her prominent cheekbones. Model and coke addict. Just what I don't fucking need. She places a kiss on my bare cheek.

"I'm the new Lexi," she says by way of introduction.

The fuck you are, I want to spit out at her.

"I haven't agreed to this," I say to Raven instead, ignoring this Ella completely. Raven shrugs helplessly.

"I'd better still get paid," Ella snaps, sending visual daggers towards Marlena. This is who Pete wants to set me up with? What a fucking delight she seems to be.

"You'll get paid if the photos make the press, now let's stand you up Hayden, and pose as a foursome," Marlena says, hands on her concave waist, as she pulls myself, Ella and Jordan together to form a group. "Loving the clean-shaven look, Hayden," Marlena smiles at me, her green eyes glinting under the fluorescent lights. "It takes years off you."

Literal fucking years. I look about fourteen.

I plaster a half smile on my face, and look emptily into several phones and cameras before flopping back down in the stylist's chair. This night is getting more ridiculous by the fucking minute.

"We don't wear suits," I state to Jordan. He shrugs as a woman scoops the offending item out of his hands and starts steaming invisible creases from it.

"It's the new look."

"I wasn't told about this, mate," I say to his reflection, as the chair is spun back around from the doorway. "You look fucking ridiculous."

"At least we'll match," Jordan laughs. I'm failing to see the hilarity. They'll have us sat on fucking bar stools next, standing up at the key change.

"We're not in a fucking boyband!"

"Hayden, it's a suit," Jordan says, rubbing his

forehead. "What does it matter?"

"It matters, because when we signed a record deal, it was for our fucking music. I didn't realise I was signing away my clothing preferences and musical direction."

"Pete said you might kick off about this," Marlena pitches in, like a tin whistle in a fucking string quartet. "Though we were also expecting a bigger fight about Ella, maybe Lexi isn't as important to you as we thought."

"Last time I checked, Marlena, you weren't in this band, so will you kindly shut the fuck up?"

"Mate!" Jordan snaps. "Don't take your pissing bad mood out on her."

"There won't be a band for either of you if you don't embrace this," Marlena spits out.

The fuck? "If you put in half the effort with this rebranding as Jordan has –"

"I didn't want to be fucking rebranded!" I shout at her.

"You should have thought of that before you messed up the reputation of your precious band by walking out," Marlena says, her arms crossed across her fake boobs. The sticky looking pink lips and eyelashes stretching from her eyelids, modelling her into a real-life doll.

Fuck's sake. I am not taking career advice from a woman playing beauty pageants.

"Can I just have five fucking minutes with Jordan," I say to everyone and no one in particular.

The room clears and Jordan plops down on the bench, littered and lined with make-up and water bottles.

"I hate this, mate," I say. "This isn't what we're about –"

"She's right, you know?" Jordan says with a sigh. "It's this or nothing. I hate to say this, trust me. But this is your fault. We wouldn't have to reinvent The Halcyon if you hadn't wandered off."

I try not to roll my eyes at the whole reinvention shite. It was apparently discovered after my walk out, that the fans, according to the polls, wherever the fuck Pete had got those from, would wholeheartedly embrace a new chapter. A step or five away from the increasingly in scale bad boy image, which I was dragging Jordan and The Halcyon into, would be the only way to keep us on the press and fans' good, money spending, record buying side. Whatever. I wasn't in the least bit supportive of it.

I ignore him. I am not about to take any words from Marlena Racer's trout pout as fucking gospel. Nor am I going to take full responsibly. I didn't invent these polls and opinions which we now had to follow. Sure, I left. But I felt I had no other fucking option.

"Are you happy with changing everything we're about?" I ask him.

"Yes."

"Pete's not here, you can be honest, Jordan."

He sighs again, and his fingers go to fiddle with his nose ring, something he does when he's nervous. But of course, it's been removed. His face looks strange without the splices of metal glinting in it. He starts indicating to the corner of the room with his head, and subtly covering one side of his face, before mouthing incomprehensible words to me.

"What the fuck? Are you having some kind of stroke?"

He shakes his head, and sighs.

"Never mind. I want to be in The Halcyon. I want make music, but most importantly, I wanna do it with you. This was our dream!" He spreads his arms around the room:

posters of The Halcyon stuck to the walls, tables piled high with any requested item we want, stacks of signed merchandise just waiting to be sold. “We’re still living it, Hayden. It’s just taking a detour. Think of it as a challenge.”

I feel my back pressed straight against the chair, with a force like I’ve been shot. I pull my fingers away from my chest expecting to see red blood. I look at Jordan, my best friend. He’s animated, smiling, excited. That’s how I should be feeling. Instead I just feel trapped, caged in.

My hand goes to my lovebird tattoo on my shoulder. The one that I was ‘strongly advised’ to cover up. Apparently, no fan wants to know their favourite singer has a matching tattoo with his first love. I toed the line with it, but only just. I placed the bird inside a thick lined cage, ensuring that the ‘LB’ on its chest was concealed by the lock. They’ve covered it up in layers of foundation and concealer now. Fucking stupid, as my arms will be hidden by that fucking awful suit.

“We’ve got to go in this direction to put a distance between any issues we had,” Jordan continues.

“You mean me?”

“I mean, the carnage you caused when you abandoned me, if you want specifics,” he smiles despite trying to frown. “You left me with no choice but to push forward. You may be the front man, but it’s my band, my dream too, mate. Pete’s pushing us to do this; we need to be on the same page together. Whatever that page may be.”

“I know, and for what’s it worth, I do appreciate it,” I say, scrubbing my palm over my now smooth chin.

“You just hate my songs.”

“I resent them, the fact we have to change the sound.

I don't hate what you created,"

I mean it. Jordan is immensely talented, but I can tell the sound and lyrics have been distorted, to fit into this mould The Halcyon now have to fill.

"Are you in this with me? Or is this a waste of time?"

The door pushes open after a brief knock. It's Ben, our hairdresser. He smiles, but I can tell it's forced. No doubt he's following orders.

"Sorry guys," he says to us gently. "But I need to get a move on with your hair, Hayden."

"Hayden?" Jordan prompts as he stands up, he looks nervous too. This is his dream, our shared dream. Who am I to take it away from him? I might be fucking good at my job, but I'm not a god.

"Fuck off, Jordan, some of us have to get ready," I smile, and hope it reaches my eyes. He pats me on the back and laughs as he saunters out the room.

My eyes glance to the mirror in front of me, I see the suit I'm meant to wear on stage hung over the back of the door. *It's just a suit.*

"Ready, Hayden?" Ben asks, I see the glinting scissors tucked into his pocket, his hand wrapped around a shaver. No guard.

I shake my head.

"No," I feel stupidly emotional. "I just need a fucking shot first," I say to my reflection.

A whiskey bottle is placed in my hand instantly from someone anonymous. I gulp the burning liquid down. I wipe my mouth and pretend I'm not about to cry. It is just hair. It will grow back.

"Do it," I say, flatly. I close my eyes, and feel the

buzzing against my head, it resonates through my skull. Echoing in my ears, down through to my teeth. I feel the cold hit my scalp. The soft falling curls, like leaves from an autumn tree, brush against my bare arms. *Fuck*.

"You look," Raven stammers, I can see his mouth moving like a ventriloquist's dummy to try form the correct word. "Different. Young."

I look like a pissing child in an older brothers' hand me downs. The cuffs on the suit come down to nearly my knuckles. The leg length trails on the floor, luckily hiding most of the boring, so unlike me, tan shoes. The remnants of Hayden Fucking Coulthard stare, lifeless back at me from the mirror. My sky-blue eyes aren't lined in kohl. The necklaces, rings, bracelets and beads have gone from round my neck and wrists. There's not even a silver loop in my ear lobe. There's no sign of my trademark curls. I'm void of anything that made me, me.

"What have I done to myself?" I ask my dulled reflection.

"Followed orders," Raven's eyes meet mine in the full-length mirror, they are full of pity, of apology. "Welcome to the club, kid. It pays the bills."

I can't even attempt a smile. The last thing I want to do was walk out on stage and perform, let alone when looking like a shrunken skeleton drowning in an oversized suit. I need another drink.

All week, we've been rehearsing. Each run through I've hated it more. The sound, the songs, the act we have to follow: everything. Unlike in rehearsals though, I've now lost my curls and short beard. I feel naked.

The last miniature bottle of whiskey has given me newborn foal legs. Yet unlike usual, it's made my confidence plummet to my toes. My hands are shaking so violently I feel I could start an earthquake. I've cracked my knuckles so much they hurt. It hasn't calmed me down in the slightest.

One of the women from wardrobe plops a curly wig on my head, I feel like a clown.

I see Jordan and Marlena smiling into another camera. They look happy, but I can tell that their smiles are salt pretending to be sugar. Someone else hands me a guitar, luckily not my own. Jordan swaggers off, spring in his fucking step, and takes his place on top of the cajon drum. I look around, still no sign of Lexi. It's what I expected, but the weight of disappointment sits heavy in my heart.

"Good luck, Hayden," Marlena says, as she smooths down the boring grey lapels, and places a kiss on my naked cheek. I try to smile, but instead I sigh with nerves and trepidation.

"Good luck," Ella says to me. I regard her with a look of suspicion. Is that really my type? Ella brushes her ash blonde hair off her, admittedly pretty, face and kisses me full on the lips. I feel her hot tongue trying to wind its way into my shocked mouth, and I see the flash of a camera resound in my eyes. That's the fucking money shot I guess. I push her away and serve her a look of fucking disgust. She shrugs and wanders away, her pert arse attracting my sexual attention for a split second.

A lady from make-up appears, dusts my face with more powder, and smoothers lip balm over my ambushed lips.

20

I walk out, stand on the x and wait behind the curtain. I can hear Raven counting down in my ears. I focus on breathing and nothing else. Inhale. Exhale. I do my best to ignore the shakiness of the air entering and exiting my lungs. I try to force the dark clouds to lift up from my shoulders, my eyes, my brain, my heart. I think of Lexi, the only girl I've ever loved. The only woman I want to love. *Fuck.* I miss her so much. I blink rapidly, like hummingbird wings to stop the tears from falling.

I look over to Jordan, who is double checking his suit. He looks so – normal, conventional. It's so fucking weird, to see him like that. At least we'll both look like fucking idiots.

The anticipation of screams and shouts washes over me like a summer breeze. I'm used to it, I can almost block it out. Not even the thought of Lexi with her silk white skin and eyes as large as saucers can brighten the heavy clouds in my mind. They cover me like a shroud.

I want to run away. I can't do this. I don't want to do this. Fuck Jordan's dream. He'll have to do it without me.

I turn on my heels, raise my hand to rip off my sound pack.

"Good luck, kids," Raven's voice echoes into my brain. Our cue is here. I've missed my chance.

"No going back!" Jordan exclaims, bouncing from foot to foot, like he's about to enter a boxing ring. I already feel like I've been pummelled beyond recognition.

"No going back," I parrot back to him, though it feels flat on my tongue, like a weight I can't shake off.

The curtain is raised and the light around me is bright, before only the spotlight halos me. I raise my hands holding the guitar and hope the shakes aren't visible through the white veil between me and the crowd.

The show must go on.

There's no music, just screams and shouts from the crowd. Pete claimed it would cause more of an impact if we opened in silence. It's fucking deafening.

I meet Jordan's eyes as I stretch my guitar towards the lights. He throws me a wink and nods his head encouragingly. Waiting for the light to flicker, as directed, I slam down the guitar. It meets the wooden boards on the floor at the exact time an explosion blares from the speakers.

Two unnamed people run out from the wings, brushes in arms. Secretly clearing the wreckage from the audience's eyes.

Like a programmed robot, my hands reach up to my head. I pull the curly wig away and throw it into the wings. My hands smooth down over the shape of my head.

The silky white curtain is lifted, and I turn to face the crowd. The audiences squeals of excitement have morphed into shock, almost horror. I guess that was too much to take. I fucking agree.

The whole crowd has taken on the appearance of a shoal of fish on dry land. Silent, gaping mouths. Wide, bulging eyes transfixed on my figure taking up the spotlight. Arms flailing uselessly out of the water. Struggling to catch their breath.

I raise the microphone to my mouth. Before I can stop it, a shaky sigh reverberates around the theatre. My eyes track across the rows of people, stock still as if frozen. Anticipation etched alongside panic, on expecting faces.

"We are The Halcyon!" I hear Jordan's voice jolting me, as if waking me from the dead. "Thank you for joining us on our next chapter. Here's *Join The Dots*."

A tinkling backing track of strings and piano keys fills the space. The crowd act like Jordan has injected happiness directly into their veins. They jump, stamp, cheer and shout. Their hands meeting above their heads like a prayer, each time Jordan slaps the cajon drum box. He looks fucking strange, perched on the wood. His usual first choice of instrument, the bass guitar, nowhere to be seen.

Like the true performer that I am, as if it's embedded in my soul to put on a show; I start singing. The lyrics come to me as easy at water from rain clouds. Without the dancing coloured lights or riffs of the original track, I feel exposed. The lyrics feel more raw. Like I've cut myself open, showed my feelings to the world. Each word sung is coated with emotion, it drips from me like honey.

The fans who have stayed with us sing along, joined together in one voice. The words may mean something else to them, to me they're a soliloquy to Lexi. I start to smile as lines flow from my voice box. Jordan and I glance at each other. He looks so happy, his mouth stretched into a smile. It's infectious, I feel my body swaying, my feet twirling underneath me. Maybe it's not so bad. Singing with my best mate every night, still living out the dream. My hand smooth down my chest to grasp at my necklaces. After finding nothing there but an open collar, I clutch at suit lapels instead. My heart stuttering at the unfamiliarity. *It's just a suit.* I swallow and start on the next line, hoping no one noticed my momentary falter.

As the song ends, the lights rotate around the crowd, like beams from a lighthouse.

I use the darkness to pull myself together. I step backwards to grab a drink, pleased to find bottles of water to quench my thirst.

Jordan, who has strict instructions to do the majority of the talking, is interacting with the front row. He's leaning forward, hunched like fucking Quasimodo, over the stage. They stare at him like a god on a pedestal. He appears so happy, so relaxed. I feel distanced from it all.

I take the time in the darkness to focus on my breathing. I stare at the setlist, the letters jumbling, as if they are anagrams. I need to focus, so I don't let Jordan down.

"All together now, let's sing Happy Birthday to Selena!" Jordan's voice spirals down in my ears, over the generic squeals of the crowd.

The jovial tune, a melody that should only bring happiness, swirls around the theatre. I am transported to my tenth birthday again. I internally berate Lydia for bringing the buried memory back to the surface, like a once dormant volcano. Tears leak from my eyes like splashes of scalding lava. I wipe them away with the cuff of my suit, but it's no use. I watch as the fabric turns darker with fat, salted tears. *Fuck.*

As the last few notes of Happy Birthday ring out, I feel like I've left my body. As if I'm watching as the escaped balloon at the party, I see myself running off the stage. I push the curtains back and weave through an obstacle course. Over wires, boxes filled with amps and lights, rows of suits and beige shoes. I squeeze past decks of knobs and switches, and guitars propped against the walls. People wearing CREW t-shirts try to stop me, but I thrust their hands away. I hear Raven's voice questioning me, in my ears. I block it all out as much as I can. I don't know where I'm going, but I know I can't stay here.

I'm running, picking up speed as I tumble over wires and leads. I shoulder the door and relief encases me. I breathe in the air in the shadowy night and look up to the sky. The navy clouds blanketing the stars, the wind picking up and imbedding my tears into my skin. The yellow beams of cars circling the roundabout nearby highlight the path, a fleeting moment of light in the dark. I run across the car park, weaving in between the parked cars. I duck down behind one as I hear the shouts of Higgsy and the team, floating out from the stage door.

If I just stay here, I might disappear. I might vanish, shrink smaller into dust. They'll all forget about me. I'll be swept aside into the bin. Discarded and forgotten about. It's what I deserve.

"Hayden?"

Fuck, now I'm turning delirious. I thought I could hear

Lexi. Which is fucking nonsense as she hasn't been to any of my shows since school, why would sh –

"Hayden?"

In slow motion I turn my head in disbelief. I see the pity in Lexi's hazel eyes, looking down at me from the rolled open car window. Great. I am now at that level of pathetic. I almost don't want to see her. There's a thread connecting Lexi and I, though. I can't ignore her, even if I want to.

Her eyes, wide like craters, stained with tears. But also with love. I can see it now, as I blink away my own tears. Fighting for space next to the pity, there's love in her eyes.

"What are you doing here?" I ask her, trying and failing to wipe away the constant tears from my cheeks.

"I think I should be asking you that," Lexi replies, as she leans her chin on her denim clad arm looped out of the window. "What are you wearing?"

"A suit."

"I never thought I would say this, but I miss your ridiculously impractical boots."

I tap the boring shoes on my feet together, like Dorothy. I wish I could go fucking home. Or even hide out in Oz until the storm blows over.

"My Gucci ones?"

"The black pointed ones," Lexi shrugs. Fashion has never interested her. "The ones that I told you are not suitable for walking dogs in."

"Proved you wrong, didn't I?" I half smile. I refused offers of wellingtons. Hayden Fucking Coulthard does not wear wellies.

"They are scuffed and covered in slobber beyond recognition. You just won't admit you're wrong."

"Hayden! Where are you?" A shout booms across the car roofs. *Fuck*, its Raven. Unlike my last escape from the stage, the team have followed me. Maybe last time they thought it was an empty threat. Or perhaps there's more to lose this time. Either way they've started to hunt me down like an extinct species.

"Do you make a habit of running out of your shows?" Lexi asks, a perplexed look on her face. I don't miss the way her face contorts into disgust as she takes in my brand spanking new bald head.

"Looks like it," I sigh.

"I hate to alarm you, but there's hundreds of hysterical teenagers heading out the doors," Lexi says to me, a note of unease in her tone.

This time they've realised I've left, but can't have got far. It may turn into a manhunt.

The released crowds are moving in messy concentric circles, bodies packed in tightly surrounding the backstage door. I watch the sea of crazed fans as they break off against the tide. Some swimming towards the car park, throngs heading to the paths. All hyped up by confusion, panic and admiration for the band they love.

"Fancy giving me a lift home?" I ask, flashing her the best smile I can muster.

I hear the mechanical click of the locks. I pull open the car door, the handle slipping under my slick palm.

"Get in the back," Lexi says. "Christ, I feel like I'm harbouring a fugitive."

21

"What's the deal with your hair then, or lack of?" Lexi asks, looking at me in her rear-view mirror.

"New image and that shit," I shrug, going for nonchalant. I'm still feeling the loss of my hair as if I'm mourning the death of a faithful friend. Or perhaps my mother. I'm so fucking pathetic. Jordan's right, it is only hair. Easy for him to fucking say. He suits his new short hair. I look ridiculous.

"Bit drastic, isn't it?" Lexi asks, brows furrowed. "You look about fourteen."

I snort, we've always been on the same wavelength, Lexi and I. Well, mostly.

"It's good for the band."

"Yes, I've heard that having short hair correlates directly to the ability to be successful in the music industry," Lexi says, her voice dripping in sarcasm.

"Sometimes, Lex, we have to make sacrifices, for the sake of the band," I snap out way too defensively to be sincere. "You wouldn't understand,"

I see her bronze eyes roll in the mirror as they follow a sigh. Her life is a pissing doddle compared to mine.

What's the most pressuring thing in her life? Scooping up dog shit?

"So, you got a plan?" Lexi asks turning around in the seat. I shake my head. I couldn't stay on that stage any longer. I had to get away. That's as far as my thoughts took me. Now I'm stranded on a dark path. Twisting away from everything I know. "Thought not," she says, and throws a blanket in my direction. "Get under that and wait it out."

I hear the gentle hum of the radio and the muffled cries from outside the safety of the car. It must be fucking carnage out there. The security will be going ape shit. At me and the fans. They'll assume I'm backstage, so hopefully will disperse back to their poster lined bedrooms pretty quickly.

"Why are you here, Lex?" I ask her from under the blanket. It smells of dog, a scent I've weirdly become used to. And a tropical lingering scent of coconuts is woven in the fibres too.

"Turns out, I missed you," comes the quiet reply. It's said almost begrudgingly. It still makes my heart start to dance. She missed me!

"You missed me?"

"Yeah, I did."

"You didn't get out of the car though."

"No," Lexi replies after a long pause. "I found it all a bit overwhelming, to be honest, Hayden." I laugh bitterly. *She's* overwhelmed. She should've spent the last few hours in my fucking shoes. "It brought back a lot of memories," Lexi snaps out above my brittle laughter. "I'm not comparing lives here, Hayden. I'm just saying I found it more emotional than I expected, and yes, that was before I got out of the car."

"You used to love watching me," I say with a smile. I loved having her stood watching me, singing along to each and every word I'd written. I still searched crowds for her now, even when it was fucking pointless. In a twisted way, I liked the torture, the pain that she wouldn't be there. I channeled it into making the show better. Myself better. Maybe, I thought, Lex would watch it back online, or read about the fucking awesome show I put on. I snort. I wanted to make her jealous, even across hundreds of miles.

"I did," I can hear Lexi's smile even though I can't see it from my tartan hiding place. "You always had that star quality, that showmanship."

"I think I've lost that now," I say and try to stop tears from splashing down my face.

The screams and sobs outside have been replaced with chattering, and the starting of engines. I don't know how long I've been under the checked blanket. I have no idea what time it is. I only know I've never embraced the silence so much.

"I've been to all your shows in London." Lexi's words make me inhale sharply.

"What the fuck?"

"Aggie moved down there a year after you," I hear Lexi swallowing loudly. "Every night The Halcyon has played in London, I've been there. Well, usually sat or stood outside, if I'm honest. I've never made it in, never handed over my ticket."

"You got all the tickets I sent you?"

"Course."

"Why didn't you tell me, Lex?"

"Our lives went on different paths, but I still wanted to support you, to see you."

"What stopped you?"

The pause rings out as if it were a song. The dark cocoon of the blanket makes my heartbeat sound as loud as a bass drum. My lungs feel like they're filled with heavy thunder.

"I couldn't bear it. I couldn't watch you so happy, without me," Lexi chuckles humourlessly. "Pathetic, I know."

"But you were with Callum," I state. She broke up with me. She didn't want me.

"I always loved you."

"That night I walked off stage, were you there?" I ask, I knew I'd seen her. And she lied about it, right to my fucking face.

"No, not then, I swear. Aggie's son had a music recital. I was nowhere near KOKO."

Ironic, that the show where I thought I'd seen Lexi, was the only one she wasn't at.

"You've been at my shows?" I repeat like an annoying riff.

"Technically just outside, if we're going to be pedantic. I've heard you, just never witnessed The Halcyon on stage," I hear her gulp loudly in the enclosed space.

"And you never told me? You never rang me, never wanted to meet me?" I fire the questions out at her like machine gun fire.

"What was there to say, Hayden?"

I push the blanket off my face and sit up, twisting my

body towards Lexi.

"You could've said hello at least, Lex!"

The passenger door is pulled open, making us both jump as if shocked with a taser.

"Isn't this cosy?" Jordan snipes as he clambers his tall frame in the small car. "What the fuck is going on?"

I watch as security from the venue, and our own, surround Lexi's car. Raven shakes his head at me. His mouth talking rapidly into a headset, his fingers tapping frantically on a tablet.

"Mate –"

"Do not fucking 'mate' me," Jordan says, anger lacing his words like cobwebs. "Are you fucking incapable of doing a full gig?"

"Jordan –"

"Pete is literally going to rip you limb from limb. I hope you're ready for it."

"I'm sorry."

"Sorry doesn't cut it, Hayden," he shakes his head, still jewellery free. "Our career is as good as over. I hope you're happy."

I shuffle myself up onto the seat, and stare at the car's ceiling.

"I'm not happy," I sigh out. I pretend Lydia is here, encouraging me to be honest. "That's the point, mate."

"For real?" Jordan snorts out. "What's the problem, Hayden? The immense amounts of money rolling in each month, the designer clothes you live in? Or is it the fact that we're lucky, and talented enough to be able to sing our songs, on stage to thousands of fans each night?"

"Mate –"

"You're right, what is there to be happy about?" Jordan says as he folds his arms. "This is all we ever wanted, mate! I know things have changed, trust me, I hate the suits as much as you. But we are under contract. We have to do this shit, if just to get out of the messes you're making. It won't always be this restricted."

"You ok, Hayden?" Lex asks, her eyes meeting mine in the rear-view mirror.

"No," Jordan barks out. "Don't pander to him, he needs to hear this. He needs to be fucking honest with me, for once. I don't know where I stand."

"It's just a bad day," I mumble, not being honest like Jordan wants.

"A bad day? You think that's gonna wash with me?"

"It's my mum's birthday," I shout, the words bouncing back towards me. "It would've been her birthday," I correct with a gulp.

Lexi reaches a hand back and pats my leg like I'm Mavis.

"I'm so sorry, Hayden," she soothes. "Birthdays are tough."

Jordan spins round in the seat, and blinks at me. He grits his teeth and winces. "Mate, you should've said," Jordan says, scratching at his naked ear. "I feel awful. Here's me having a go at you, and you're dealing with this shit."

"You weren't to know," I shrug. "I didn't exactly talk about her when she was alive, let alone now."

"We're best mates. You can tell me anything, talk to me about anything."

"I'll give you guys some space," Lexi says.

"No, Lex," I scrub a hand over my face. I hate the way it feels without my scruff of a beard. "I want you to hear this."

"What is it, Hayden?" Lexi asks.

"I killed my mum."

22

Might as well get straight to the fucking point. The root of all my problems.

"No, you didn't," Jordan says, incredulous. "Pete said she fell down a flight of stairs. Fuck, did you push her?"

"I didn't push her! But I might as well have. It was all my fault," I confess into the cramped car. Sometimes I think it would be easier if I had pushed her.

"Hayden, what do you mean?" Lexi asks as she looks into my dancing eyes. The shadows of the bare trees nearby, creep silently into the windows. The gnarled branches start morphing into my late mum's hands. Grappling for gin, or me: the one who killed her. I close my eyes tight in a bid to block it out.

"My mum brought a fuck ton of gin to my house in Camden. I told her to finish it all, and then leave. She did just that, first time she's ever listened to me. She drank the whole fucking lot. Tripped down the stairs on the way out and broke her neck. It was pretty painless apparently. Almost instant," I state the facts, void of emotion, as if I'm reciting a recipe.

"Shit," Lexi sighs out.

"Mate, you never said," Jordan says, as he turns to face me. Anguish on his piercing-free features. "Why didn't you tell me?"

Stringy blonde curls spiralling around her creased face, blue eyes like my own dulled with the alcohol always in her system, looked up at me. A wonky half smile, once painted a pale pink with lipstick, now smudged around her mouth, leered at me. A handbag slung low over her bony shoulder, stained jeans, an oversized jumper that was clearly never created for women to wear unless they were farming, and scuffed, worn out trainers that I imagine were once white and clean completed her outfit. And of course, always accompanied by clanging bottles of gin: the must-have accessory. I sighed at her. Fuck's sake. "Son, help me up."

She was slumped outside my flat door, as I returned from the gym. I pulled her up, with more force than necessary. She fell into my chest, she was so fragile. She looked like a flightless bird. Easily broken and useless. No good for me, or anyone, unless there was a gin shortage of course. I saw the bottles tumbling from flimsy plastic bags by her feet. If there was a gin shortage, I was pretty sure my mother was behind it.

"What are you doing with like, ten bottles of gin?"

I had always liked a drink. A bottle of whiskey interspersed with a couple of shots was a standard night out for me. I guess I get my liver strength from my mum's side. My fridge was always full of champagne. But that was for parties that inadvertently happened.

"Thought we could have ourselves a party, Hayden. A little mother/son session," mum slurred, dribble made purely of gin running down her chin. I looked at her with

pure disgust.

"You are a fucking mess," I mumbled as I ushered her inside. The last fucking thing I needed was the neighbours, and thus the press, all over this.

She turned and bent down to collect her transparent liquid treasures.

"I'll get them, go and sit down," I felt like the parent. I wondered briefly if my dad felt this way. Was his life in Scotland like being a parent to two children? I sighed. I should have phoned him. Asked for advice if nothing else. But of course, I didn't.

She looked a fucking mess. She was a fucking mess. She stank, her clothes were stained with fuck knows what, and I looked on in pure horror as she wet herself right there on the wicker chair.

"You need to go, I can't handle this," I told her, avoiding all eye contact, and staring out of the window instead. Luckily, I was four floors up so no peeping toms could sell photos of inside my flat.

"I've just got here, I brought us all these thinks."

"Thinks?"

"The gin, drinks of gin," she attempted to enunciate. It was pathetic.

"Take them with you, I'll call you a cab," I said, rubbing my forehead. I could feel a headache brewing behind my eyes.

Mum jumped up, with a sudden burst of energy and anger. Her curls flailing like mine do when I'm on stage. Her blue eyes wild and fiery. She clenched her bony fists, her knuckles white. "You can't kick me out!"

"Watch me," I sneered, as I dialled for a car to come and remove her from my flat, my life. I didn't care where,

as long as she was out of my sight.

"You never do anything for me," she shouted at me. She hit me feebly on the chest, and threw her precious bottles at the Farrow & Ball painted walls. The clear liquid glistening against the teal colour.

I grabbed her by the shoulders, focussing on her spirals of hair as opposed to her bleary eyes, "I pay your fucking rent, and all your bills each fucking month. I am the one funding your fucking drinking habit," I spat out at her, disgust oozing from my pores. "I have done so for the past six years, since you rocked up drunk at my gig."

"I wanted to see my son."

"No, you wanted my money, which you get."

"I'm sorry, I know. Just let me stay here and finish my drinks."

"You have your own house to go to."

"One night, Hayden," she sighed as she sat back down. "I'm here now, we don't want to waste the gin."

"Drink every single fucking drop of your gin, then get the fuck out," I seethed as I headed into the sanctuary of my bedroom, grabbing a bottle and taking it with me. "And then don't fucking come back."

My confession trembles around the car. I go to tug at my curls to provide some form of relief, but of course, they're not there. Lexi and Jordan are both staring straight ahead, looking out of the windshield at the empty car park. They're both so still I wonder if I haven't actually just bared my soul to them. The branches of the nearby trees swaying in the wind, the night kissing the evening away.

"So, it was my fault," I conclude to the stunned silence of the car. "All my fucking fault."

Lexi turns to face me. Her palm returns to my knee, and she squeezes it gently. The pressure is reassuring.

"Your guilt is misplaced, Hayden," Lexi says to me.

"Lexi's right, mate."

"Your mum died as a result of her actions and choices. It was an unfortunate incident, and you are not to blame," I see a sheen on Lexi's eyes.

"I wished for it. As I lay in bed, I could hear her mumbling on, bottles smashing and whatever else. And, fuck, I wished she'd just leave and I'd never have to see her again."

"Mate, everyone has fleeting thoughts of things like that. It doesn't make them true, and it doesn't mean it was your doing," Jordan's eyes bore into me. Is he convincing himself or me? This may spell the end of the band, if not our friendship. Who wants a mother-killing mate in their life?

"It was my fault!" I hit my balled-up fists on my thighs, like an ungrateful child at Christmas. "It was my money that bought her the gin, it was my flat, my fucking stairs. My shouting at her to leave."

"You didn't force her."

"I know people hail you as God's gift to music, Hayden, but that doesn't mean you have the same power as a deity. You did not control your mum's actions," Lexi says, a small smile creeping over her mouth. I return it. I can see she's trying to help.

"It wasn't your fault," Jordan repeats.

"I didn't even find her," I cry, the same tears trickle down my face, leaving traces of their guilt behind, "I didn't even check on her. I shut the front door, triple locked it and fucking drank the gin. A bottle of the gin *she* brought.

Then I fell asleep. It was the best sleep I'd had for ages. The police officer woke me up hammering on the door, at some fucking early hour."

"At the risk of sounding like a broken record, it still doesn't make it your fault."

"If it wasn't for me though –"

Lexi cuts me off, almost too quick. My mouth gapes like a fireless dragon. Useless. Like always.

"We don't know the answer to any 'what ifs'. Don't torture yourself, H. Please."

Silence encases us again, at least from the interior of the car. Outside I can hear Raven talking into his phone. Jordan's right, Pete will fucking kill me after this.

"Is this what it all links back to?" asks Jordan, his face turning to mine. "The drinking, walking off stage?"

"I guess," I shrug, my shoulders lifting a tad easier now I've shared the load.

"Look, I know little about your world, right," says Lexi, her head dancing from Jordan to me. "But you need to deal with these issues, Hayden. The alcohol dependency and the death of your mum; you need to address them and accept them, before you can continue with your career."

"Who made you Little Miss Therapist?" smirks Jordan, as he ignores Lexi's point. A point which I agree with. I think.

"My university degree, actually," Lexi purses her lips together.

"It's just bad timing," I say pathetically, trying to diffuse the situation. I can tell that emotions are running high, and the confined space isn't helping.

"You know I'm right," Lexi says folding her arms. "You

can't go on like this, either of you."

"When you've lived a week in this industry, Lexi, I'll maybe pay attention to you," Jordan snorts.

"You two cannot carry on like this, Jordan,"

"Maybe you're just using it as an excuse to get Hayden back," Jordan counters. "Now Callum has binned you off."

"I ended things with him," Lexi says, her teeth gritted.

"I wonder why?"

"Not that it's anyone else's business, but there were many reasons."

"I bet. You were just waiting to get your claws back into Hayden and keep him here, weren't you?" Jordan snaps, his voice increasing in volume with each word.

"Claws?!" I see Lexi smiling in amusement, she's both tickled by the phrase and annoyed.

"Keep him away from his life in London, and all that it has to offer."

"Is that right? Is that my only goal in life?" Lexi says followed by a sigh. I watch her nails subconsciously scratch at the tattoo on her shoulder. She chuckles quietly. "You're pathetic, Jordan. Taking out your frustrations on me."

"I bet you've spent the last ten years pining over Hayden. First sign of him back in Cumbria, and you're suddenly single and willing to look after him."

"Jordan –" I put in, but they both ignore me.

"Pining?! Yes, I've achieved nothing in the last decade. Just running my own business, nothing important like a number one single. That's the only pinnacle of success, right?" Lexi fires to Jordan, who ignores her.

"Wanting to keep Hayden all for yourself, just like old times. Sorry to break your romantic bubble Lexi, but he hasn't given you a thought."

"Jordan –" I try to cut him off.

"Different bird every night, and not once has he mentioned you,"

"I've been pretty busy myself, actually," Lexi says casually, but I can see a hint of hurt in her brown eyes.

"No doubt you'll run straight to Callum once Hayden's back in London."

"You're deluded, Jordan," she shakes her head, in disbelief I assume. Even to me, Jordan is pushing it too far. "But if it makes you feel better then, carry on. I'll be your punching bag."

"Note how you didn't deny it. You're living in a fantasy world, Lexi, thinking things can be how they were when we were teenagers!"

"Shut the fuck up!" I shout out over the bickering running in endless circles. "Jordan, I need to speak to Lexi –"

"You always do. It's always Lexi over me," Jordan sneers.

"You sound like a spoilt brat. He's not a toy to fight over," Lexi sighs out. I can tell she's getting fed up, of Jordan and his comments, and possibly of me saying nothing.

"You'd pull him apart to keep him with you."

"Look at him, Jordan!" Lexi snaps, fire burning in her eyes. "He's already broken, and you're ignoring it to focus on the band!"

"This band is our reason for living," Jordan states. I feel another wave of guilt. It's not my reason any longer.

"It will be the thing that kills him, at this rate," Lexi hisses. I feel like she's punched me in the gut. Fuck, she might be right.

"Jordan –" I say, as I watch him tug on his bare ears, elongated from years of wearing stretchers in the lobes.

"I'm going, to clean up *your* fucking mess," Jordan opens the car door, then leans down to stare at me, bitterness and anger colouring his eyes. "Again."

The slamming of the door echoes in the car. Punctuated only by Lexi's fast, angry breaths.

"This is madness," she snaps out, and unclips her seatbelt. She follows Jordan out of the car.

23

I watch through the frosted windows as Lexi and Raven stand with their taut backs against the car, deep in conversation. Higgsy nearly rips the door off the little silver car. I brace myself for his huge arms to drag me out. I prepare to kick and scream like a fucking toddler. Instead, he piles blankets, buckets, towels and bottles of water in next to me, along with a pile of neatly folded clothes. Someone else throws me a six pack of cheese and onion crisps.

"Look after yourself, mate. It's not worth making yourself ill over, it's only show business," Higgsy half smiles before shutting me in the car. Away from the world, away from cleaning up the mess I've left for Jordan. Guilt pools in the corner of my eyes, then leak out like an annoying dripping tap. Why does everyone think it's so fucking easy? I'm not working in a fucking nine to five office job here. Pete can't just replace me with a fucking temp.

Lexi climbs back in the car and starts the engine. A look of steely determination etched on her features.

"Where are we going?" I ask, confused, by the lack of instruction or demands.

"I'm giving you a lift home."

"They're really just letting you take me away?"

"You're hardly in the right emotional or physical state to do anything else tonight," Lexi says to me in the mirror.

"They don't need me," I state, darkness beginning to fill up my lungs once more.

"This isn't a pity party, Hayden," Lexi says, a pout on her red lips. "You need to help yourself first. Plus, Jordan is fuming."

"I got that much," I snort. He sounded so angry. I bet even several rounds of killing zombies on a screen won't diffuse his aggression.

"Raven said Jordan would tear you apart if you went back into the theatre."

"Fuck."

"Maybe he needs some time, too," Lexi shrugs. "Does he know how you feel?"

"About what?"

"About your mental state –"

"I'm not a fucking nut job."

"Didn't say you were, chill your bones," Lexi says into the mirror. A no-nonsense look on her face. "You're not happy, Hayden. Maybe Jordan is struggling to comprehend why."

"I'm sorry about him, the things he said," I tell her. Bringing up my sexual conquests and shit, what is his game? And his blatant lies at me never giving Lex a moment's thought. She must know he was just saying it to cause a fucking scene. Callum pops into my head and travels around it, meandering. He lodges himself like a stray peanut in my throat. Will he always be hovering on the side lines, like the referee waiting for things to go wrong? Is Jordan right? Will Lexi forever have Callum as a back-up? I swallow, try to wash the lump away. The lingering taste of peanuts remains, despite the water rinsing him away.

"Did you tell him to say them?" Lexi eyes me in the mirror, when she isn't concentrating on the road.

"Fuck, no!"

I watch as Lexi's narrow shoulders shrug up and down. I spot the edge of our once matching tattoos peeking out from her top. Kissing the creamy skin with black ink. My heart skips a beat, or eight.

"Then it's not your place to apologise," she smiles. "This is tough on Jordan too, he's obviously not in the same place as you."

"I guess not."

"He lives for The Halcyon, like he says. But I think you've outgrown it. Or at least need a break, but that's your call," Lexi sighs. I hear a quiver on her breath. "And despite what Jordan may think, that is your decision, for you to make, and you alone."

The rumbling in the car, over the potholes and loose gravel, is strangely comforting. Unlike Jordan and our band, I always revelled in being on the tour bus. The patterns and rhythms of roads lulling me to sleep, making me feel relaxed. It was easy to enjoy the ride, and not worry about anything else.

The darkness of the night encases us, the eerie orange

glow and occasional glare of white lights our only jolt from the bubble and safety of the car.

"Did I kill her, Lex?" I ask, the first time I've ever voiced that question. I've been too scared to say it out loud. Was my mum's death my fault? It must have been me. It was *my* money that paid for all the gin. It was *me* who told my mother to drink it all. I was the one who gave her an ultimatum to leave. It was my wish, however fleeting, that she'd never come back.

"I did, didn't I? I killed my own mother."

"No, Babe, no," Lexi says in her soothing lullaby lilt. I don't miss the term of endearment nestled in her words, I hope it won't be the last. "It was an accident, an unfortunate incident."

"I didn't even fucking like the woman, and yet I miss her," but I suppose you would miss someone who you killed. Responsibility on the fucking shoulders and all that.

"You don't have to like someone to love them, H," Lexi says into the car. I let the words bounce around.

"Is that a song lyric?" I ask her, I recognise it from somewhere.

"You said it to me when my dad left," she replies. I remember now. She was angry and hurt, but missed her dad too. The juxtaposition made her feel lost. I wrote her a poem, used words to try and ease the pain.

"Say it again," I implore.

"You don't have to like someone to love them."

Lexi knows just what I need. She says the right thing, always has. Maybe I don't quite believe her, yet her words penetrate my skin – unlike my own which run off and away like raindrops down a window. I sniffle and focus on the wind turbines dotted on the hills. Graceful like ballerinas performing sweeping moves in the dimmed sky.

"Me and you, Lex," I say out loud, closing my eyes so I can't see her reaction. "Do you think we're meant to be?"

"Let's tackle one thing at a time," she says gently. The phrase reminds me of Lydia. I smile, a little. "First, let's get you away from here and back home."

I down a bottle of water and a small smile pulls my lips upwards.

Lexi's talking about all sorts now, her conversations jumping like fleas; anything to lighten the mood. Her tone is light, trying to act as a life ring to my sinking thoughts. *Fuck,* I've missed that voice. Any and all riffs and licks of notes I create come up short: they're never as tranquil, or idyllic, as the timbre and melody of Lexi's voice.

24

I tumble out of the car as we pull up to Paws2Heal. Confused, yet relieved that my dad and his disappointing glare aren't waiting for me.

"They'll be expecting you to go to Jock's, or mine," Lexi explains. "But I thought you could do with time to mull things over. Before the inevitable madness kicks in. I don't know how you live like that, Hayden."

"It's not as fun as I thought," I mumble. "Not now."

A bat swoops low above our heads; it makes me jump. I'd forgotten about wildlife while I was in London, or living out of suitcases on the road. Unless it was a mangy fox scavenging in the bins. The fresh air, cooler and almost lighter, fills my lungs. The towering trees nearby, and the quaint churchyard give me a sense of serenity. It's the calm after the buzzing and screaming of the theatre. The stars sparkle like diamonds, like dreams waiting to be realised. I look at Lexi. I feel free and almost calm, despite the evening's events. I feel happy.

"I don't want to be on stage anymore," I admit to the stars, to the zooming bats and fluttering insects, to myself. To

Lex. I want to be free to be who I want, who I am. Whatever the fuck that is. I want to be a better man. Someone who I can be proud of, who my dad and Lexi can be proud of. The thirst, the craving of whiskey dissipates at the relief of my confession. I killed my mum, maybe it wasn't all my fault, but I'll always carry the weight of it.

I don't want to return to stage. I want out of London, out of the celebrity world. I want this; right here.

"What's the solution to that, H?" Lexi asks, as she holds my hands in hers. The keys nestled between our palms like a secret.

"There isn't one," I could fucking cry.

"Of course there is," Lexi smiles. "Stay in The Halcyon or leave."

"It's not that simple, Lex."

"I bet you it is."

"Marry me, Lex," I say, not for the first time. Her response is the same; blushing and a short laugh. A shake of her head, a dismissal.

"Now is not the time for bold statements," Lexi chides, as she fiddles with her keys in one hand, mine in her other. The moon offers little light, but she steers me around a plant pot of hydrangeas, to the main door of Paws2Heal.

"I love you Lexi," I blurt it out, it is a step down from the marriage proposal which keeps dancing on my tongue whenever I see her. Perhaps she'll accept this testimony more readily.

I turn Lexi to face me, my legs still wobbling like I've just ran a marathon. Yet my mind as clear as the moonlight from betwixt the dark clouds. Her hazel eyes are wide, tears sheen on them, magnified by her glasses.

I pull her into my chest, her head nestles, as I knew it would under my chin. I inhale her perfume, it's mingled with my stench of another drink-fuelled disaster of mine, of course. Yet the notes of coconut, citrus and crushed petals pushes through to ignite my senses. My heart fills with love. Dark thoughts are cast aside by the sunlight Lex brings through the smiles, the kisses she showers my lips with. I place my hands on her neck, trace the hollow of her throat. My stomach flips; the one flat note of the melody is the missing necklace on Lexi's skin. I knew she wasn't wearing it, who wears jewellery from an ex anyway? Making love to her without the sliver chain and little etched heart glimmering against her pale skin. Fuck, it's going to tear a chunk from my pitiful, battered heart.

"Where's your necklace?" I ask her. Wanting to sob like a child about its absence. I'm so pathetic.

"You don't want to know," Lexi smiles sadly, her chocolate brown eyes misting over behind her glasses.

"Bottom of the river?" I suggest.

"Someone stole it."

"What? Who?" I ask. I bet it was fucking Callum. Callum and his pissing short hair that looks good.

"Pete."

"Pete? Pete Morris-Turner?"

"The night you were signed. Ripped it from my neck. Said you weren't mine anymore," Lexi shrugs, resigned. If it's true, then she's had ten years to deal with that fucking revelation. It's like a punch to the fucking gut to me right now.

"Fuck, Lex."

"Don't think about that now, ok?"

I want to. I so fucking want to. But then, Lexi's hands

caress my face, neck, my ridiculously sad bald head. I am such a vain fucker. She kisses me, her tongue dancing with mine, and all thoughts of my manager are forgotten.

The nerve endings on my skin under her touch stand on end, firing rockets to my brain, and more predictably straight to my cock. I don't want Lex to think this is just a physical thing. Fuck knows it's so much more. Though she doesn't seem to be put off, and her nails scrape down my back and she pulls me towards her body more, and kisses me with so much force I nearly fall over.

I hold her flushed cheeks in my hands, feel her baby soft skin, like silk under the callouses and ridges of my fingers. I stare into her eyes, feel myself falling into the chocolate heaven that they are. My heart and body screaming at me to kiss her again. To stop with the distance, the idle chit chat. Yet, I need her to know that I mean it, that my words count. That after all this time, my past secrets spilling out from the gutters to break us; that I do love her.

"Lex, Lex, I love you. I love you so much, it's always been you. Marry me."

Lexi stares deep into my eyes, as if searching for answers. A frown passes over her dark eyebrows, momentarily hiding them behind the frames of her glasses.

I have no other words to say. I've told her countless times since I left Cumbria how I feel. Each lyric I've written and sung, is a declaration of my dedication to her. She must know this, surely she must. Yet, as my head leans down towards hers, blue eyes meeting hazel, I put everything into imploring with her. *Please, Lexi, believe me. After all the shitty, fucked up things I've done, you've gotta believe that I do fucking love you.* Her frown relaxes, and a smile makes my heart beat like a snare drum playing double time.

"H, I love you so much."

My heart almost bursting with relief and happiness, the two of us stumble and tumble through the door at Paws2Heal. Lexi's deft dainty hands discarding my suit jacket. I hear it land with a splash into a nearby puddle as the door swings closed behind us. Best place for it, what a crime to fashion; though right now Lexi could be shredding my Gucci suits, and I'd happily stand back and watch her.

My bones and muscles have regained some strength, and I scoop Lexi's lithe body up and push her against the wall, the Reception area still drowned in darkness. Like our own secret slice of paradise, hiding from the harsh lights of reality.

It's passionate, physical, just like it always was. We never did the whole vanilla sex; it was all or nothing. Clothes flying, teeth biting, moans filling the room, sweat dripping, skin slapping together like we were on a time limit.

The passion still remains, but this time I look into her eyes, watch her features, feel the weight of her, the feel of her skin. I want to thread my fingers through each strand of her once Snow White hair, kiss her so deeply, so full of tenderness that I forget my name. I repeat over and over again, as we fit together like melody and lyrics, that I love her. That everything I do is for her, that Lex is all I'll ever need, and all I'll ever want. This woman, whose eyes lock onto mine as she bites her lip and joins me in the most intense orgasm ever; she's my one and only. With her love, I can conquer all my demons.

I'm ecstatic yet exhausted. Lexi takes my hand, and leads me what I expect is an office, but is a simple bedroom piled high with coats, dog food boxes and reams of paper. Framed photos of dogs grace the walls, and all the staff certificates.

"What's this? Your sex room?" I laugh, hating how slurred I still sound, my throat parched from the sting of the whiskey. Sweat clings to my skin, and not just from the physical exertion.

"Yes, Hayden, I run a prolific sideline of prostitution. The smell of liver dog food really gets the punters going," Lex laughs. I join in, creating a beautiful melody.

"Who can resist a liver snap?!" I kiss her, again, because I can. Because I want to. I never want to stop. "Did I mention that I love you?"

"You did, yes. And I love you, Hayden."

"So when are you going to marry me?"

"Ask me when you're not drunk."

"Deal."

With shaking hands, from adrenaline, tiredness or alcohol, I'm not sure; we undress completely, almost shyly, and then giggle as we slot together in the small bed. Fingertips connecting freckles and moles, following veins and tattoos. We lull into a blissful sleep, only to be woken up again by the other with kisses and shared dreams, old memories and hopes full of new adventures.

25

It's still dark when my eyes creak open. The unmistakable feeling of whiskey swirling in my stomach, along with my battered liver protesting against my choice of liquor. It makes me feel like I'm swimming through quicksand.

Fuck, I'm going to hurl.

I struggle to sit up, a weight holding me flat against the mattress. I look to my chest, the ink of my tattoos blending in with a fan of blonde hair seamlessly. I inhale sharply, who is this faceless woman? The hair slides off a bare shoulder, revealing the love bird ink staining the skin. The bile mingles with dancing butterflies like tambourine bells as I recall the events of last night with Lex. I smile, despite the queasiness of my insides. Relief floods my veins like the river bursting its banks.

"Lex, I need to get up," I half whisper. She rolls away, mumbling about it still being dark and way too early. I stagger to the toilets, ignoring the pulsing in my head. I'm a pro at dealing with hangovers.

I loathe being sick, my hair always gets in the fucking way, and the chains around my neck sound dull and empty as they jangle against the porcelain bowl. I never learn to take them off. My hand goes to my chest as I throw up. Bare skin. My thought process is punctuated by vomit. When did I take off my jewellery? I don't even have any rings on. My hair isn't escaping from the bun I must have put it in. Fucking weird. I don't usually tie it up before bed as it gets too tangled. I watch the swirling water flush away all evidence of another alcohol-infused night as my hands run across my hair. *What the actual fuck?*

I scream. Memories from yesterday fire at me like the pounding bass of an underground nightclub. Melding into one large mess.

"Fuck," I shout as I heave myself off my bare knees.

"Hayden?" I hear Lexi's concerned voice from behind the door.

With both hands on the cold sink, I can just about stabilise my shaking legs. I can't bear to look at myself in the mirror just yet, nor do I want to see Lexi until my heartbeat has slowed.

"Give me a minute, Babe," I say, and despise how my voice wobbles.

"You sure?"

"Yep. Just feeling rough," I sigh and exhale deeply.

Both hands automatically make their way towards my scalp. They're met with spiky stubble. The whole shape of my head underneath them. Dull dry blue eyes are staring back at me in the pockmarked mirror. Not a hint of mascara or my ever-present kohl liner. No dangling curls firing out at odd angles. The three silver loops gone from my left ear. An image of the nondescript grey suit flutters past my eyelids. Why did they do that? Why did I fucking let them?

There's nothing of me left. If they could've skinned me of my tattoos, I'm sure they would've. Fuck. I hate my management team, the whole brand image that I have to comply to. All the fucking contracts that I'm tied up in. The controlling puppet masters who sit in swivelling leather chairs. Pete and his band of minions, deciding how to mould me to gain them the most money, as if I'm clay. My heart stutters as I think of Jordan. I'm doing this for him. I wish I could stand tall and tell him that I've had enough. That last night was the final fucking straw. The last note of that melody of my life. My swan-song.

But I won't. I can't. I can't ruin this dream for Jordan. We've been in this together since we were teens; I can't abandon him now. Especially as he's finally found his own fucking voice. Fuck, I'm stupid. Too weak, too afraid to say no. I want out of this life. But I can't do it to Jordan.

"I was drunk." The justification, or rather the excuse leaves my fucking mouth. I watch my lips form the words, like they have many, many times before. "I was drunk."

Lexi taps on the door and pushes it open, a sheet wrapped around her naked frame.

"Hayden? Are you ok?" She rubs a hand down my arm, my eyes still haven't left the mirror. I can't bear to look at her, I'm so fucking ashamed of myself.

"I was drunk. Last night, I was so fucking drunk."

She rests her head against my back, her hands gripping around my empty stomach.

I can feel Lexi gulping in silent sobs, feel her tears rolling onto my skin. I'm furious with myself, that I drank so much, that I was so fucking self-indulgent that I didn't stop the gig, let alone the whole image change. Look at the fucking state of me. How the fuck can I get back from this? It's like I never fucking existed.

"It was all a massive fucking mistake," I say to my reflection. They've changed me beyond recognition, and I did nothing to stop it. Look what you let them do to you, to your whole being! I scream internally. I shake my head, and release my grip from the sink, watching my white knuckles return to pink. *Fuck.* I need a drink. Water, not whiskey.

"Lex, can you bring me a glass, Babe?" I look behind me in the mirror, noticing the door swinging gently.

Silence.

***

It feels as if a brick has lodged itself in my throat. I'm parched, my tongue as dry as a drum skin stretched taut. I creak my eyes open, and scrub my hands down my face. The shock of bare skin, with only a touch of stubble makes me sit bolt upright. *Fuck.*

Last night was a mess. A smirk pulls on the corners of my mouth, until Lexi and I got here of course.

I have no idea what the time is, but I can see daylight creeping through the blinds. Lexi isn't curled up next to me, nor is there any trace of her. I down the bottle of water by the bed, and pull on the clothes that I assume Lexi has left for me on the chair. My skin feels grimy, my face tacky with the remnants of foundation smeared into my pores. I need a fucking shower.

I pull the door, the florescent lights of the corridor

instantly making me regret not putting on shades. My eyes squeeze themselves shut. I lean into Lexi's office, but find it empty.

My phone buzzes against my thigh. I've already ignored every call and text, bar my dad. I sent him a quick message saying where I was and that I was safe. Probably the only time I've been a considerate son since I fucking left home. First time for everything.

The buzzing is persistent. I wrench the phone from my jeans in annoyance. Pete. Time to face the music, so to fucking speak.

"Pack your bags, I'm coming to get you tomorrow," Pete barks down the line, reverberating in my ear like an echo in a blackened cave.

"What?" I ask, confused. It's not like him to dive right in without a hello. I haven't even finished this rehab stint.

"We need a strategy meeting, back in London. You need to be away from any and all distractions, man. This is a monumental disaster."

"Distractions?" I ask, though I think I know where this is heading. He's going to blame it all on Lex. It's always someone else's fault. Never his own, although it was his idea to get me back on the fucking stage before I wanted to.

"Lexi, for one," Pete hisses like a cobra. I roll my eyes. Those two have always clashed, any excuse and they'll throw insults at one another like a constant thrum of bass booming from speakers in a club.

"She's done nothing but brought positivity to my life," I reply, the words jumping out of my throat in defence.

"You didn't give two shits about her before you

clapped your eyes on her five weeks ago, man."

I sigh out in frustration. That is so not fucking true. What is it with him and Jordan? Have they elected to forget that every song I write is about Lexi? That every woman I end up in bed with has at least one similarity with her?

"She's making you lose focus. I was wrong to think she could help with the image, I hold my hands up to that. But, now we've got Ella Egan on board –"

"No, I'm not having anything to do with Ella," I interrupt, I've had enough of her already, and the whole farce of fake dates.

"We'll see. She can open up a whole new branch of publicity for you, for The Halcyon. Plus, may I remind you that your precious Lexi didn't even attend your gig last night?"

"Lexi's shifting my focus, I agree, Pete," I voice out, my words echoing back at me. Choosing to ignore his incorrect information, and refraining from fucking correcting him.

"I'm glad you agree, more trouble that she's worth."

"I didn't say it was a bad thing," I half laugh, Pete missing my point, yet I'm still too much of a fucking coward to correct him. "I've been writing, so many songs, Pete. Lex has really inspired me."

"Are they better than the ones you showed me?"

I gulp. He hated those, regarded them as being emotionally and lyrically weak. He even kept my fucking notebook as 'encouragement' for me to try harder, write better. Stick to the fucking new direction The Halcyon is apparently heading in.

"I think so."

"We'll look at selling them off, they're not for The Halcyon."

"Pete, I –"

"Forget about the songs, Hayden. I don't think you and Jordan understand how serious this is, man. You have broken contractual ties, again. Those fines are coming straight out of your bank account."

"I can't get into my fucking bank account anyway, you've fucking seen to that," I mumble.

"I'll send you a copy of the statement, quit your whining. I will ensure that the money won't be there for long, after these disasters you keep inflicting on yourself. Jordan won't be out of pocket, as you'll be covering the costs on his behalf."

"You're having a fucking laugh!" I spit out.

"Do you hear me laughing, Hayden?" I picture Pete in his black leather chair, behind his obsessively tidy desk. Speakers lining the room instead of pictures, his ear always tuned into the sounds resonating out.

"Fine, take my money and pay me out of these fucking contracts too," I snap out as I rub at my forehead, the headache beginning to pool behind my skull. "I'll hang up the microphone and just write."

"Don't talk nonsense. Your current songs aren't good enough for reality show winner album tracks, man, let alone anyone half-decent. We will discuss all this once we're all in London. You, Jordan, my good self, the team."

"Set me free, Pete, I'm not worth your time," I say, defeatism colouring my tone, I just want out. I want to stay here. Away from the madness.

"I signed The Halcyon for a reason, man, I am standing by you, as a band," Pete says.

"I don't want you to."

"I am not standing back while you ruin this for

yourself or indeed, Jordan. You and him are in this together, until the bitter end, man. 'No going back', that's what the two of you say."

The words Jordan and I say to each other before each and every gig come back to haunt me, as if they are a boomerang. They were always so positive, now they are tainted with blackmail and fucking misery.

"Can you not get him a solo contract?" I shrug, trying to be a problem solver, and failing. No one tells Pete Morris-Turner what to do.

"His reputation will be in tatters after this, no one is going to touch him for a solo deal. It comes down to this Hayden, what's more important: Lexi or Jordan and the band?"

Lexi. Lexi. Lexi. My heart pounds. Her name flows through my veins, as easy as the water rolls down the riverbeds passing through the town.

The devils dance on my shivering shoulders. One with glasses, dressed in a white and blue dress, a love bird etched on her skin. The other with zombie tattoos and piercings, a bass guitar in his hands.

The woman I love, and my best mate.

"Be careful how you answer that, man," Pete warns, sounding like an American and more unforgiving version of my dad.

The silence on my end of the line stretches out. I hear Pete tapping on his keyboard, his other phone line ringing, and the constant thrum of music hovering in his office. Lexi's name pounds through my veins, keeping time of the passing seconds.

"I have it on good authority that she's getting back

with that Callum dude, anyway," Pete breaks through my heartbeat.

I laugh out loud, a brittle sound bouncing off the walls, covered in polaroids of four and two legged companions. My eyes scan the colourful squares for Lex. Like I'm playing my own game of Where's fucking Wally.

"No fucking way!" He's talking nonsense, just lies. Yet as I swallow, a salty, nutty flavour appears on the roof of my mouth. Grains of peanuts feel like they are lodged in between my teeth like grout.

"Be a shame to throw it all away for someone who isn't as invested as your good self, man. I'd hate to see you get hurt by her, again."

As if I've just climbed aboard a time machine taking me back to a decade ago; the stab in my heart when I found out Lex had cheated on me raises its painful and ugly head. I stumble back into the room where I spent the night, and sit down with a bump on the bed. The force of the blow still as strong as it was then. The past and present battle in my head. Screaming at me to let it go, to leave it locked up. Roaring at me to remember I can't trust her. Once a cheater, always a cheater and all that shit. Surely Lex and I have moved past that, it feels like another lifetime. I don't even feel like I've needed an apology for it, since we've been reunited. My neck prickles in unease. Though, it would maybe be nice. Fucking courteous, perhaps. Can the two of us move on, start afresh; when our foundations are cracked and waterlogged?

"We have lots to discuss, man, be ready in the morning. Nine am, sharp," Pete says, cutting into my thoughts.

"Fine," I say out on a sigh. What's the fucking point of arguing?

"And Hayden?"

"Yeah?"

"Bros before hoes, man, always. Don't leave Jordan stranded."

The line clicks dead. Like my hopes of being free.

26

Lexi is not back with Callum. Pete doesn't know what the fuck he's banging on about. I shake the demons from my head as I down another glass of water. Lexi cheated on me ten fucking years ago. We've both moved on from it. It doesn't matter. It shouldn't matter. My head thuds like the bass in a club. I scrunch my eyes tight. Maybe all I need is one tiny apology from Lex and then I can forget about it all. That should be enough to paper over the cracked foundations. An easy fix. Shove a bit of gold leaf on it and it'll be as pretty as a kintsugi vase again. Perhaps I don't even need that apology I thought I longed for, as if I were a kid with a Christmas wish. I'm happy with the empty box instead.

I walk past Lexi's office, again, and glance in on my way to track her down. My feet freeze as if I've stepped in wet concrete. Callum is casually slumped on the sofa opposite her desk. One trainer-clad foot resting on his thigh. A rolled-up newspaper tapping out a rhythm on his palm. I slink against the wall and strain to hear his words drift out of the half-closed door.

"It makes sense, like," he says, casually, as if he always chills out on the sofa in Lexi's office. Which, I guess, he fucking did. "It's a whole other world for these celebrities. Me and you, Alexis, we're one and the same."

As if I'm carved from stone like the opulent angel on top of an old grave, I feel myself freeze, the breath stuck in my lungs. My features appear calm and unmoved, yet I've been battered by extreme weathers and seasons since I was created. Like my stage persona, until fucking recently that is, nothing shows on my face. Smooth and still, never changing, just as the sculptor envisioned. The image of Lexi and Callum leaving the local church passes through my mind. Hand in hand, confetti fluttering around their smiles like butterflies. Her hazel eyes pass over my stone features before disregarding me and walking away, feet as light as feathers as they enter married life. *Fuck. That escalated.*

A dry chuckle from Lexi breaks through my nightmarish daydream, and I'm brought back to the present. I push myself flat against the wall, the cold plaster sticking to my lower back, where my jumper has ridden. It's fucking freezing, but I grit my teeth to stop me from shouting out.

"Think about it," Callum says in response to her laugh. "I'm serious."

I hear the leather sofa squeak and wait. I hold my breath as Callum walks away from Lexi's office, and out towards reception. He walks assuredly, slowly. Legs splayed wide, as if he's just fucking dismounted a horse.

Think about what? Has he just fucking proposed? Again? He cannot take a fucking hint. Lex obviously does not want to marry him. Why would she suddenly change her mind? Is he a fucking glutton for punishment?

I peer around the door and watch as Lexi flicks open the lid of a square green box. Callum *has* proposed, the fucking prick. The glinting gold band sparkles under the strip light above her desk. The light shining off the diamond in the centre. Be fair to the bloke, that's an impressive rock. My eyes jump to Lexi's face. She's smiling. My heart starts beating double time. Is she considering accepting? What can Callum offer her that I can't?

A distinct lack of personality. I snigger. The humour dissipates as facts hit me square in the jaw, like a punch.

Stability. Consistency. Reliability. No mother's death guilt issues. No alcoholism, substance abuse, or whatever the fuck issues I'm tarred with. No constant intrusion from the press or fans, or someone wanting a fucking selfie. No bickering band mates, sniping managers trying to start an argument, or ridiculous schedules to contend with.

My shoulders slump and the almost positive feeling I awoke with sinks, with weighted negativity to my toes. There's always something, usually fucking reality, ready to bring down my good mood.

"Two proposals in less than twenty-four hours, Lex," I say as I saunter into her office as casually and confidently as I can. "Who knew you were in such demand?"

Lexi jumps, her shoulders meeting her ears as she fumbles with the box. It clatters onto her desk, the ring rolling free from its cushion and swirling in circular motions before rattling to a stop.

I watch it, mesmerised by the polished gold.

"Both of which I'm ignoring, thank you very much."

The ring box taunts me like an emerald in a mine of

coal. I haven't even bought a fucking ring, and Callum rocks the fuck up with his stable job and diamond ring. I sigh out. I'm pissed at him, at myself. At the world. I can't shift Pete's words from my blackened brain.

"Want to talk about last night?" Lexi asks in her professional therapist's voice. It pisses me the fuck off, that she dismisses my proposals, yet is clearly considering Callum's. Perhaps Pete is right. I must be more invested in this relationship than she is.

"No," I laugh. Is that it? Is Lexi just going to talk to me like a fucking basket case, and not as her, what? Lover? True love? Fuck this. Maybe it was a pity fuck last night, the depressed devil whispers into my ear. I want to swipe the horned fiend away like an annoying fly, but the thought sticks like glue.

"I really advise you speaking to Lydia today, Hayden."

"Whatever, I don't wanna deal with this shit now," first Pete barking demands at me, then Lex purposefully ignoring the only positive parts of last night, in favour of her being Miss Goody Fucking Two Shoes.

"I can't just ignore it, Hayden! You're still a client, there's procedures in place –"

"What do they say about shagging your client?" I sneer out like the bitter wind whistling in the dark winter's night, extinguishing the fire.

"Hayden!"

I'm such a dick. I know she's only trying to help. I know Lex has got a duty of care and all that shit. The dark clouds have enclosed me like the stage curtains. I can't find the energy to fight through and see the light on the other side. It's easier, I've found, to push people away. To just remain isolated in the darkness.

"Fuck this, I'm going for a drink."

"You won't find any better answers at the bottom of a bottle."

"Well, I'm sure as fuck not getting any sense out of you," I mutter like a petulant teenager.

"You are, you just don't want to hear it!" Lexi snaps out, making Mavis, her ever present canine shadow raise her head from the snug beg she's curled up in. I think of Anoushka; she would have let out an echoing bark at Lexi's raised voice.

"You don't understand my life, Lex," I say dramatically, arms flailing wide. Enjoying Mavis' saucer like eyes following me round the room.

"Talk to me, help me understand," Lexi pleads, tears line her eyes. I look away from her. My heart shatters when I see how I hurt her, intentionally or not.

"Callum's right. You're better suited to him than me, and all my shit."

"Hayden –"

"I was drunk last night –"

"When are you not?" Lexi mumbles. I don't think she meant to say it out loud. She stares out of the window, watching the clouds float on by. I'm not even sure she's aware she's voiced her thoughts.

"Let's write it off, all of it. You should marry him," I say dismissively, pushing the box and the ring towards her. I nestle the ring back into the cubed padding and tap the lid for emphasis. She ignores it. I can feel her trying to catch my eyes. Bronze and blue. Like the picturesque sand and sea image. But I ignore her. My eyes dance over objects, the clouds, anything.

"You don't mean that."

"Don't I?"

"Hayden, please. Don't use it as an excuse, you weren't that drunk," Lexi reaches for me, grasping to make contact. I dismiss her with a wave of my hand and hope that my voice doesn't crack under the bravado I place on it.

"I can't even remember what happened," I add a half laugh on to it, to try and play it down.

"Hayden –"

"It's all a fucking blur, Lex," I smile with a shrug, to mask my real emotions.

"You can't remember anything? Nothing we talked about?" she asks. I know she's upset with me. But the lies come thick and fast like a heavy snowstorm on the mountain tops.

I shake my head dismissively, and sniff.

"Nah, not really."

"Nothing?" Lexi asks with a voice crack. It shreds my soul like a shard of razor-sharp ice. Mavis stands herself up and pads across to her owner. I reach down to stroke her, but she hurries her black legs past me and places her snout against Lexi's leg.

"Let's just forget about the whole thing," I shrug. "Me and you, let's just forget about it."

"Hayden."

"I could've done anything, said anything. Just nonsense drunken shit. I do it all the time."

"Hayden," Lex repeats, like a lyric stuck in my brain, circling endlessly. "You can't mean that, I –"

I shake my head to cut her off, cracking my knuckles.

I'm still missing the jewelled rings on my own fingers.

"I need to go back to London. Pete's coming to get me tomorrow." Thats the crux, I suppose. I'm leaving, I've had my orders and I must obey. It's best for the band, for my friendship with Jordan. I have to leave Lexi behind. Again. It'll be ten times fucking easier to leave her if we part on bad, bitter, broken hearted terms.

"You need to finish this rehab programme," Lexi says, her head snapping up to mine.

"You just want to keep me here, like Jordan said." Even I can see that I'm jumping from point to point, making little sense but following whichever train of thought travels on the line of most destruction the fastest. I feel like my thoughts are akin to *Bohemian Rhapsody*, dancing from genre to genre, never deciding which to focus on. It worked for Queen. I just feel like I'm drowning in my thoughts.

"Not at all!" Lexi looks exasperated with me. I should just fucking leave anyway, without making an excuse of a fight, yet I can't stop myself. "For your sake, not mine, you need to stay here and start addressing your issues."

"Are you wanting to stop me from going back to London?" I know I'm searching through the rubble for an argument. Lexi seems to be resisting, cleaning away any attacks in neat piles.

"I have never in my life, stopped you from doing anything."

"You asked me not to go to London, Lex!"

"Like a million years ago," she throws her arms up wildly before they settle, running long strokes on Mavis' salt and pepper back. "And I only meant it for a split second."

"You didn't want us to sign with Pete, either."

"I still wanted you to have a record deal; I just didn't trust him. I still don't. Do you honestly not remember anything I said about him last night?"

The dogs bark outside, breaking up our conversation and thoughts. Giving me a moment to fucking consider my response. I recall her words. Every word we shared. Every touch felt. I shake my head to clear it.

I believed her last night, clung to her like she was my beloved guitar and I was the strings, wound tight around her. Together it all made sense; her fear of Pete which she hides under jibes and snipes. How she still loves me, never stopped, yet how she believed I'd reject her for whichever pretty model was apparently waking up in by sunken bed.

But today, in the bright, glaring light of day, I'm faced with the reality. Was Lexi telling me these things to keep me close? Did she think I wanted, needed my ego stroked? *Fuck,* of course I did. I'm only fucking human. I wanted to discover that her candle always burned just for me. I needed to know that it's not just been me pining after her, still holding her in my messed-up head and heart.

Maybe she read me like I was a copy of *The Strange Case of Dr Jekyll and Mr Hyde*, my favourite book. Told me what I wanted to hear. I swallow. I'm so confused, and this hangover isn't fucking helping.

I have two choices, I can be honest with Lex, or I can keep my poker face on. It's easier to go back to London, to the band. It's a job, a job that I fucking wanted. I'm being a fucking ungrateful prick by wanting to throw it all away. A decade of playing a role sits easier on my face, though it threatens to slide off my heart, like a drip-glazed cake. My heart's already in pieces over leaving, I might as well twist the knife and leave some real, lasting damage in my wake.

"It didn't matter anyway, you'd already slept with Callum," I shout at Lexi, who flinches at the volume of my words.

"What the fuck?" Lexi snaps out. Her harshness jolts me, I wasn't expecting her to be so aggressive about it. She was always the one at fault.

"You're really going to deny it all these years later?" I snort. This is actually the first time I've confronted her about the cheating. Lexi's been on the receiving end of anger-fuelled lyrics and scribbles, both that I've sung and kept hidden. I've referenced an ex cheating on me in interviews. I've had emotional, tear punctuated arguments, and bitter, hurtful confrontations with her in my head while I've been on the road. Sometimes they've ended in my romantic mind envisioning a woodland wedding in the Lakes. Other times I've woken up hungover and hollow in a woman's bed, who has a similar coconut scent lingering on her skin, or the same raven dark hair I associate with Lex. Occasionally I've paid for the pleasure. But I've never challenged Lexi about cheating face to face. I wanted to. If I was a betting man, I'd have put my inaccessible millions down on it, that I'd have brought it up by now. But I never found the inclination to (possibly) ruin the love blossoming between us again. Now though, might as fucking well go hell for leather.

"Damn right I am!" She takes her glasses off and rubs her eyes, the late night must be catching up on her too. "Where did you get that idea from?"

"Pete."

"Pete is a fucking liar. I told you that already."

"And Jordan. He saw you with someone else, I'm assuming it was Callum. Though do correct me if I'm wrong."

Lexi laughs out a little and shakes her head, she avoids my eye contact. Fine by me, it makes it easier to argue.

"He was in on it too? I thought Jordan would have had more sense."

"What do you fucking mean?" I narrow my eyes at her, and perch myself on her desk, the legs wobbling like a cymbal.

"Is there any point?" Lexi shrugs. "You'll never believe me over Pete."

"Why should I believe you over him? He's always got my best interests at heart."

"Has he? Putting you on stage last night – that was the best thing for you to be doing?"

"It was for the band's benefit."

"What about *your* benefit? Like I said last night, Hayden, you cannot carry on like this. You need a break from The Halcyon, from that mad world you exist in."

"Pete didn't break my heart, you fucking did!" I shout out, pointing a shaking finger at her, I feel like I'm sidestepping the point she's trying to make. Lexi exhales loudly.

"Pete told me to break up with you, ok? He advised me that it was best for you, for your fucking band. I didn't want to, flat out refused," she says quietly, like it pains her. First I've heard of this shit.

"You cheated on me!" I jump up and walk towards the window.

"I did not! Why would I? I loved you!"

I stagger a little on my feet, as if a litre of whiskey has already been emptied down my throat. This doesn't make sense. Pete and Jordan witnessed her betrayal. Why is she straight up fucking denying it?

"Then why didn't you tell me, Lex? Why didn't you correct me? You didn't even fucking fight for me! For us. You didn't tell me this last night."

"I thought –" Lexi flicks her fringe out of her eyes. Her glasses abandoned on her desk. She looks like she did ten years ago, my heart starts to melt like the morning frost. Her fingers flutter by her throat. Was she telling the truth about her necklace? "I thought you couldn't remember anything about last night?" Lexi asks, an eyebrow raised. I open my mouth to respond, but she continues regardless. "I was convinced that maybe, I *was* holding you back. That you wanted to be young, free and single. I believed Pete, in the end."

"You never listened to anyone back then. You used to do the polar opposite of what you were told to do. You were a fucking nightmare at school!"

"He was fucking terrifying, Hayden. You know I never trusted him. He said so many things, threats to me – I couldn't tell if they were empty or not. I didn't wait to find out, maybe that was wrong. But when you've got someone telling you the same fucking thing every day, several times a day, you start to believe things that you usually wouldn't." Lexi sounds defeated, not defiant as I expected.

"Pete threatened you?" I ask. I don't know if I'm scared to know the truth, whoever I decide to believe, but my hands have started shaking. My heart feels like its beating so fast it might explode.

"What did he say, Lex?"

"It was just mind games, H, looking back. I was stupid to believe him."

"What did he say?" I repeat. Is she stalling for time? Thinking of things to say? Or are the memories too painful for her to voice out loud? Lexi scoffs a little and shakes her head.

"He said he'd fix it so my car got stolen, so I couldn't visit you. My scholarship and university place thrown out so I couldn't be in London. Said he'd find out my most treasured possessions and take them from me. He said the necklace was the first thing I'd lose that was important to me."

"You're just saying that," a laugh escapes my throat, but its dull and discordant. "You felt guilty for cheating on me."

"Whatever, Hayden. Keep thinking that if it makes you feel better," Lexi's brown eyes meet mine fleetingly, before she turns her head away with another sigh. "I didn't believe him, all his threats, ok? I didn't. But when he tore the necklace from me at the signing party, I was scared, Hayden. He got to me. I didn't know what else he was capable of. So I let you go, when it came to it."

She's such a fucking liar. Pete wouldn't meddle with me and Lexi, not back then. He saw how happy we were – everyone could fucking see it. Yes, I recall he did say it would be better if I was a free agent. Better for my future adoring teenage fans to be daydreaming about a single pop star than a happily committed one. But I told him I wouldn't lose Lexi for the sake of anonymous teens' fantasies. The decision was taken out of my hands when Lex cheated on me. Jordan witnessed it, and though Pete may be "just" a manager, my best mate would not lie to me about Lex. He knew he'd have to break my heart by telling me. Lexi must be spouting this shit to ease her own guilt.

I don't allow myself to believe that I may be wrong. I won't be. Though my heart feels like its shattered. Like I've thrown it against the wall in a drunken rage. I can almost feel smashed whiskey bottle confetti sticking to my skin. Cutting through things I've never known. Making me bleed red droplets of newfound understanding.

I cannot fucking cope with this. Pete wouldn't do that. He fucking wouldn't. He can't even kill a wayward spider in his office, he has to set it free. But Lexi. She wouldn't make this shit up. *Fuck.* My fucking head is pounding.

I can't look at Lex. I won't look at her. I step into the spotlight of being someone else and push her words to the rear of the stage. Lock them in a forgotten about dressing room.

"Didn't take you long to get over me though, did it? Straight into Callum's bed, weren't you?" I shout at Lex, ignoring the bared teeth of Mavis at her side. Time to get back on the fucking track. If I can't rely on Pete, then what do I have? Jordan needs me. Pete needs me to be on his fucking side. I swallow down bitterness creeping up my throat.

"No, I –"

"Bet you couldn't wait, could you? How long had you been seeing him? You always were a bit of a slag."

"What the hell, Hayden?" Lexi's voice is raised, her lip curled in anger. Mavis is flanked by her legs, ready to protect her owner.

"Flirting with Callum at school, and even Jordan," I

carry on regardless. Might as well cut all ties while I'm here, got fuck all to lose now.

"Jordan? Are you joking?"

"Any male with a pulse. Would flash a smile and a bit of cleavage at anyone who'd buy you a fucking drink on a Friday night,"

I'm exaggerating of course. Who doesn't become a little flirtatious after a few bevvies, especially as teens? But still, the poison pours from my tongue as if water cascading down a waterfall. It's easier to ignore anything Lex says against Pete. I won't have to deal with her once I get picked up tomorrow anyway.

"Why are you saying this?" Lexi cries out, anger and hurt bouncing around her office like a butterfly trying to escape the confines of inside.

"Desperate for attention from any man who could try to replace the hole your dad left when he fucking abandoned you for his new family."

"H," Lexi inhales sharply. I know I've hit a fucking nerve with the dad bomb, but I can't stop myself. Her eyes mist over, and I can see her chin and lips starting to wobble like jelly, despite the lack of tears falling. Mavis whines, trying to comfort Lex, or maybe picking up on her hurt.

"Is that the thing with Callum, he's a good father figure? Reliable and steady? Always around, unlike me."

"What? No!" Lexi's fringe dances across her forehead as she vehemently shakes her head.

"Don't deny it, Lex. I know you cheated on me with Callum."

"I did not. And I didn't date anyone for five fucking

years, Hayden."

I pause, the next words laced with stinging nettles hang silently from my open mouth. The snarl falls from my features, and I try to find comfort in grasping my chains. My hands return to my sides, empty and shaking.

"I don't believe you, Lex. Pete says –"

"I don't care what Pete says, or Jordan, or right now, you. Pete is a liar, Hayden! He's been lying to you for years, and you're too blind to see it," Lexi hisses at me as if she's a viper coiled to strike.

"Pete wouldn't lie to me. He's my manager; he has my fucking back! Which is more than I can say for you."

Lexi slams her palms on her desk, the pine-coloured tea jumping from her mug. Mavis lets out a bark, feeble compared to Anoushka's, but it still makes me jump.

"I have done nothing but look out for you since you arrived home, and you fucking know it, Hayden," Lexi is seething, her eyes are like stones in the river. Cold and unforgiving even with the shimmer of tears that dance on them. I'm reminded of our bitter arguments from years ago. Although this time, I know we won't be rounding them off with kisses and apologies. My heart stutters at the realisation, even if it's for the best.

"Pete has always been there for me, and he always fucking will be," I say to her coldly.

"He wants you to keep his pockets lined, don't kid yourself. You're nothing more than an income to him. You deserved better, always did. But he blinded you with promises of champagne and awards in London."

"Fuck off, Alexis."

Lexi looks like I've slapped her. I think that might only be the second time I've used her full name. It felt alien in my mouth. I feel a bitter tang in place of my tongue.

I watch as she places her glasses back on her face with shaky hands. All remnants of her teenage years wiped away, like her black mascara tears.

"Shut the door on your way out," Lexi says calmly as she starts to pick up papers and looks set to continue on with her working day. Leaving me, our argument as a distant memory. A fleck of dust on vinyl, easily removed with a gentle, almost indiscernible wipe. Unlike a scratch. A deep groove which ruins the melody, the lyrics.

"See? That's my point proven," I say as I push myself off the edge of her desk, anger stomping through my veins like a constant electro beat. "You don't care enough to fight for this, for me and you."

"You're not listening to me!" Lexi says in exasperation. Desperation. Or just defeat. The hangover is making things unclear.

"You're not saying anything I want to hear," I admit in a mumble. I rub over my head with my hands, the short stubble making a scratching sound.

"That's the truth, Hayden," Lex starts writing in a notebook, the pen scratching aggressively. "Sometimes it hurts, but that's life – you need to deal with it."

"Whatever," I snort, ignoring her bare neck, the sting over the lack of necklace and confusion over Lexi's version of its whereabouts spiralling around my skull. "Do us all a favour and marry Callum. Then we can both fucking move on, and finally stop this pathetic back and forth between me and you, Lex."

The pen stops scratching, and though Lexi doesn't show me her face, I know I've hurt her. This is what it comes down to. I'm willing to destroy all hope for the both of us as a couple. Burn our happy endings, and leave fragments of memories smouldering like used matches.

"Are we done here?" Lexi says, she may be going for calm and collected, but I hear the quiver in her response. I swallow Lexi's easy acceptance down with guilt, she's thrown the fire over our flammable ruins.

"Are we?" I ask, begging internally that she'll tell me she loves me. Even though I'm the one pushing her away and gagging for a fight. The whiskey hangover jolts me from emotion to emotion as if I'm the scales on a piano.

This is what I wanted. What I need. I can't leave and head back to London, to my normal life, if there's even a sliver of hope for Lex and I. It needs to be tied up. All blood flow cut off. Left to dry up, wilt away in this secluded Northern corner of the country.

"Yeah, I think so. Off you fuck then," Lexi dismisses me with a gesture of her head towards the door. She holds my eye contact. I can see the pain in her eyes, how her lip wobbles, and her throat bobs with the force of swallowing sobs silently. Yet I also see her features become hard, defensive and impassible. My heart cracks as I realise I've hammered the last fucking nail in the coffin for us. Kept us preserved in the past. Decaying over time until there's nothing left.

"You should marry Callum," I repeat, cursing myself at the voice crack as I speak. I have one palm flat on the door and turn to face Lex. She can't even bear to look at me anymore. The pen she holds in her delicate fingers, hovers above the notebook, shaking with emotion travelling through Lex's body, her train of thought forgotten.

"I should, shouldn't I?" she asks, though it's unclear whether she's asking directly for my advice. Lexi's eyes are trained on the holly leaf green box, the ring inside the reward, like rich red berries. "It would help me forget about you, wouldn't it, H?"

I slam the door in response.

27

I answer my phone to Jordan by taking a swig of whiskey. People talk at me, whether I speak or not. He doesn't even wait for me to say hello.

"Mate, I've just heard that Lexi's back with Callum."

News travels fucking fast, who needs social media when you live in a small knit community? Still, hearing it makes my throat contract around the pungent liquid. I wipe my mouth on my sleeve and am grateful there's no press to take photos of me stumbling around the park.

"Who told you?" I cough out, my words dry like crushed, fallen, rose petals.

"Pete."

"You remember when Lexi cheated on me?" I ask, ignoring how Pete knows anything about Lexi. He can find out everything, that man.

"Yeah, what about it?" Jordan almost chuckles. He must think I'm a fucking nut job raking over the past. He is certainly one of those for living the moment, blah blah.

"You sure about it? Sure it was Lex?" I ask. I drop an empty bottle in the bin, and hear the tinkling bottles jangle like my chains used to against my neck, in the rustling plastic bag at my side.

"Mate, it was years ago. Why are you questioning this now?"

"I dunno," I shrug even though Jordan can't see me.

I pause as I walk up the wooden steps, cut into the steep bank, surrounded either side by towering, skeletal yet strong trees. I turn around and look down at the path below. I feel a sigh escape from my lungs, my soul. The cool air clings to my exhale, making it swirl in front of my face. I hear the river, hidden behind the wall, nestled in its rocky bed away from my prying eyes. The sound of the water dancing, darting over the rocks instantly makes me feel like I'm home and welcome, despite feeling like an imposter, an outsider. A total fucking lost cause.

"How are you?" He asks, his voice crackling as the trees interfere with the phone signal.

"Shit," I answer honestly as I reach the top of the steps. The town's highest bridge splayed out before me.

The irony isn't lost on me, though. I told Lexi to marry Callum. I pushed her away. This is what I wanted. For Lex. Not for me. My feet kick up the loose stones, I watch them skimming the path, darting all ways, like my thoughts. I feel like a stowaway, hiding out and jumping from ship to ship as quickly as the tides change. Never knowing where to drop anchor.

"Where are you?"

"In between a rock and a fucking hard place, Jordan."

***

The empty glass bottle smashes against the black wrought iron railings. The sound is gentle yet abrupt. Tinkling chimes wrapped round a dull thud, a clang. Sounded better than the first one. I wonder if I could write a song based on it? I shiver. What's the point, who would hear it?

My manager? Great, he'd make me perform it wearing a fucking suit, auto-tune me beyond recognition, ensure each verse was written in fucking rhyming couplets, and probably get Jordan to sing lead. I'd be stood at the back doing fucking harmonies.

Jordan? He would rewrite it to fit the fucking new image, and dedicate it to Marlena. Another lie to add to the CV.

Lexi? Why would she listen when she's got a fucking wedding to plan?

I should've taken the glass and sliced my wrists.

Fuck.

The thought scares me.

I shouldn't have pissing stopped. It's all my own fault. If I hadn't walked off stage in London and left Jordan. Then I'd be blissfully unaware of Lexi and Callum. I'd still be performing songs I wanted to, wearing what I liked. Making music I felt passionate about. Lexi's face fades into all recesses of my whiskey addled brain. It was all for her, and there was never any fucking point. We can't be together. It won't work. *Pete won't let it.* That's a new thought. Where the fuck did that come from?

I shake my head, the image of Lexi and her negative words against Pete, rattle inside my skull, as if they're ice in a whiskey chaser.

If only I had battled through the gig at KOKO, I could still be hiding under the dazzling glare of the spotlight. Paint my mask on each night. Hide my demons in the bottom of bottles. In the beds of faceless women. Smother images of my mother's corpse and coffin with lines of white powder. Pretending the sweat pouring from me was from the bright lights, not the alcohol.

My best mate would still be that, not picking up my slack through stares of disappointing disgust. Not being instrumental in changing our band so we still have a fucking wage each month.

I could just be doing my job; posing as Hayden Fucking Coulthard from The Halcyon. Nothing more, nothing less. Just an image. The brand of a man on posters and screens. Lyrics shielding my heartbreak.

But I fucked it all up when I stopped.

I lean back against the cold bench, the early morning fog not lifting yet. I barely feel the frost on the bench against the bare strip of skin between my Prada jeans and ever faithful Gucci leather jacket.

I've been sat here for hours. Wandered, or more accurately, slipped up and down the bulbous paths around the park until collapsing here on this bench for a sleep fuelled by alcohol. It was filled with nightmare images of my mother coming to take me with her to the fiery circles of Hell, and Lexi and Callum rolling around in bed together, diamond sparkling on her finger.

I sat watching the sky streak from dark indigo to pale grey, mist kissing everything in its wake. Counting the hours with half bottles of whiskey.

I haven't performed for ages, the longest ever I think since I first picked up a guitar. I'm not counting the disastrous gig in Carlisle – that wasn't me performing. That was a replica, a false god.

I start humming, toe tapping, fingers drumming as my knees shiver beneath them. I hear the words of my songs whispering over my tongue, can hear the melody fill my ears.

At that moment I'm back on stage, strumming my beloved guitar, which I haven't picked up for weeks. I can hear, almost feel the rhythm bouncing from the drumsticks hitting the skins. Jordan strumming his bass with pure dedication. His vocals backing mine up when I need it, one ear of his always listening to everything, feet on the pedals. Following my compositions, winking at me during each chorus we wrote together. Strobe lights highlighting his zombie apocalypse tattoos, his nose rings glinting.

I twirl, singing into the next whiskey bottle, stumbling but styling it out, like the showman that I am. Caught in the memories, the music thrumming through my head. I stand on the bench, stepping onto the lower wall, before clambering up to the bridge top. Shaking my hips that makes the teenagers squeal, I click my fingers as I have no strings to play, lyrics pouring from me, my volume increasing as I get lost in this make-believe concert. I spin, one arm out, feeling invincible.

"I would die without you", I sing out then stop, taking in the surroundings: an empty bridge, no fans, no band, just me, alone, "here."

My arms drop, the whiskey swings back and forth, like a pendulum. I feel the wind rush past me. See the bare branches waving at me, my only crowd. I look down and instantly feel awake. Grey-tinged water topped with creamy bubbles flows far beneath the bridge. Just like last time I stared at the river, my mother's wrinkled face floats by. My eyes widen as her body dressed in a lilac silk sheet hovers up to my level then reaches a hand out, enticing me to join her. I shake my head, and with that she's vanished, back into the mirage.

I sit down, the damp soaking into my jeans, through to my boxers and my skin. It makes no difference. I'm already cold to the marrow of my bones. I visibly shiver due to the cold. The wind up here is relentless. There's no shelter. I thought was freezing on the bench. Up here it's like the pissing Arctic. The bridge nearest to my Camden flat is like a tunnel, no exposed tops or sides. Narrow and enclosed, like an alleyway on stilts. Here everything is more open, more at one with the landscape. Built to blend in, to enhance.

I unscrew the top from the bottle, my skin white with the effort. The burn warms my throat, but doesn't dull my senses.

Lexi is going to marry Callum, at my insistence. I killed my mother. I let my dad down, have done for years. My manager and best mate have me cornered into a band I've started to hate. I leave a trail of destruction wherever I fucking go. The weight that is always pressing on my skull, my shoulders, my heart – it's heavy, pinning me to the bridge.

"You're not thinking about jumping are you?" Jordan's lilting voice floats up to me from the path. I don't turn around, despite being startled to know he's here. I can't bear to see another disappointed face caused by me just being fucking me.

"Would you care?" I spit out. I look down at the full

drop. That would probably fucking do it. The river would easily drag me under, like clutching hands pulling me down. My lungs turning to water. The wind howls past my ears; my stupid bald head is fucking freezing. My feet bump against the iron railings, thudding a rhythm that echoes my heart. I try not to look down again, try to block out the gushing noises of the water.

"Fuck off, Hayden, you're my best mate," Jordan laughs, the sound dancing on the clouds like birdsong. "Of course I'd care."

"What's more important to you, Jordan?" I ask, honestly, prepared for an answer I don't want to hear. "Me being your band mate, or best mate?"

"Best mate, every time," Jordan's reply comes instantly. As easy to him as finding chords on his bass.

"Pete says the band is more important. That it's not over yet. No fucking going back and all."

"Please mate, do not let him twist our words. And for fuck's sake, do not jump off that bridge to get out of a fucking contract," I see Jordan's hands grip around the black railings, knuckles inked with skulls turning white. My hands grip onto the stone plinth I'm sat on. My fingertips push into it with such force that I wouldn't be surprised if it cracks in two and sends us tumbling into the water below. I've never gripped so hard onto anything, not even the Gravity Max rollercoaster in Taiwan, and that was pissing terrifying.

"The Halcyon means more to you than me, than our friendship. That's what Pete keeps telling me. You'll never forgive me if I leave," the words, my worries, bumble like the water flowing over the rocks far beneath me.

"I'll never forgive myself if you jump," Jordan says, all

traces of humour gone from his tone.

I'm too much of a selfish prick to jump, to actually end it all. I mean I would go down in history I guess, keeping company with Michael Hutchence and Kurt Cobain, but, fuck, no. I'm too much of a shit bag to even top myself fucking right.

"It's your whole life," I shrug, helplessly. I still feel such guilt about not enjoying living out our dreams, for ruining it all for my best friend. "The Halcyon is your reason for living."

Jordan sighs as he fiddles with the silver rings in his nose. It makes me feel better seeing him almost back to normal, in his flared jeans over battered boots, and vintage band tees that he orders by the bucket load off fucking eBay. Thank fuck he's got shot of that suit.

"If it's a choice between you being alive or the band, you know it's you every time, mate."

"It is?" I ask, wondering if he's just saying what he thinks I need to fucking hear, in case the temptation to jump becomes more than a passing thought.

"Of course! It's just a band, innit?"

"You've changed your fucking tune," I spit out. He needn't fucking tell me that The Halcyon means fuck all to him, not after everything I've sacrificed.

"Get your skinny arse down here, and I'll talk to you about it."

My feet land with a bump, and I stumble on the solid ground, into Jordan's waiting arms.

"Did you want to jump?" Jordan asks as he guides my shaking legs to the chipped wooden bench, carved with initials from years gone by. "Are things that bad for you, mate?"

"For a split second, maybe. Not seriously," I shrug, it's true.

Jordan raises an eyebrow at me, holding me at arm's length and trying to see if I'm lying.

"I swear it, Jordan, I don't want to die," I pull him into a hug, and talk into his shoulder, the leather jacket as smooth as butter. "But I'm so unhappy."

"With everything?" Jordan asks as we both sit down, our thighs touching. He smells of cigarettes and spicy cinnamon aftershave. Like a Christmas party.

"Pretty much," I shrug and go to run my hands through my curls and groan in frustration that they're not there. "I know I should be happy, I know it. I hate that I feel like this. I'm such an ungrateful prick."

"You're happy being back with Lexi though?"

I snort. What does that matter? I've ruined that. Not only have I missed the boat on a relationship with Lex and I, I've blown a hole in the fucking hull.

"She's with Callum, again."

"Forget about him, just for a minute," Jordan clicks his tongue. "She makes you happy, doesn't she?"

"Yeah," I'm embarrassed of the tears threatening to fall, but don't swipe them away. Jordan's seen me in worse states.

"Even a decade down the line, like a proper love story," Jordan adds, not a question, but a statement. I look over at him, his eyes gaze across the river, lost in thought.

"Maybe she's just meant to be with Callum though," I sigh with a shrug, resigned. I always thought Callum was the spare part, the percussion in the strings section. The towering wall between our love. But maybe I'm the one in the wrong place. Perhaps those two are the sweeping strings and I'm the solitary drum, breaking their concerto of happiness.

"So, I should have told you this back then, but I didn't," Jordan's fingers fiddle with his nose jewellery, a sure sign he's nervous. "I just wanted the band to work, more than your happiness with Lexi."

My hands, though flat against my thighs, start shaking, stuttering like they're tapping out a rhythm I can't keep up with. Concepts and ideas of what Jordan could be about to say bounce around my mind like notes without their staves to keep them in line. I wonder fleetingly, if he's going to confess to being the one who slept with Lexi. I think I might throw up at just the mere suggestion of the possibility of that being true. I don't know which one I'd be more fucking angry at. Jordan's my best mate, he knew, knows, how much I love Lex. He wouldn't do that to me.

28

"Mate?" I ask, my heart stuttering with nervous anticipation. The sinking feeling in my bones and my soul knows that I'm not going to like what Jordan has to say next.

"Lexi didn't cheat on you."

Despite not being atop the bridge, the wind still whips across my face, blowing my tears away. They stop sliding down my cheeks, in shock and confusion. I feel like I'm free falling into the icy water running below us. My head jolts up as my brain catches up and realises I'm not plummeting to the water. My mouth falls open, and I feel an awkward bubble of laugh in my gut. Part of me, all of me, my whole being actually, is fucking relieved he didn't sleep with her.

"What the fuck?"

"We made it up," Jordan's eyes glance at me then away again. "Pete and me, we made it all up."

"What? Why?"

"So you'd be more focussed on The Halcyon. Mate, it was stupid. I knew the band was your everything. I just listened to Pete when he said it would be better all-round if you didn't have to think about anything else," His face is contorted into anguish, it looks alien on his usually carefree features.

"You lied to me? Broke my fucking heart?"

"Yeah, Hayden, I did," Jordan raises his head to the clouds. "I can't apologise enough."

"Fucking hell, Jordan!" I shout out, the words bouncing back towards us on the wind, as I push myself off the bench. "What made you do it? Keep up the facade for ten fucking years?"

"It spiralled," Jordan says, shaking his head in despair. "I honestly thought you'd get over Lexi once we left."

"I didn't," I state, though Jordan fucking knows this more than anyone. Days, hours, weeks and months, fucking years, if we're being honest, of heartbreak. It wasn't always raw and bleeding. It scabbed over and occasionally itched. Until I saw her, or thought I saw her in a crowd. Slept with a woman who had skin the scent of coconut, eyes that reminded me of hot chocolate. Walked past a Clinique Happy bottle, or heard an INXS song on the radio. Then I'd scratch incessantly at the scab until it oozed and hurt once more. It was a vicious cycle, but I fucking indulged in it. Maybe I revelled in it so much as I could lay the blame with Lex. It was her cheating that broke my heart; I was the innocent one. I could blame her for it all. Each and every time.

"No, you didn't," he sighs and shifts on the cold bench under my gaze. "You did write some great lyrics from that heartbreak though." Jordan smiles, but I wipe it off with a fucking hard stare. He's fucking right though. Especially after each slip back to the pain, the lyrics would flow from me like the red wine blood stains.

"Why are you telling me this now?"

"Because, even though Lexi is a feisty, sassy cow," a smile tugs at his lips. "I can see she's good for you. She's always ready to put your best interests first. Which is more than I can say."

"No one else puts up with me like you do," I counter.

"I'm not here for you to stroke my ego, mate. Though I do appreciate it," Jordan says as he runs a hand through his now cropped hair. Until yesterday it ran the length of his back, strangely though, he suits the shorter style. It doesn't drag his face down, he actually looks better. Lucky sod.

"So you're telling me this now, after Lexi's fucking engaged to Callum so I can, what? Write better songs?"

"Mate, I spoke to Pete. He said he knew it was your mum's birthday yesterday. I'm furious with him on your behalf. You should be ready to string him up. He knew how much you were struggling with it, how you didn't want to be on stage anyway, let alone on her fucking birthday. He should not have pushed you, us, so much. You're meant to be in fucking rehab!"

I shrug. There was zero fucking point arguing with Pete about it.

"I got back on stage for you, for The Halcyon," I say to Jordan. He was my driving force, even if I careened off at a hairpin bend before the end of the second song.

"You shouldn't have. Hayden, if you'd told me, I wouldn't have let you. I knew you were a mess, but I just thought it was one too many whiskeys, I didn't think it was anything else," he clicks his tongue again, I hear the metal running through it clanging against his teeth. "I didn't ask you if it was anything else, anything more serious, and I should have. I should've known."

"I didn't want to be a fucking burden, but in the end I made it worse."

"Mate, quit the band."

What the actual fuck? I almost laugh. What a three sixty change of direction this is from my best mate.

"I still want this, you don't," I see Jordan's shoulders shrug under their shelter of smooth leather, a carefree gesture but said with such conviction.

"But we're in this together. We made a promise –"

"Fucking hell, mate!" Jordan laughs, jumping up to stand opposite me, "We were fifteen. It doesn't still stand now." His white teeth gleam like stars, the humour spreading across his features like the clouds covering the grey sky.

"I can't, Pete won't let me. He won't let us," I shake my head, again, missing the spirals of curls dangling in my eye line.

"Hayden, get a fucking lawyer! You can have mine! People quit bands all the time."

They do, I guess. McCartney left the Beatles. Johnny Marr left the Smiths. Robbie left Take That. Geri left the fucking Spice Girls. Gabriel left Genesis. Even Smokey fucking Robinson quit his band, despite it being named after him. Still, where does that leave Jordan? I muse, possibilities starting to step into the spotlight flickering in my head.

"If only we could leave HeadScan Records, and Pete, as a band then –"

"So why don't we?" Jordan shrugs, carefree. As if he's not balancing the weight of his, our, career on his shoulders. "I would've said this to you yesterday, but Pete was watching us."

"What? He was in London."

"Mate, he had cameras in our rooms to check we were toeing the fucking line."

He did? That's wrong on so many fucking levels. Though I guess I was a flight risk. Not that it stopped me.

"Is that what you were trying to say to me?" I think back to Jordan's incomprehensible mumbles and gestures. That must be why Marlena was so vocal, eager to please King Pete on his throne of press coverage and sponsorship deals.

"Yes! I meant what I said, though. I want to be in The Halcyon with you more than anything, but only if you're in it with me. It's our band. I'm not going to make you leave then fucking replace you, am I?"

"If I quit, then where would that leave you?" I ask, and despite the serious tone of the conversation, I laugh.

"I will fucking smash it as a solo artist," Jordan laughs too, sounding like sleigh bells. "I'll be like Robbie, but better, and obviously more attractive."

"And more talented."

"Goes without saying," he winks. I'm not sure which of them have the biggest fucking ego, mind. I admire Jordan's self-belief and optimism. He stands up and starts singing Take That songs, he could not be further away from a boyband image if he tried. I love him for it though. We laugh, our bellies shaking, the whiskey dancing in circles in my stomach like I'm a washing machine. Tears streaming down our faces, only a few of mine representing relief and desperation.

“Pete said you won’t get a contract though,” I say, as past conversations run through the beam of clarity in my mind. We sit back onto the bench, catching our breath after a few minutes of crazy dancing and singing as if we were a boyband tribute.

“He’s a liar, mate. I’ve had solo offers sent to me daily since you left at KOKO,” Jordan says, swallowing a mouthful of my whiskey. He wipes his lips on the back of his palm, and smiles at me. Like we’re just two mates sat drinking on a cold bench in our hometown. Which, I guess we are.

“You have?” My eyebrow raises as I regard him. Is this true?

“I’m in talks with people,” Jordan says mysteriously, pretending to straighten an imaginary tie. “Meetings left, right and fucking centre.”

“Does Pete know?”

“Of course not, I’m not that stupid,” he rolls his eyes.

“You make it sound so simple, Jordan,” I sigh, watching my breath curl in front of us like a boiling kettle.

“It is. You’re the one complicating it, mate.”

“Am I?”

“It’ll be easier to understand once you’re sober,” Jordan places a large hand on my thigh and pats it.

I rub my forehead, it’s starting to pound now, like I’m being attacked by a woodpecker.

“I’m a mess, mate,” I confess.

“You are, if I’m honest,” he looks into my eyes. I feel like I’m seeing him properly for the first time in years. “Luckily, we both know a woman who can help you.”

I snort. Considering Jordan has never met Lydia, I assume he means Lexi. I remember her facade cracking, as I cut her down with my words. I sliced her over and over, until just bare bones remained. Ruining everything we'd ever had. No masses of shining gold can repair that shattered kintsugi vase. From the lingering look in her hazel eyes, the shards of ceramic are nothing more than dust.

"She won't help me."

"Lexi will always help you. She'd walk over hot coals for you, mate. Did you not hear her last night? Every attack I launched at her," Jordan holds a palm up to halt his train of thought. "I owe her a massive apology; I was a dick. I took my bad mood out on her. Anyway, every single thing I threw at her, she served me right back. If we were tennis players, she'd have beaten me game set and match, as well as tying me up in the fucking net! She's on your side, Hayden."

"I was so cruel to her," tears of regret sheen on my eyes. I scrunch them closed to try and erase the guilt. Another slab of wrongdoing stacked high on my shoulders.

"She'll get over it," Jordan shrugs, struggling to light a cigarette. The flame from the lighter sparks pathetically in the wind before refusing to catch. He delves into his pocket and strikes a match, cupping a hand around the flame. He smiles as it catches. His optimism is starting to fucking grate on me.

"Why is it all so easy to you?" I snap out. He laughs, finding humour in my irritation. He was always the laid back one. Sailing through exams and tests with no revision, wandering around school with shirt untucked and bright green trainers on and never getting detention.

Even these days, he strolls through the airport, pace as slow as a tortoise. Whereas I am always dashing, practically sprinting to make a connection, our team bustling around us like we are in a group race. My curls springing free from my hat, curling like tornados around my sweat-drenched face, arms aching from my guitar and bags weighing my shoulders down. Jordan would always make it in time. Ice cool, not a hair out of place, usually with a duty-free purchase swinging from his relaxed arm. He would slide into his seat, moments to spare, like ice in a cocktail: smooth and easy.

"You should know this, you wrote a song about it," he smiles around his burning cigarette.

"What the fuck are you on about?" I snap at him again, my head pounding like I've a team of roadworks drilling into my temples.

> "*Love can mend it all*
> *rebuild the walls that fall*
> *Cement the broken bricks*
> *Love can be the simple fix,*"

Jordan sings a bridge from *Love Can,* a song I wrote a few years ago. Fuck. He's right. I did say that, I did write it.

"Trust yourself, mate," Jordan smiles. "You're Hayden Fucking Coulthard, you've got this."

"I don't know where to start, mate," I say, pleading like a child needing help from a responsible adult.

"That's easy, you start with Pete," smoke exhales into the frosted air surrounding us. "Then you go to Lexi."

"Easy as that?" I scoff. Confronting, even talking to

either my manager or my ex, feels like it will be anything but a simple task.

"Easy as fucking pie, mate," Jordan nods his head in the direction of the path. "Looks like you're starting now."

29

Pete reminds me of a fucking shark. The ultimate villain, like Jaws. Two notes and you know instantly you're fucked.

I turn my head to follow Jordan's eye line and see my manager striding towards us. He's flanked by two security guards, no sign of Higgsy or the others who we usually have in close proximity. Pete's pale blue, almost silver suit glistens under the winter sun. Like he's swimming confidently through clear waters. His eyes are narrowed, and although a smile graces his face, it's vicious and suspicious. Menace threatens on his features, though he shows no signs of being apprehensive or frightened himself. Like the shark slinking below the surface of unsuspecting swimmers, he's got the upper hand. He holds the power.

I stand up and puff out my chest like a peacock. Ready to dazzle him, blind him with my bright ideas. Pete regards me with a look of uncertainty. He was clearly expecting to find me as a broken man, a shell of the star he's moulded me into. Crabs change shells to grow, now is it my time for a new home? One without the luxurious fittings I've become accustomed to. My eyes leave Pete's, and I take in the tall, bare trees. Even in their wintery state, they are beautiful. I inhale the clear, fresh air and feel a little strength enter my lungs and soul. Jordan stands next to me, his body rocking on his battered boots. Confidence oozes from him. I feel like hiding in his shadow. How the tables have fucking turned.

"We got this, mate," Jordan says quietly, while looking at our approaching manager.

"No going back?" I repeat our traditional band saying, but pose it as a question. Jordan winks at me.

"No going back," I wish I had half his fucking confidence.

"Jordan, Hayden. At last, I've found you," Pete says as he reaches us. I feel like we're about to have a standoff in a Western. I don't think I could pull off a Stetson, although it would cover up my lack of hair. My eyes dance over Jordan's battered boots, he would totally suit a pair of squared toe Western boots.

"Pete," Jordan nods in acknowledgment. "Where's Higgsy?"

"Gone. Got a whole new team in place for this next chapter," Pete replies dismissively. Guilt settles low in my stomach. Weighing me down like I'm about to plummet to the bottom of the ocean.

"What? Why?"

"They did a frankly, appalling job of running things smoothly last night. Although I think we all know who is at the root of that problem," he fixes me with a stare that makes me feel like a child. Or more like a helpless fish, about to be trapped in his gleaming jaws.

"It was a nightmare, Pete. We know that."

"So what are we going to do about it?"

I shrug. Jordan stands, motionless, waiting for me to say something.

"Guys, wait for us in the car, please. Make sure the champagne is chilled, and that there's wild jacu coffee ready and waiting." The burly giants turn, and Pete watches them retreat down the path. "Right, let's be frank. This is what we're going to do. We will regroup, away from here. Put some distance between The Halcyon and last night. Rebrand using this new look, the new sound. This may come as a shock, Jordan, but we're not using your songs. I've got a team of songwriters in."

"What?" Jordan shouts out. I can tell he's furious. I'm shocked too. Pete has been practically salivating over Jordan's demos as if they were chateaubriand cuts of steak.

"It's not personal, man. This way you two aren't arguing over who wrote what, the usual issues that can break a band."

"You mean we miss out on royalties?" Jordan says with a snort.

"Jordan, man, you don't need to worry about finances. I've seen your bank account. Hayden, however –"

"So this is a ploy to punish him?" Jordan has always been rankled about Pete having authority over my money. He pleaded with me to get a lawyer or similar involved. I didn't listen, couldn't be fucked to cause a fuss.

"Showbiz isn't all champagne and awards, man. There are consequences to your actions."

Champagne and awards, that's what Lexi said yesterday when we were arguing. Or more accurately when I was barking at her in anger, and she was trying to calm me down. She used that exact phrase when slagging Pete off, how he tempted us to sign with him. He was the best The Halcyon could ask for. Realisation hits me like a fucking tidal wave. He *was* the best, *is* the best: for the band. Not for us. Not for me.

"Jordan has done nothing wrong," I say, and hate how fucking feeble my voice sounds, despite the conviction resounding in my lungs like thunder.

"Jordan was meant to ensure that you," Pete jabs a finger into my chest. "Did not leave the stage last night. You didn't even make it through the first half, Hayden. I am bitterly disappointed in you, both of you."

Jordan lights another cigarette as he looks towards the sky. I know he's had enough of this argument.

"I take all fucking responsibility, Pete. It wasn't Jordan's fault."

"I appreciate that he's your buddy, Hayden. But from a managerial perspective, from my perspective man, I need to start treating you both exactly the same. You two are meant to be a team. I hold my hands up, I should have always kept you together. Placed you on the same level footing. That's another reason why we're scrapping your songs, Jordan," Pete says smoothly, as if he's outlining the weather. Not delivering blows to our beloved music.

"I want the songs," Jordan states, arms folded. Cigarette smouldering in front of him, acting as a barrier, almost a warning. One step closer, and the burning tip will singe Pete's Amarni suit. "I want my songs. The masters, demos, rights, the lot."

"They're yours, man. Though, I don't know who will sing them," Pete's tone holds a hint of a chuckle. Has he always been that blunt? "Right now, man, no one is going to touch either of you with a barge pole. You're lucky I'm still fighting your corner. Let's hope we can get past this. Come on, the car's waiting."

"We want out," Jordan states, taking words I want to say from my mouth. My voice box remains locked, like a forgotten treasure chest. Rusting on the ocean floor, sand stuck in the lock.

"I'm sorry?"

"Hayden and I, we want out. We want to dissolve our contracts, end The Halcyon."

Pete laughs. The sound is laced with sarcasm, bitterness and disbelief.

"You guys," he says, chortling, hands on his stomach, as if performing a sketch. "You almost had me there."

"Pete –" I try to interrupt his flow, but like a single plankton, I'm swept away by his current of words.

"This is a new chapter for us. A new, different, more interesting book to add to The Halcyon franchise."

I want to tear the pages from their bindings, melt the glue and alight the crisp pages, until they're nothing more than curling ashes and a lingering scent of the past. I don't want a new fucking chapter; the same life but under a different heading. I want a blank page. I want a new start, not a continuation. I should take note of the steely determination radiating off Jordan, he wants this too. I must have been too blinded by my own issues, and by Pete, to take so little notice of his needs and wants.

"You're not listening to us, Pete," Jordan says loudly, talking over Pete's American accent. "I've got a lawyer back in London. We want out. Both of us. I've got offers for solo deals flying into my inbox weekly. Just let us go."

Pete freezes, like he's been sculpted from ice. His narrowed eyes dart from Jordan to me, like seaweed hitting a rock. His upper lip raises in a snarl, showing his pearly shark-like teeth. I shudder under his gaze, from dread or the cold seeping into my bones, I can't be fucking sure.

"Hayden, you're awfully quiet about this."

"Pete, be honest with yourself for once," Jordan answers for me. "Hayden wants this more than me."

"You want a solo deal too, man?" Pete asks me direct, ignoring Jordan completely. He plucks his phone from his suit pocket. There's a smile painted on his face, but I can see the cracks behind the front, like an ageing clown. "We can sort that. I can get you a deal with HeadScan records today, right now. Just let me make some calls."

Jordan laughs. The sweet tinkling sound is still there, but it's flanked by flat notes.

"You wonder why we want out," Jordan hisses, bitterness sticking to his words, like salt in the air blowing from the sea. "You've just given us a fucking speech about treating us as equals, yet you only want to fight for Hayden. He doesn't even want a solo deal! Fuck you, Pete. I deserve better than this. We're done. We give up."

I swallow a lump in my throat the size of a fucking mountain. Jordan, my best mate before my band mate, needs me to step up to the fucking plate. I feel his shoulders slump beside mine. He feels he's on his own in this. He's taking my silence as defeat.

"We're not giving up," I say, finding strength from

somewhere inside me. Even the smallest of fishes can move water. "Giving up implies we've failed, and we haven't. We're leaving, on our terms. Jordan and I don't want this anymore; we want different things. He wants a solo deal. I don't. I want a different life."

"Hayden, don't throw this away, man," Pete says, almost pleading. I notice sweat bubbling against his darkened hairline. "Tell me this has nothing to do with Lexi."

The mere mention of her name on his lying lips sparks a fire of anger in my soul. Jordan must hear my sharp intake of breath, as he steps his frame in front of me, and tries to look in my eyes. I look through him towards our manager. The person who was meant to have my back. I recall the hurt, pain, lies, that Pete has inflicted on me. Mainly linked back to Lexi, but also how he didn't listen to my pleas for a break, to not perform on my mum's birthday.

"Take a moment, mate. He's not worth it," Jordan says to me, clearly he remembers my fighting stance from being on the school yard. I don't think anything can fucking stop me. Ten-foot walls, fire, a swarm of fucking wasps, certainly not my best mate.

"Lexi is not worth you giving this up. I told you, she's back with Callum," Pete says with a shrug and a fake smile. "It's time for you to really move on. Let's head back to London and talk this through. You're better off without her. Remember how she broke your heart, man?"

Like an abrupt crash of a cymbal, my anger snaps in two. I will tear Pete Morris-Fucking-Turner limb from fucking limb. The alcohol fuzz lifts, and I feel the weight of the empty whiskey bottle swinging from my hand. I take a step towards Pete, the man who has been my puppet master for too long, and puff my chest out. Maybe it's the alcohol and anger, but I reckon I could take him. He's got the advantage of strength and width, but I've got rage coursing through my veins.

"Did you take her necklace?" I shout out. I note Jordan looking at me like I've lost the fucking plot. But I need to know. It's been burning at the base of my spine. An itch I can't get rid of. Did he threaten her? Lie to me about Lex? I can't fathom why Lexi would make it all up. But I hate myself for not believing her outright. I need to hear it from Pete too.

"What, man?" Pete scoffs, his eyes dancing from mine towards Jordan, who I see shrugging.

"Lexi's necklace that I gave her, did you take it? Rip it from her neck?"

"Hayden, man."

"Did you tell her to end it with me?"

"Yes," Pete stands tall, confident within himself. "Yes, I did. The same way I told you to end it with her. It wasn't right for the image of The Halcyon, man. The band had to come first."

"What did she tell you?" I ask. I know Lex. Know how much more stubborn she was as a teen. I know she'd never let someone tell her what to do, without putting up a good fight first.

"It doesn't matter, man. She cheated on you anyway."

"Pete," Jordan says, exhaling smoke in his direction. He shifts on his feet, awkwardness still lingers on his stance after his confession. "He knows. I told him we made that shit up."

"What did Lexi say to you, when you told her to break up with me?"

Pete rubs his forehead with the heel of his hand. Rain running off his hair dancing on his face.

"Honestly? She told me to fuck off."

I hear Jordan giggle. He throws a smile in my direction. He knows too, how feisty Lex was. And still is. I knew Lex wouldn't have paid any attention to Pete at first. He really must have fucking worn her down.

"Then what? You didn't give up there, did you?"

"Mate, where is this going?" Jordan asks quietly. I ignore him.

"I hold my hands up, man. In hindsight, I perhaps put too much pressure on her," Pete admits, his palms raised. I want to punch them.

"What did you do?" I ask him again.

"I warned her."

"Threatened her you mean?" I ask, Lexi's words circling my head. I've been dancing round the truth for too long. I believe her, always have. Why didn't I just fucking listen to her? "The necklace."

"Yes, I made a poor judgment, man, a moment of violence. Very out of character for me, you'll agree. I took her necklace and told her I'd –"

Pete stutters. At a loss for words for once. I tear my flaming eyes from him to glance at Jordan. His mouth dropped open in shock tells me he didn't know this either. That's a fucking relief.

"You told her the necklace wouldn't be the last thing you'd take from her. Perhaps her car would go missing, told her you'd fuck up her scholarship at uni. Destroy pieces of her one by fucking one. Until she gave me up."

"Empty threats, man. I did it for the band."

"Did she know they were empty threats, Pete?" Jordan asks, his face wincing at this confession.

"Did you say you'd hurt her?" I ask. Lex is a strong, warrior of a woman, always has been. There must be something she's not telling me. I take a stab in the fucking dark, that Pete threatened her with violence.

"I can't recall, man. They were just words. Words that didn't mean anything. But look, I'm sorry. Ok? Now let's get things sorted, come on. The car is still waiting. Man, she's back with Callum. Let's leave this mess here."

The rain batters down from the sky, darkness enveloping the bridge like my anger. Rain drops pelt down like they are in a hurry to escape from the clouds. They sting my face, my arms, they bounce off the path. He fucking *can* recall. I know he can.

Words. Just fucking words. Words, lyrics are my life. If I never get back on stage again, I know I'll write for the rest of my days. Words mean everything. They can mean so much depending on who hears them and when. Where. They can be a matter of life and death. The start and end of relationships. Of everything. And here's Pete, fucking dismissing them? Fuck this.

"Lexi's really back with Callum, is she? Did she tell you that herself?" I chuckle bitterly, my voice catching in my parched throat, stale whiskey painted on my mouth, teeth, tongue. I prod the cool bottle into Pete's Armani suit. I think of the shining gold band in Lexi's office, and hope she hasn't slotted it into place on her left hand's third finger.

"Sure," Pete replies, but I know he's lying. "Let's get

away from these distractions and plan for the future," I can see that he doesn't know where I stand; he's unsure of how things are going to pan out. He won't like this. He needs to be in control.

"Pete, he doesn't want this!" Jordan shouts out, his words echoing and startling birds from the bare bones of the wintery trees. "Especially not now, after all this shit."

"I am not talking to you, Jordan. It's clear you're a lost cause."

"No. I'm not leaving," I say through gritted teeth.

"Hayden, Jordan, you're both still under contract. This is your whole life, your career. Get in the car."

"Speak to my lawyer, I've had enough of this shit," Jordan says as he lights another cigarette and steps away, talking into his mobile in hushed, yet hurried tones.

"Don't mess your life up for Lexi, man," Pete says. He leans towards me, with rain running down his forehead, his strong nose, that I want to break in fucking two. "She'll ruin your life, just like your mom did."

I see my arm rise and smash the clear glass bottle over Pete's head. No drum roll, no planning. Straight up and straight down. Fragments of glass cover his head and shoulders like snowflakes. Pete stumbles and I raise the shattered bottle again. More snowflake shards scatter around us. Pete pushes me backwards and I land with a bump on my arse. He pounces on me, I'm reminded momentarily of rugby at school, how tackles always got out of hand. I feel the blows from Pete's fists rain over my ribs and nose. I splutter as cardinal red blood fills my mouth, spraying Pete's face with splatters.

I feel Jordan's arms around me, he pulls me off our

manager, but I don't leave it. Jordan's throw to remove me from the situation fires me towards the iron railings of the bridge. I use them to push myself off from and I charge at Pete's shimmering ice blue suited back. I leap onto him and pull, twist, grab his hair his ears, punch at his face. Anything I can do to try and cause him pain, even if only temporary. Pete's strong, and a lot broader than me. I cling to him like a koala but he shucks me off, my nose and jaw receiving more punches from his ringed fists.

Jordan manages to hold me back again, and so I shout. I fill the air with my voice; words loud and obnoxious, yet pleading. Begging. Enough of this fucking farce of a life I'm trapped in.

"I want out! I fucking told you I want out! We both want out! End our fucking contract! I'll fucking pay you double!"

"I will make your lives hell, drag you through the courts," Pete spits, blood; his and mine dripping down his face, staining his pale blue suit.

I didn't want this, I don't want this. I wanted to write music, perform it worldwide, make a living from it. I didn't want to be controlled like this; trapped, suffocating slowly into a mould that is a million miles away from who I am. How can Pete not see this?

I'm kicking out, my arms waving madly like a toddler having a tantrum. Jordan holds my arms behind my back and kicks my legs from under me. Fuck him and his martial arts.

"You don't need to do this, Pete. My lawyer can get us out of any contracts. You know it, I know it. Stop fucking bluffing," Jordan says calmly as he pins me to the ground. His knees on my back. He holds me down, with pressure but not enough to cause pain. I know he's trying to calm me down. To protect me. The side of my head against the cold, damp, solid ground. It makes my heart rate slow. I breathe slowly.

"Just let us go. For once, give us the fucking easy way out. I am fucking begging you, Pete," tears stream down my face, I'm so frustrated, so fucking done. I feel defeated, at the very end of the tether. Playing out the same, repetitive notes on a loop, until the melody becomes lodged in a frustrating, endless riff.

I look towards Pete. I see the fear in his eyes. This man doesn't trust me to obey him, not anymore. The strings have been cut. He knows I'm a lost cause too. A battle he cannot win. The Halcyon are now unable to be controlled and moulded. Jordan and I are in this together. No fucking going back.

30

The clouds of despair, of anger have faded. My eyes feel as bright and awake as the sky reflected into Ennerdale, on the crispest of spring mornings. The rain still runs down our faces, but both Jordan and I have smiles to give away for fucking free. The relief almost floors me again, as Jordan pulls me to my feet. My legs threaten to buckle underneath me.

"You thought that was easy?" I laugh at Jordan, as I spit blood from my mouth. My stomach feeling queasy, after the punches thrown have jolted the whiskey. It feels like there's a fucking tornado inside of me.

"Well, mate," Jordan shrugs. "I wasn't anticipating quite as much bloodshed." Me neither. I prod at my tender nose. I hope it's not fucking broken. "What matters, though, is that we did it."

I'm drunk, well hungover, not fucking naive. "Pete's not going to let us go that easily Jordan. He's fucking livid."

Jordan lights another cigarette and shrugs. Easy for him to be so carefree when he hasn't been pummelled like a fucking punch bag. "He knows we want out. Sure, he might be a right dick about some things, but I promise,

Hayden", he places a reassuring hand on my shoulder, "our lawyers are on it."

"Our lawyers?" I ask. I guess I don't believe it really is nearly over. I'm almost out of the birdcage, balancing on the edge tauntingly close to freedom, but all it would take is a nudge and I'd fall backwards, back under lock and key.

"You're my best mate, I'm not going to leave you to sort this shit on your own."

I smile and feel my lips twinge in pain with the gesture. I hate how much of a vain fucker I am, but I hope Pete's fists haven't done any lasting damage.

"I wouldn't blame you. If you left me in the fucking lurch," I admit. Jordan slaps me on the back, I only wince in pain slightly. I pull him into a hug, ignoring the soreness of my bruised body.

"I'll always, always have your back, Hayden. You need to have more faith in people. Stop pushing us away."

I rub the back of my neck, missing my hair to pull at in frustration, "Yeah, I've got some shit to work through," I confess. "Pete fucked us over, didn't he?" I ask, for confirmation, and reassurance.

"He tried, mate. But we fought back, eventually," he smiles, and I'm reminded of the boy who was my first friend when I moved to Cockermouth. His head raised in question and acceptance as he kicked the football across the schoolyard to me. I kicked it back, as I shucked off my backpack and joined in with the other lads. There was no going back. "We've lost the band, but you weren't happy – "

"Were you happy? Truly?"

He exhales smoke at me, just to be an annoying prick,

"I don't think I was, now I think about it."

"Plus, you looked awkward as fuck in that suit."

"At least I still look half decent, mate. You'd better hope those damn curls of yours grow back quick."

"Twat," I laugh.

"So," Jordan says, as we both sit down on the bench, our feet kicking at the glass remnants of my night drinking. "What's the plan for you, mate?"

I blow air out of my cheeks. I'd love a fucking hot shower right now, and probably need a ton of arnica smothered over the patchwork of bruises on my face; but I don't think that's what he means.

"I think I might write," I shrug. "Trade in the stage for a studio."

"I read your stuff," he says, as our eyes take in the surrounding views. We watch a bird, hopping from branch to branch in front of us. Happily chirping then spreading its wings and flying high to the clouds, fighting against the wind and circling our heads, before it disappears, lost to the freedom of the sky. "They're really good, like, Ivor Novello good, mate."

I shake my head. He's just being kind to me after the fight and trauma of the last day or so.

"They are, Hayden. Pete gave me your notebook, I couldn't resist looking," he raises his shoulders in a casual apology, but I know he's not really sorry. He's done nothing wrong anyway. We've lived literally in one another's clothes for a decade, we have no issue with privacy. "You should do something with them, for sure. Sell them to me if you don't wanna sing them yourself."

"Fuck, they must be good," I laugh, still not quite

believing him. Pete told me they were shite. That Jordan's were better. I've heard his stuff, it's good. Not what I'd create, but definite number one singles.

"I don't wanna be on stage anymore, Jordan. I can't do it. I don't want to do it."

"I guessed that much," Jordan squeezes my thigh. His cold palm pushing the rain through the denim onto my goose-pimpled skin. I put my hand on top of his and pat it. I can feel the shape of his hand, his knuckles even though I feel numb. I should invest in a pair of fucking gloves. I love Jordan like a brother, it feels fucking alien to know we're not going to be sharing the same lives after so long. "Ten years though, more than we ever imagined."

"Beyond our wildest fucking dreams." We high five one another in a wee celebration of the band we created. We dreamt of waking up to champagne and caviar. To while away our days making music, absorbing every scream from fans. But living it, it was indescribable. Amazing, so fucking amazing. "And it's not over for you, mate."

"I hate to quote our almost ex-manager, but it really will be a new chapter for me." Jordan's gaze drifts off to no doubt solo concerts and interviews. Marlena was right, not that I'd ever tell her that. Jordan does deserve this. It's his time to take centre stage, have the spotlight solo on him, and let him fucking revel in it.

"If you mean it, I'm more than happy to give you my songs. The words to kick off your new chapter."

"Yeah?"

"It would be a fucking honour, mate."

"You gonna buy a house up here, or build one? Or just

move back in with your dad?"

"Dunno," I reply non-committal. Jordan seems to know, better than I do, that I'm not returning to London. I can't imagine it, now. Not after the peacefulness of Cumbria. Plus, it will be good for me and dad to spend some time together, without me either dashing off to do a gig, or sniping at him with whiskey infused words. I swallow a lump in my throat. I want to spend time with him too. That's a fucking first. "I guess it depends."

"Depends on what?"

"Lexi," I answer, without any thought. Her name being my response before reason kicks in. My heart falters as I recall our, my, harsh words yesterday. I don't know if she'll forgive me. I pushed her away as if my life depended on it. I thought it did, in one fucking way. Despite my bones feeling they're rattling with cold like a wooden kokiriko instrument, my veins feel like they're flooded with lava. The burning heat of love, and hope covers the guilt and regret making my blood run cold. I need to at least fucking try and apologise to Lexi, to make her understand how I really feel. "Jordan, I need to go speak to her."

"I thought you might say that," his heavy eyebrows raise, the raindrops bouncing off the piercings. He winks at me and smiles. I think he understands that I'm not choosing Lex over him. I never would, they're two separate people. Two different choices.

"I don't mean to abandon you, it's just –"

"Go on, mate. Who am I to stand in the way of true love?"

31

"Lexi!" I shout as the door swings behind me. I'm fucking thrilled to see her, standing behind the desk in Paws2Heal. Her blonde hair tinged purple under the neon sign on the wall.

A sigh escapes from my chest, this could be it. This could be the last chance I ever get to make things up with Lex. To put things right, to be honest and open, to strip myself of the pop star label and just be me. Just be us. I would wait another ten years; I would wait forever for her.

"Marry me."

"Don't be ridiculous," Lexi hisses out quietly, pulling me to one side. She throws an apologetic smile towards the waiting room.

"You said to ask you when I wasn't drunk. I'm not drunk," I smile, my lips still smarting from the fight.

"You're hungover," Lexi says with a raised eyebrow and a no-nonsense tone. "And you look like you've gone five rounds with Tyson Fury. What the hell happened to you?"

"Might have had a fight with Pete," I shrug. In the adrenaline rush of running from the bridge to Paws2Heal,

I'd forgotten that I must look a right fucking state. Blood drying in rust red splatters over my beloved Gucci jacket, and fuck knows what my face looks like. My knuckles are raw and open, yet I feel no pain. I scoff to myself, they'll sting like hell when the numbing effect of the whiskey wears off. "The ending of our contract didn't quite go to plan."

"What?"

"I'm free. Jordan too. The Halcyon is no more," I smile, feeling a spring bounce back in the balls of my feet. "It's not official, yet, but the lawyers are sorting it out."

"About time," Lex smiles gently. "Seriously, good for you."

"Marry me, Lex!" I ask her, shout it loud. The dogs bark, and the people sat in the waiting room gasp. I turn round and smile at them all; they return my cheer with a look of awkward dislike. I guess I'm not exactly the polished pop star I usually present to the public.

"Hayden, I'm not going over this again," she says as her eyes flit around the room. Colour rising from her chest and blooming on her cheeks like rose petals.

"You're right. Fresh start and all that," I watch as she shuffles on her feet, and wiggles her glasses on her nose. Her professional persona threatening to slip, under her obvious embarrassment. "Shall we go into your office?"

"I think that might be best."

I sit, legs swinging on the edge of Lexi's desk, waiting for her to return with a first aid kit. The aches from the fight are spreading, increasing in pain with each second. If I wasn't buzzing on being given a second, third, or fucking fourth, chance with Lex; I'd be in fucking agony.

With a bottle-green box and a blanket nestled under her arm, and a dripping flannel in her palm, Lexi regards me with a look of disheartened joy. I'm pretty fucking sure she's pleased to see me, even if I must look like I've been in a pub brawl on Mad Friday. But, as always, she's not giving much away.

Lexi peels the ruined Gucci jacket off my arms, apologising as I wince; the scent of coconut filling my senses with love and hope for the future. She wipes my knuckles with the flannel and then the sting of antiseptic has me jolting as if stung by nettles in the park.

"Sorry," Lexi says with a slight wince. "How are you feeling?"

"Pretty fucking good," I smile and try to send her a wink, but the spasm makes my cheeks ache.

"Well, you look terrible."

"You should see the other guy," I try to laugh but it sounds forced.

"Be serious, Hayden."

"I am serious," I shrug. "I feel better than I have in, fuck, so long," I mean it. I feel a sense of relief, of freedom. I feel like me. Or more fucking accurately, not a moulded shape of what someone else wants me to be. I feel weightless, like I could run up Scafell Pike, swim the length of Windermere. The millstone around my neck falls to the floor, smashes, then crumbles into dust.

"Physically then, how are you?"

"Bit sore," I say, not being entirely truthful. Play the alpha male and all that shite. The muscles and bones send tap dancing pains to my brain, but I try my best to ignore them. This is more important.

I move my eyes around Lexi's desk, studiously. I can't see the golden ring or luscious green box anywhere, I try to lean subtly over towards the bin, but just find crumpled pieces of paper.

"What are you looking for?" Lexi asks, a smile breaking through her nursing seriousness. She might be putting on a front of being professional, but the tenderness in which she touches my skin extends from caring to loving. At least I fucking hope so. I zone in on her left hand. All fingers bare. I breathe out a sigh of relief. I shake my head. I don't want to waste my precious breath on enquiring about Callum.

"I owe you an apology."

"Just the one?" Lexi asks with her head tilted to the side.

"Too many to count," I say through a mumble, as Lex dabs at my split lip. The water dripping onto my jeans, another colour to add to the patchwork of mess.

"You were horrible, Hayden," Lexi says, her expression stony. I reach out to hold her face in my bruised hands. I have the fucking audacity to blush in embarrassment. My thumbs stroke at her smooth skin. I rub over her lips. Her eyes glance to mine and towards my own mouth before she can catch herself and frown. "Horrible."

"I know, believe me," I say imploring to her. "I am so sorry. I was a dick. A total dick to you."

"I shouldn't even hear you out," Lex says with a shake of her head, as she steps away from me.

"I said things I didn't mean," I scoff, I didn't mean any of them. "Everything I said was a ploy to push you away, to make you hate me."

"You did a good job."

"If I could take them back, I would."

"What would you say instead?" She asks as she rinses the flannel in the sink. I watch the red liquid swirling away. I note how her back is rigid, stiff. From her posture I assume she hasn't accepted my apology, start of the apology, yet.

"I'd beg you not to marry Callum. I'd tell you that I love you. That last night, being with you was just like heaven."

"You don't believe in heaven." She says flatly with an eyebrow raise.

"Fine," I sigh. "I'd tell you that being with you was the best thing that could've happened to me, that I've missed you: physical, emotional, friendship, sex, all of you. Every part of you, even your stubbornness and short temper."

Lexi opens her mouth, to fire an insult or cutting remark at me, but then pushes her lips together. I want to kiss them.

"Have we established that I'm sober enough to propose?" I ask instead of placing my lips on hers. As tempting as it is.

"I wouldn't exactly go that far," Lexi says as she holds a wet flannel to the bridge of my nose. "But I will confess that you are of more sound mind than I first thought when you barged in here. Throwing marriage proposals about like confetti," a smile dances on her lips, closely followed by an eye roll.

"Nice words, Lex, I must use that in a song."

"I'll sell it to you for a price," Lexi replies, deadpan.

"So, will you marry me?" I ask with a smile. If I had a ring, I'd present it to her. If I could, I'd cover all her fingers in rings, tokens of my love. But, it's just me. Empty handed.

"Maybe we should take it slow. We've been apart a long time, Hayden."

Lexi was always feisty. Stubborn. Had an answer for any and everything. Ready at the drop of a fucking hat to start, or finish an argument.

But she was also always more cautious. Reserved when it came to feelings. I was the first to say 'I love you'. I was the first to want to talk about our intertwining futures. I knew she agreed; I could tell she wanted it too, to be with me. To be us. Yet it took her much longer to say it.

I know that Lex loves me, and that's not me being fucking arrogant. I can see it in her bronze eyes, even now as she tries to throw me an irritated look, her lips pursing in a pout. I can see the corners of her red lips trying to pull themselves into a smile. Feel it in her touch, as she cups my jaw with one hand, her fingers gently rubbing soothing caresses onto my prickled skin. Her other hand patting dry my cuts and scrapes.

"Then let's date. Will you go on a date with me? Actually, fuck that. I don't want to date."

Now I'm faced with the prospect of waiting; I can't wait. In typical me fashion, I've changed my fucking mind. Abandoned my previous concerto and started another, as if I'm Beethoven.

I've waited, wasted years without Lex in my life. I don't want another fucking second to pass me by without her with me. Lexi laughs a little, her eyes closed gently. She shakes her head and her shoulders drop, helplessly. The lovebird tattoo visible through her white top. My own one seems to sting with the agony of being almost hidden, now that its mirror image is within touching distance.

"Hayden," she says as she pulls her glasses off her face, her arms swing helplessly by her side. "I am exhausted with this back and forth. You propose in one breath, then tell me to marry someone else the next. What do you want?"

"I want you, all of you. Wonderful, stubborn, beautiful, feisty you. I want us to argue and make up, kiss like we're running out of time, talk about everything until the sun sets. I want to fall asleep together and wake up next to you every fucking day, then watch your face scrunch in frustration, as you feel about for your glasses on the bedside table. I want to squabble over what to watch on the tv, I want to bore you rigid when it's fashion week. I want to curl up together and live off your mum's sandwiches!" I spread my arms out wide, enjoying being dramatic, but loving that Lexi is my only audience. Lex laughs loudly as she puts her glasses back on. She turns to look at me, her hair framed by the sun coursing through the windows, the rain now moved on, leaving cotton wool clouds in its wake. The raindrops send patterns of circles over her bare arms; she looks like a dream. The best fucking dream I could wish for.

"I want you, Lex. I've loved you since I walked late into Maths class in Year Seven. I've loved you for the last ten fucking years we've spent apart. I will love you for the rest of my life. If you marry Callum, if you don't, if you marry me, or someone else, it won't change things. You could marry Jordan for fuck's sake, and I'd still love you." I stand next to her, pushing my cold hands against the radiator, our shadows stretching out before us.

"I don't want to marry Callum, or Jordan or some

random man, stop palming me off with people." Lexi says with a scowl. The way she glances at me then away, and how her hand covers her mouth, tell me that she's smiling, or at least battling against it.

I push myself off the radiator, missing the warmth against my palms and legs. I encircle Lexi's wrists with my fingers. Feeling her pulse beneath my touch. I bend down and push our foreheads together. She sighs, but doesn't sound exasperated. Her warm breath tickles my face. She meets my eyes over the top of her glasses then closes them. Her eyelashes kissing her cheeks. She extracts her hands from mine and loops them round my neck. I stand myself up and pull our bodies together in a hug. Lexi feels warm, safe. The hug feels like love.

"Lexi, I'm a mess. I'm an unemployed alcoholic. I'm going to be living in my teenage bedroom until I can get hold of my money and buy a house. I have fuck tons of emotional baggage, issues, shit to deal with, to work through," I admit. Here I am, laid bare.

"H," she says out on a quiet gasp, taking a step backwards. "You said it," I watch her wipe a tear from her glistening bronze eyes.

"Said what? You kind of interrupted my flow there," I half smile, a gentle frown passing over my features.

"I don't want to ruin your flowery words," Lexi sniffles and smiles, her face looks happy. Her eyes dance merrily across mine. "But, just know, that in a professional capacity too, I'm so proud of you," she sniffs again and I kiss her on the nose.

"I can't offer you much right now Lex. Except my unconditional love, and words. Words, melodies and lyrics written about you, as quick as my hand can write them."

"I am partial to a nice lyric, truth be told. I mean, you're no Michael Hutchence, but you're pretty good," Lexi says, as our hands join. Fingers intertwining without either of us realising. Like instinct.

"I will spend the rest of my days trying to write you a song that you'll adore as much as you love *Tear Us Apart*, Lex,"

"Alright," she flushes. "Enough of your lyrical prose, Hayden. You're not writing a song now."

"I want to write a song about every moment with you, Lex." She snorts and I chuckle. "Putting the wash on, walking Mavis, arguing over forgetting to put the bins out, make up sex," I flash her a wink. She meets my eyes and smiles, a genuine smile. Her eyes sparkle, like jewels.

"You are ridiculous."

"Ridiculous or romantic?"

"Repetitive," Lexi smiles. She tilts up her head and places the lightest touch of a kiss on my lips. It stings, but it's fucking worth it.

"I love you, Lexi Blackwood."

"I love you, Hayden Fucking Coulthard."

Acknowledgements

I have endless gratitude for everyone who has supported, encouraged and helped me on this journey with Hayden and Lexi.

Richard and the Beans, family, friends, friends that have become family, and writing buddies near and far; thank you. You know in your hearts who you are.

To the inspiration behind Hayden's name- Hayton Coulthard Haulage based in Twynholm.

A huge thank you to all at Atmosphere Press, who have been a joy to work with.

I always write with a *Roget's Thesaurus* to hand, and *Staged* would not be what it is today without it. An extra special thanks to my Hubs for being the one to buy it for me; and for his constant belief and unwavering support.

A final note for the dreamers, creative souls and romantic hearts in the world; never give up. You can and you will.

About Atmosphere Press

Atmosphere Press is an independent, full-service publisher for excellent books in all genres and for all audiences. Learn more about what we do at atmospherepress.com.

We encourage you to check out some of Atmosphere's latest releases, which are available at Amazon.com and via order from your local bookstore:

Twisted Silver Spoons, a novel by Karen M. Wicks
Queen of Crows, a novel by S.L. Wilton
The Summer Festival is Murder, a novel by Jill M. Lyon
The Past We Step Into, stories by Richard Scharine
The Museum of an Extinct Race, a novel by Jonathan Hale Rosen
Swimming with the Angels, a novel by Colin Kersey
Island of Dead Gods, a novel by Verena Mahlow
Cloakers, a novel by Alexandra Lapointe
Twins Daze, a novel by Jerry Petersen
Embargo on Hope, a novel by Justin Doyle
Abaddon Illusion, a novel by Lindsey Bakken

About the Author

Finding teaching to be more about paperwork than expanding the minds of young children, and refusing to pay extortionate childcare costs, Elsie G Beya started writing stories and chasing her dreams of being a writer.

Elsie has attended several writing workshops and courses in her home county of Cumbria. She runs a local book club and writing critique group, and looks good in any and all hats.

She loves writing, reading, shopping, biscuits and tea, boybands, and being by the sea.

Staged is Elsie's first novel.

Made in the USA
Columbia, SC
07 October 2021

46454206R00164